P9-DFT-730

THE

RECOLLECTION

GARETH L. POWELL

SOLARIS

First published 2011 by Solaris
an imprint of Rebellion Publishing Ltd,
Riverside House, Osney Mead,
Oxford, OX2 0ES, UK

www.solarisbooks.com

ISBN: 978 1 907519 98 7

Copyright © Gareth L. Powell 2011

The right of the author to be identified as the author of this work
has been asserted in accordance with the Copyright,
Designs and Patents Act 1988.

All rights reserved. No part of this publication may be
reproduced, stored in a retrieval system, or transmitted, in any
form or by any means, electronic, mechanical, photocopying,
recording or otherwise, without the prior permission of the
copyright owners.

10 9 8 7 6 5 4 3 2 1

A CIP catalogue record for this book is available from the
British Library.

Designed & typeset by Rebellion Publishing

Printed in the US

THE
RECOLLECTION

ALSO BY
GARETH L. POWELL

The Last Reef
Silversands

SOLARIS

For Edith and Rosie

PART ONE
UP AND OUT

Who has gone farthest?
For I would go farther.

— Walt Whitman, *Excelsior*

CHAPTER ONE
LONDON

THE TWO SERBIAN butchers had Ed Rico pinned to a
table. They were getting ready to break his wrists with
the flat edge of a meat cleaver. He'd been playing cards
with them since yesterday lunchtime, in a store room
above their shop in Bethnal Green. Now it was late
afternoon and he couldn't afford to pay the four grand
he owed them.

The room was dark and squalid, with meat-filled
chest freezers humming against the walls, and a single
brown light bulb overhead. The Serbs had him face
down across the wooden packing crate they'd been
using as a game table, his arms stretched out, hands and
wrists dangling over the crate's edge. He felt the pile of
betting chips digging into him through his shirt. The big
guy holding him smelled of coffee and stale cigarette
smoke. His name was Pavle and Ed could feel his hot
breath on the hairs at the nape of his neck.

"Time's up, Ed, my friend."

Ed struggled. Through watering eyes, he watched
Grigor, the smaller of the two men, hefting the cleaver
from hand to hand.

"He'll be here with your money," Ed said, "I know he will."

Grigor looked up at the clock on the wall above the sink. He shook his head and his tongue clicked behind his gold teeth.

"He is already late."

He placed the cleaver carefully on the top of one of the freezers and rolled up the sleeves of his polyester shirt, like a backstreet surgeon preparing for the first incision. He had crude tattoos on both of his forearms, and fat gold rings on his fingers. His bald head shone like a bullet.

"It was a good game," he said, smoothing his thick moustache with the index finger and thumb of one hand. "And I am genuinely sorry it has to end this way."

Ed tried to pull free, but couldn't. Pavle's hands were like iron clamps.

Grigor leaned down. "Ed, you are a good taxi driver. I also know you are an artist, and for whatever it's worth to you, I very much like your work. But you must understand that this is a matter of honour."

Grigor cleared his throat and spat. Ed squeezed his eyes shut and gripped his hands into fists. His heart thumped against the wooden crate. He'd gone into this game hoping to hustle a few hundred quid for rent and art materials, but as usual, he'd pushed it too far. He'd been stubborn and reckless and dug his heels in when he should have folded. Now he could almost feel the flat edge of the knife striking his wrist, shattering the bone. Bile rose in his throat. He squeezed his hands until his fingernails dug into his palms.

This was really going to *hurt*.

He heard Grigor lift the cleaver. The floorboards creaked as the Serb took up position, shifting his weight from foot to foot as he prepared to deliver the first blow. Stretched over the crate, Ed winced in anticipation, every muscle tensed against the coming pain. He heard Grigor grunt as he lifted the knife high above his shoulder, ready to strike—

Thump! Thump! Thump!

The noise from the door startled them all. Still holding Ed's arms, Pavle recovered first.

"For your sake, I hope that's him."

Ed opened his eyes, blinking away tears. Hardly daring to breathe, he watched Grigor lower the knife, stalk to the door and crack it an inch.

"You have the money?" The Serb demanded.

"I do."

Grigor took a step back, making way. Beyond him, standing beneath a dusty bulb on an uncarpeted landing, stood the one person Ed had been praying for: his brother, Verne.

Verne worked for the BBC as a war correspondent. He was a well-built man with thinning hair, rimless glasses and an expensive olive trench coat. He stepped into the room as if afraid of getting his shoes dirty.

"It's all here." He pulled a fat envelope from his inside pocket. "Now, let him go."

Grigor snatched the envelope and tore off the end. He thumbed through the contents and then, obviously satisfied, muttered something to Pavle. The pressure on Ed's forearms eased.

Ed slid to his feet. He felt like crying. He rubbed his wrists, reassuring himself they were still okay. His legs were shaking. He stumbled over to his brother, who caught his arm, holding him up.

"Are you okay?"

Ed gave a nod. There were tears in his eyes. He swallowed hard.

Grigor slid the money into the pocket of his butcher's apron.

"Okay then, we are quits." He brandished the meat cleaver. Its sharpened edge flashed in the pale brown light from the room's solitary bulb. "But if we ever see you or your cheating brother again, we fuck you both up, you understand?"

Verne looked down at him, clearly unimpressed.

"Perfectly."

And then they were out of the room, stumbling down the narrow stairs to the front door, Ed's weight resting on his brother's shoulders, and a wild laugh bubbling in his throat.

HALF AN HOUR later, Ed sat hunched in the back bar of a high-ceilinged Tudor pub in Holborn, a few short steps from the Chancery Lane tube station, in a carved wooden booth that reminded him of a confessional. Verne was at the counter. He came back with two pints of bitter and a glass of brandy, and pushed the brandy across to Ed.

"Drink that. It'll stop you shaking."

"Thanks." Ed did as he was told. Then he coughed, and wiped his eyes.

"It wasn't my fault," he said. "They were cheating. They kept talking in Serbian. I knew they were up to something."

Verne heaved a sigh. "Then why did you stay? Why didn't you just walk away as soon as you realised what was happening?"

Ed shrugged. He'd been pushing his luck and he knew it.

"This is typical of you, Ed. It's just one disaster after another. When are you going to grow up?" Verne took off his glasses and rubbed his eyes. "You know, I had to call in some pretty big favours to get that money."

"I'll pay you back."

Verne shook his head. They both knew Ed hadn't sold a painting in months, and could barely afford to buy the materials he'd need to paint new ones. Since his mother's funeral, he'd been at work on a triptych depicting the half-scavenged hulls of oil tankers being broken up by gangs of ship-breakers on the grey mud flats of Chittagong in Bangladesh. Put together, the three panels formed a panorama showing fourteen, maybe fifteen ships. Yellow sparks flew in the twilight. Gangs of thin, grimy men clambered over the wrecked ships, like crabs attacking beached whale corpses. He'd layered the mud in thick daubs of brown and grey paint. Most of the men were stick figures. It looked like hell on Earth, and of course, no-one wanted to hang it on their wall.

Ed looked miserably at the office workers crowding the bar. It was only five o'clock, but it was already dark outside and felt much later. The pub itself dated back to the 1920s; it had a high pitched roof and a long bar counter sitting beneath a row of large oak vats. Many of the fixtures and fittings had been rescued from the previous building to stand on the site, the latest in a long line of ale houses, dating back as far as the seventeenth century.

"I'm sorry, Verne. I mean it. You've always been there for me."

His brother waved a dismissive hand. Today was the first time they'd spoken since their mother's funeral, six months before.

"Look, forget the money, okay? I've got more important things to worry about right now." He replaced his glasses and sucked the froth from the head of his pint.

"I was going to call you anyway," he began. "There's something I want to ask you."

Ed raised an eyebrow. "What is it?"

Verne put his glass down and hunched forward, resting his weight on his elbows. "It's Alice. I think she's having an affair."

Ed's drink tried to go down the wrong way. He coughed and wiped his mouth on the back of his hand.

"What makes you say that?"

Verne looked over the top of his rimless spectacles. "I don't know. Has she said anything to you?"

Ed dropped his hands out of sight and squeezed them into fists, knuckles brushing the smooth denim of his worn jeans.

"No. No, she hasn't."

Verne's fingernails rapped against the tabletop. "She's been different since I took that assignment in Somalia. Distant. And she's been taking more photo jobs here in town. You know she kept her apartment in Peckham? She spends two or three nights a week there now. Or says she does, anyway."

He let out a long, ragged sigh.

"I know she came to see you, Ed, when I was away. Did she say anything...?"

Ed shook his head. What else could he do? He couldn't forget the night Alice had shown up on the doorstep of his first floor studio flat. She'd been lonely and restless, looking for company. He'd asked her in and opened a bottle of wine, and they'd sat drinking by the window. The night had been warm and he'd left the blinds and windows open, letting in the lights and sounds of the city.

He remembered her auburn hair and the print her lipstick had left on the wineglass.

"It's not like Verne and I don't love each other," she'd said, looking down at her drink. "It's just that we don't know how to live together."

Ed had been sitting on the edge of his work table, beside his easel.

"I'm sure you'll work it out."

Alice had her legs crossed at the ankle. She wore black stockings. Her shoe dangled carelessly.

"Sometimes I think I chose the wrong brother."

Ed shifted position. He looked down at his hands.

"Don't say that."

She twirled the stem of her wineglass between thumb and forefinger. Her cheeks were flushed.

"Why not? It's true."

His mouth suddenly dry, Ed turned to look out of the open sash window.

"Okay," he said, "but you don't have to say it."

Outside, the streets were hot and quiet, and bathed in electric orange light. He watched a car slide past, its tyres making a soft ripping noise on the warm tarmac.

Ordinarily, he would have jumped at the chance to be with a girl like Alice, married or not. She was clever and funny, and fiercely independent. And he'd known her longer than Verne had. Yet he couldn't get away from the fact that she was his brother's wife. That was one line he didn't want to cross. He didn't want to be that kind of guy.

He drained his glass and rose to get another bottle. As he did so, Alice slipped the wedding ring from her finger and dropped it into her handbag. She sat up straight and brushed a strand of auburn hair behind her ear, and started to unbutton her blouse.

"I know how you feel about me, Ed."

THAT HAD ALL happened over a year ago. Thinking about it now made Ed's hands shake all over again.

"She didn't—I mean, she didn't say anything to me." He could feel his cheeks burning.

Watching him, Verne's eyes narrowed the way they did when he caught the scent of a really good story. He sat back and used an index finger to push his glasses firmly back onto the bridge of his nose.

"Ed? Is there something you're not telling me?"

"No."

Verne leaned across the table, almost out of his seat.

"What is it, Ed?"

"Nothing."

Ed's eyes were watering. He bit his lip, fighting back a nervous laugh.

"I know when you're lying, Ed, and you're lying now. Look at you. Come on, if you know something, anything, you have to tell me."

In his peripheral vision, Ed saw faces turning their way, drawn to the brewing confrontation like sharks scenting blood in the water. He brought his hands up.

"Verne, please—"

He looked up and saw his face reflected in his brother's specs.

"I'm sorry, I can't. I don't know anything."

Verne frowned. "Don't lie to me, Ed. I can tell there's something—" He broke off, eyes wide.

"Oh *shit*," he said. "It's you, isn't it?"

Ed looked down at his hands.

"Shit. She told me she'd seen you. I should have known." Verne raked his fingers back through his thinning hair. "Jesus Christ, Ed. What were you thinking?"

Ed pressed back in the booth. The smirk was gone now. His heart beat so hard he could feel it at the back of his throat.

"Look, Verne—"

Verne's mobile rang. With a curse, the older man pulled it out and checked the caller display.

"Don't say another word, Ed. Not another fucking word, okay?"

Still scowling, he pressed the answer button and clapped the phone to his ear. After a few seconds he said, "I'll be there as soon as I can. Tell the camera crew to wait for me." Then he lurched to his feet and pocketed the phone, swept an angry hand through his hair, and straightened the lapels of his trench coat with an angry tug.

"I've got to go. There's something going on by the Embankment. Some kind of emergency. They want me to report on it."

Ed swallowed. He knew that if he let his brother walk out now, they'd never have a chance to talk this through. That would be it for them. Verne would cut him out of his life again, as he had after the funeral.

"Verne, I—"

Verne turned on his heel.

"Goodbye, Ed." He stalked out of the room, down the passage that led past the oak-panelled front bar, out into the street.

For a moment, Ed sat and endured the curious stares of his fellow patrons. Then with a sigh, he pulled himself out of the booth, and gave chase.

When he got outside, he found it was raining. The shop windows were bright with Christmas lights and decorations. He splashed across the street, weaving between the buses and taxis, to the steps of the Tube station, catching Verne at the ticket barrier.

"Don't go," he said, tugging his brother's sleeve.

Verne shook him off without a word. Without looking back, he swiped his ticket and barged his way through the barrier.

Ed didn't have a ticket. He looked over at the queue for the machines. By the time he got a ticket, Verne would be on a train and gone. Without stopping to think, he jumped the barrier. Shouts came from the guards, but he didn't stop to look. Scrambling to his feet, he pushed through the crowd and tackled his brother at the top of the escalator, grabbing his arm.

"We need to talk."

Somewhere, an alarm rang. Verne shoved him away. He stepped backwards onto the moving escalator and pointed an angry finger at Ed.

"Stay the fuck away from me."

"But—"

"I mean it. Take one more step and I'll hit you."

"But Verne—"

And then two armed police officers were yelling at Ed to kneel and put his hands behind his head. As they cuffed him, Verne turned away in disgust, riding the escalator down towards the platform. Kneeling there, on the cold wet floor at the top of the stairs, with one of the officers holding a firearm to the back of his head and the other talking into a radio, Ed watched his brother's retreating back. Verne had his shoulders hunched and head tipped back, looking at the ceiling. Ahead of him, the air at the foot of the escalator rippled like a heat haze.

Ed blinked and shook his head. For a moment, he thought his eyes were playing tricks. Then as he watched, the haze solidified. A purple arch shimmered into place, filling the base of the sloping tunnel like a hungry mouth: a mouth into which the metal steps of the escalator were falling one by one, disappearing in searing flashes of actinic white light as they did so.

Ignoring the angry curses of the police officers, Ed struggled.

"Verne!"

He saw his brother's shoulders twitch. Then Verne finally looked down and saw what was in front of him.

The air pressure in the tunnel changed. Ed felt his ears pop. He thrashed against his cuffs until one of the policemen slapped the side of his head hard enough to crack his nose into the moving rail of the escalator. Then the man noticed what was happening below. Ed heard him swear. Both policemen started shouting into their radio mikes. They still had their guns in hand, but now they didn't know where to point them.

Ed raised his head. His nose felt broken. Hot blood dripped from his chin.

"Verne!"

Through watery eyes, he saw his brother trying to climb against the downward motion of the stairs, but he was too close to the arch and Ed could see he wasn't going to make it. The stairs were falling away beneath his feet.

Ed strained forward. Their eyes met for a second, and Verne stopped moving.

"Run!" Ed yelled.

Verne shook his head. He closed his eyes. He let the stairs carry him down until the wounded escalator gave a final grinding screech and collapsed. Ed caught a final glimpse of his brother falling backwards into the archway, arms outstretched, his body disappearing in a flash of white.

THE BUBBLE BELT

TIERS CROSS WAS a small planet orbiting just beyond the outer fringes of the Bubble Belt. It was icy and cold but it had been given an atmosphere, and two artificial orbiting suns that kept the surface from completely freezing up.

Only one city sprawled across its icy plains. Uptown, there were bright lights, crowds and skyscrapers, but down by the spaceport, drifters and tired hustlers worked the narrow streets. They huddled at windy intersections in flapping coats, waiting for the right deal, the big score. Katherine Abdulov moved among them, avoiding the ebb and flow of their skinny bodies. She had an appointment to keep with a potential client. Her insulated boots crunched on the frozen ground, her breath coming in ragged clouds. She wore a long grey coat over a set of stained ship fatigues, and a warm cap with fur earflaps. The glyphs on her shoulder identified her as the master of the *Ameline*, an old trading vessel currently mothballed in orbit.

She walked through the same old familiar street smells: the greasy stink of the fast food joints, the mingled reek of urine and vomit, the burned plastic tang of fuel drum alley fires. Her ears picked up the electric fizz of the illuminated signs in the windows of the bars she passed; the buzz of a tattooist's needle from a shop on the corner; raised voices and the crash of shattering glass off somewhere down the block.

Above the street, the Bubble Belt stretched across the night sky like a curtain of beads, filling the heavens. It was a Dyson swarm of bubble habitats, as wide as the orbit of Mars. There were maybe a billion individual habitats in there, each one sporting a different size, shape and internal environment. No-one knew who'd built them. Most were between one and two hundred metres across. Some had working biospheres with animals and insects. Others were tight-packed mazes of empty corridors. Some were filled with water or gas, others with nothing more than soil. But all were as unique as snowflakes, and all perfectly self-contained.

At the Belt's heart, something like a naked singularity lay wreathed in a fog of incandescent gas. As a fixed point where the rules of space and time broke down, it resisted the mind's attempts to interpret it. When looking at it, some saw a mirrored sphere, others a greasy, writhing mess of flabby tendrils. Nobody saw it in the same way twice. It had driven good men insane. It was an inexplicable gnarl in the grain of the universe and after a while, in order to preserve your sanity, you learned to stop noticing it.

Although a handful of the Dyson habitats had been settled, the vast majority remained unexplored. The crews scouting them called themselves 'bubble breakers.' In all, there were upwards of fifty breaker crews operating in the Belt at any one time. They were salvage teams and they were scavengers. They hit the bubbles, drilled their way in, stripped out anything useful-looking, and auctioned it online, to the highest bidder. It was a dirty and dangerous get-rich-quick kind of a job, and in these lean economic times it tended to attract dangerous and desperate people. People with little left to lose.

People like Katherine Abdulov.

Twenty-six years old and the estranged scion of a wealthy trading family, Kat had come to the Belt the same way so many others did: out of fuel and out of funds. She'd been hoping to score a lucrative charter, carrying a few rich prospectors and their recovered loot. Low on cash, she'd gambled everything to get here, a desperate last throw that left her with nothing, not even enough money to refuel her ship. Unable to find either passengers or cargo, she'd been forced to put the *Ameline* into storage and join a breaker crew.

She looked up, to where a green dot indicated the position of her ship on her visual overlay. Increasing the magnification in her eye, she managed to resolve a recognizable and familiar silhouette: the *Ameline* lay in a standard parking orbit above the moon. Tiny readouts flickered in the corner of Kat's eye, giving estimates of distance and relative velocity. Red and green navigation lights blinked along the ship's blunt, wedge-shaped hull. Maintenance tugs nosed around it like curious fish around a sleeping shark.

The *Ameline* had been a derelict when Kat had first found it, half-cannibalised, stripped for parts, and it had taken weeks of patient work to get it flight-worthy again. Since then, she'd worked her way along the branching trade routes that stretched, like the threads of a spider's web, from Earth to the Outer Worlds, hauling whatever passengers or cargoes were available, trying to get home, back to Strauli. Somehow, she'd managed to stay one step ahead of the wolves crying outside the airlock door. Against all the odds, she'd lurched from one job to the next, keeping the old ship flying until finally, broken down and busted, she'd reached the Belt.

A chill wind blew up the street. Kat returned her vision to its default setting. She wondered if the ship's eager, dog-like mind felt as restless as she did.

On Tiers Cross, life was tough at the bottom of the food chain. There were too many people here seeking their fortunes. Every time a ship arrived, it brought more of them. They all came to Tiers Cross looking to make a fast buck. And ninety-nine times out of a hundred, they were disappointed. If they weren't killed or crippled, they wound up broke and starving. They huddled around fires burning in old fuel drums, or slept uncomfortably beneath tarpaulins, waking at dawn to find themselves covered in frost. Some picked through heaps of scrap for saleable fragments of obsolete cyber-crap, or tried to hawk homemade jewellery to tourists. Others, like Kat, joined breaker crews when they'd spent the last of their savings. It was dangerous, but it was the only option they had left.

When Kat did it, she packed her few possessions into a bag and walked down to the yard in the chill morning air to enlist. There were two crews hiring that day, but she discounted the first straight away. Fat Keith had a bad rep. He'd lost eight men on his last expedition, and word had it that in order to save his own skin, he'd abandoned three of them in an airless bubble. Giving him a wide berth, Kat signed instead with the second crew. It was led by a known alcoholic with the name of Radford. He had a fierce black beard and hard blue eyes, and an old military tug tricked out for civilian use.

"I expect you to do your job, and to do what you're told," he blustered.

His crew consisted of Kat and two others. The first bubble they hit was refrigerated inside: all snow and ice, and nothing of any worth. The second wasn't much better, but they managed to rip out an air filter that fetched a good price when they later put it up for auction.

Before they had the chance to find anything else of worth, Radford slipped and broke his leg in the third bubble. He was drunk. He lost his footing on a ladder and fell ten metres onto a hard rock floor, which ended the expedition and left Kat back on the streets of Tiers Cross with barely enough in her pocket to cover the *Ameline*'s berthing fees.

So, for the last few weeks, she'd been haunting the port bars looking for work. Some days, she hadn't been able to afford to eat. It had been a miserable, desperate time, but now, at long last, it looked as if her luck had changed. She had a lead and, if this meeting worked out the way she hoped, she'd soon have a couple of paying passengers and funds to refuel the ship.

THE BAR SHE was aiming for lay at the end of an irregular row of prefab shelters, relics left over from the first expeditions to arrive. Their generators had powered the settlement's first, faltering steps, and their tough walls had given shelter to the colonists during the early blizzards that threatened to wipe everything else away.

She reached out and gave the nearest an affectionate pat with her gloved hand, as if acknowledging an old friend. Beneath the graffiti and frost, she saw the faded flags and insignia of long-dead organisations: NASA, USAF, ESA...

Ahead, she heard jukebox music blowing up the street and shivered. The tune was an old electric blues number, and one of Victor's favourites. She squared her shoulders. She didn't want to think about Victor. Their last fight had taken place years ago, and light years away. Since then, she'd tried her best to forget him. Now, annoyingly, he was here on Tiers Cross. She'd seen his ship arrive on the Grid this afternoon, and she'd been lying low ever since, afraid of running into him. The last thing she wanted was for him to see her like this, penniless and desperate.

She blocked the music out of her mind and kept walking.

When she reached the bar, it was the same low, scrappy affair she remembered from previous visits, some years back. Its fizzing neon sign featured a stylized skull and crossed bones, and the name: Admiral Benbow. The walls were built from old packing crates and sheets of corrugated iron. Whenever a shuttle lifted from the port, the windows rattled.

Kat pushed through into the bar's stale warmth. The place was mostly empty. This early, only the hardcore drinkers were at the bar. She walked across and slid into a vacant booth. Nobody met her eyes, although a few pinged her neural implants with their own, checking out her public profile. Ignoring them, she took off her fur hat and shook out her mussed chestnut hair with a gloved hand. The table had a chipped plastic touch-screen, and she used it to order a glass of Palinka brandy. She didn't look up when the waitress brought it over, just dropped a handful of local coins onto the woman's tray. From beneath a lowered brow, she scanned the bar, from the gaming tables at the front of the room to the scuffed cybersex cubicles at the back. The place itself hadn't changed much in the years since her last visit. In fact, looking around she was fairly certain it hadn't even been cleaned. Two tables over, a man watched her. He wore a hooded black robe, like a monk's habit.

"Captain Abdulov?"

She narrowed her eyes. "You're Francis Hind?"

The man rose. Beneath his hood, he had short hair, grey at the temples.

"I am."

"You didn't tell me you were an Acolyte."

He slid into the chair opposite.

"I didn't realise it was relevant."

Kat shrugged. She couldn't afford to be picky.

"It's not." She dismissed the matter with a flick of her fingers. "Now, how can I help?"

Hind glanced around, and then leaned discreetly inward. In this light, his skin looked as grey as his hair.

"I'm searching for passage to Strauli Quay," he said.

"For two of you?"

"Yes, myself and one other."

Kat sat back in her chair. "And the fee we discussed?"

The man patted a concealed pocket in his robe.

"I have it."

He pulled out an antiquated palmtop and transferred the money to her account. As soon as he had, she used her neural implant to order a priority refuelling. Then she shook the man's hand, gave him an estimated departure time, and watched as he bade farewell and left the bar, tugging his hood forward as he did so, to protect his face from the wind.

When he'd gone and the door had banged shut behind him, she allowed herself a sigh of relief. She'd been stuck on this worthless planet for three long months, getting cold and tired, and wondering if she'd ever fly again. Now, she could hardly wait to get airborne, to open the throttle and feel the kick of the exhaust, the giddy freedom of the up-and-out.

Two passengers weren't enough to make the voyage pay for itself, but they were enough to fuel the ship, and who knew what she'd find when she got to Strauli? Would her parents be waiting for her? Would they be pleased to see her, or would they turn her away again? She picked up her glass and swirled the contents. She would find out. Whatever welcome they gave her, anything beat being stuck in this chilly backwater.

Kat downed the remains of her drink, and rose to leave. She was pulling her cap back over her head when the door of the bar burst open and three men piled in laughing, brushing flakes of snow from their flight jackets, talking in off-world accents.

They stopped when they saw her, and the tallest stepped forward. He pulled down the scarf covering his mouth and nose.

"Ah, Kat." He seemed embarrassed. Kat's heart thumped in her chest. This was exactly what she'd hoped to avoid.

"Hello Victor." She felt her fists tense. She'd last seen Victor Luciano on a planet seven light years from here, and on that occasion, she'd thrown a drink in his face.

"It's been a long time," she said.

Victor's lip curled as he looked her up and down, obviously comparing her thick-soled boots, drab grey coat and army surplus hat to his own immaculately clean flight suit.

"Not long enough." He tried to step around her but she moved to block him.

"Get out of my way," he said quietly, looking around the bar, obviously uncomfortable.

"Can we talk?"

"No."

He moved past her. She tried to stop him but he shouldered her away, and she staggered into the arms of one of his comrades, who wrapped a thick arm around her throat. She struggled and got in a few kicks but couldn't squirm free. Her palms itched for the pistols she'd left on her ship.

Victor stood arms folded, watching her thrash about with a look of embarrassment on his face. After a minute or so, he shook his head sadly.

"Throw her out, boys."

CHAPTER THREE
ALICE

A MONTH AFTER Verne's disappearance, Ed summoned the courage to visit Alice at her apartment in Peckham. He left his taxi in a residents-only space and climbed the metal outside steps to her front door. She answered his knocks in a dressing gown, her auburn hair ruffled and flattened on one side, her eyes raw and puffy, smudged with yesterday's eyeliner. She took him in and offered to make him a cup of coffee.

"You'll have to have it black, I'm afraid. There's no milk."

Her apartment comprised a couple of cluttered rooms on the top floor of a subdivided brick town house on a quiet street. The front room had a small kitchenette at one end and a television against one wall. The walls were covered with framed prints of photographs she'd taken. They were mostly pictures of collapsed and overgrown buildings, but there were a few pictures of the night sky, taken from various locations. An Ikea sofa separated the kitchenette from the rest of the room, and judging from the half-eaten meals and sticky wine glasses on the carpet beneath it,

Ed guessed Alice had been using it as a bed for several days. A duvet had been scrunched into a heap at one end. He perched on the sofa arm beside it.

"I heard the police dropped the charges," Alice said.

Ed scratched at the week's worth of stubble on his chin. The bruises around his nose and eyes were mostly gone now, but remained fresh in his memory.

"They had better things to worry about. I got off with a fine and a slap on the wrist."

Steam came from the kettle spout. The switch clicked off.

"You're lucky you weren't shot. What did you think you were doing, jumping the barriers like that?"

"I had to stop him."

Alice poured out the hot water and stirred the coffee with an angry rattle of the teaspoon.

"I wish you had." She thrust the mug at him.

He said, "Have you seen the news?"

Alice sniffled wetly on her sleeve. She wore jogging bottoms beneath the robe, and had thick hiking socks on her feet.

"What news?"

He leaned toward her. "There are other arches now, maybe a dozen of them. Two in the States and one in Venezuela. Four in Africa. Perhaps another three in the Far East, some more in Russia."

Alice frowned. She seemed about to say something, but stopped herself, as if too worn-out to make the effort. Instead, she opened the fridge and pulled out a half-empty bottle of Shiraz.

Ed got to his feet. He'd been glued to the TV since his brother's disappearance. He'd seen the restless crowds milling on the streets around Chancery Lane and the

Embankment, with their candles and petrol bombs, unsure whether to smash the arches or worship them.

"China's closed its borders," he said. "Germany's gone for martial law. Everyone's scared. I even saw some troops on the streets of Hackney yesterday, and there are police barricades and roadblocks everywhere. I got stopped and questioned twice on my way over here."

Alice pulled the cork out of the bottle with her teeth and spat it into the sink. She swilled a dirty glass under the cold tap, shook it dry, and then sloshed the remaining wine into it.

"So everything's falling apart? That's your news? That's what you came all this way to tell me?"

Ed cleared his throat.

"A guy in America found one of the arches and went through it."

"So what?"

"He came back."

Alice put the wine bottle down with a clunk.

"*What*?"

Ed reached for her hand. "He went through and a couple of hours later, he came back. I saw the pictures on CNN. He had frostbite and bruises, and he kept spitting up blood, but he made it back."

Alice looked pale. "W-where had he been?"

"Mars."

"You're *kidding*."

Ed shook his head. "They analysed the grit on his boots. He went to Mars, and somehow he stumbled back through the gate without dying of cold or suffocation."

He watched Alice rub her forehead.

"So what are you saying? Verne's dead?"

"Not necessarily." He gave her hand a squeeze. "You see, while he was there on Mars, this guy saw more arches. NASA sent through an astronaut in a spacesuit and she confirmed it. The scientists think they're part of a network."

He slipped a battered Tube map from the back pocket of his jeans and spread it out on the kitchen counter.

"Imagine each of these stations is an arch," he said, tracing the Bakerloo line with his finger. "And they're all linked. You can get from any point on the network to any other if you follow the right route, jumping from one station to the next."

Alice bit her lip. Her eyes were damp and confused. "So, if it's that easy, why hasn't Verne come back?"

Ed cupped his other hand over hers, enfolding it.

"Maybe he's trying to. Maybe he's stuck on the wrong part of the network and he's on the Central Line when he should be on the Circle."

She slipped away from him and wiped her eyes on the back of her hand. She walked over to the window, and the thin winter light kissed her face. The front room window looked out over the bare trees of the Common. Leaves blew around on the grass.

She said, "You want to go after him, don't you?"

"Yes."

She shook her head. "Well, you're crazy. You don't know what's on the other side. And besides, you'll never get close enough to an arch if the police have them all blocked off."

Ed folded the map away and picked up his coffee.

"You may be right. But if they keep appearing like this, then sooner or later, if I'm quick enough, maybe I'll get to one before they can throw a cordon around it."

Alice turned.

"And then what? What happens if you appear on, say, Mars while he's on Pluto? How are you going to find him?"

Ed rubbed his eyes. Whatever she said, he knew he had to try. He couldn't stand the thought of his brother still out there alive, still angry at him, still trying to make his way home. He had to find him and bring him back. He had to make things right.

He walked over to Alice and took the wine glass from her fingers.

"This isn't doing you any good," he said.

He made her take a shower. When she came back, she looked better. Her cheeks were flushed and she wore one of her husband's old sweaters. Her legs were bare. She had her hair wrapped in a towel.

"Look," she said. "What happened between us, what we did, was wrong."

Ed's coffee had gone cold. He tipped it down the sink.

"So, it's definitely over?"

"Of course it's over. How can you even ask?"

"I wasn't asking. I thought—"

"Are you glad he's gone, is that it? What are you thinking? That I'll fall into your arms like nothing's happened?"

"No, of course not."

"Then shut up."

She curled herself onto the couch and pulled the duvet over her legs. She looked warm and tired, and ready to sleep.

"I think you'd better leave now."

Ed looked down at her. He stuck his chin out. "You know, I'm going to find him, don't you?"

Alice wriggled lower, eyes shut.

"I'll believe it when I see it, Ed."

WORLD NEWS

Click here to subscribe to RSS feed ■

US President calls for calm after night of rioting

Unrest triggered by yesterday's grenade attack on Wilshire Blvd arch.

Hundreds hurt overnight in clashes with Los Angeles police and National Guard.

World's oldest man dies in Tokyo, aged 143

Relatives attribute longevity to exercise and diet of rice and raw fish.

Hurricane winds batter Miami
for the fourth time in three months

Thousands homeless.

Governor declares national disaster.

Vatican: 'Arches are a test of faith'

Pope urges caution.

New water war in Middle East?

Droughts spark fresh hostilities.

Refugees flee arch sites in Midwest

Unconfirmed alien sightings spark widespread panic.

World Health Organisation fears arch-related pandemic

WHO recommends strict quarantine procedures.

Urges governments to be vigilant for 'alien pathogens.'

CHAPTER FOUR
SABOTAGE

A COUPLE OF hours after her scuffle in the bar, Katherine Abdulov found herself sitting in an office on the upper floor of a two-storey bunker on the edge of Tiers Cross's main port. The windows looked out over the landing field. From where she sat, she could see the sparks of shuttles lifting from the terminal buildings at the far end of the field.

She was there at the surprise invitation of Ezra Abdulov-Paulsen, a distant cousin on her mother's side. She hadn't even known her family had a permanent office on this planet.

Sitting behind a plastic desk with his back to the window, Ezra was a small, slight man about the same physical age as her, with a tuft of blond hair that gave his rounded face a boyish aspect.

Just looking at him made her feel old.

She'd been travelling since her early twenties, jumping from star system to star system, on one trading vessel or another; and while a jump through hyperspace felt instantaneous to the crew of the ship making it, in reality it lasted the same length of time it took light to cross the intervening distance. This, when dealing with distances measured in tens or dozens of light years, meant Kat was objectively quite a lot older than she looked, and certainly a hell of lot older than the young man on the other side of the desk.

"If you were still an employee, we could file an official complaint on your behalf," he said.

Ezra's invite had arrived less than an hour after the brawl at the bar. A few blows had been exchanged. It hadn't been a real fight, but Kat's lip was swollen and she knew she'd have a black eye in the morning.

"There's no need," she said.

Ezra opened a drawer and produced a half-empty bottle of whiskey, and two tin mugs. He poured a measure into each and slid one across the desk to her.

"On the contrary, I think you should file a personal complaint with the port authority, and the sooner the better," he said. "Anything to keep Luciano tied up here for as long as possible."

Kat sniffed the mug he'd given her.

"And why would you want me to do that?"

Ezra appraised her with a look. Then he drained his mug, coughed, and dabbed his lips with a handkerchief. He blinked rapidly and despite his bravado, Kat got the impression he rarely drank.

"We have a bit of a problem, Katherine. The family, I mean. And we need your help."

Kat put her mug back on the desk without sampling its contents.

"I should have known."

Ezra gave an apologetic shrug.

"I know you were excluded from the family because of your, ah, association with Victor Luciano. I also know that association ended acrimoniously, some years ago."

Kat folded her arms across her chest. Victor captained for a rival trading firm, and her relationship with him had been viewed with distaste by both sides. To the rest of the galaxy, it was ancient history. But to her, travelling between the stars, only a matter of months had passed, and the feelings were still raw.

"The thing is," Ezra continued, "we know Luciano's heading to Djatt for the Pep harvest."

Kat shrugged. "Don't you have a ship going?"

Ezra pursed his lips. "We had the *Kilimanjaro*, but it's been delayed. We can't get a replacement here in time to beat him. It's a logistical thing."

Kat raised an eyebrow. Prized by aficionados and epicures, and produced from a plant flowering only once every hundred years, Pep was a mildly addictive stimulant with a peppery, metallic taste. A single crate of it could fetch enough to buy a brand new starship.

"Delayed?"

"There was an explosion of some sort. Reports are patchy but, unofficially, we suspect sabotage."

Kat sat forward. The Abdulov family had enjoyed a near-total monopoly on supplies of the drug for centuries. To lose it now would be a serious blow to their reputation and prestige.

"Why not send a ship from Strauli?"

Ezra shook his head. "They're seven light years away. The first they'll hear about this is when Victor passes through the system, seven years from now. By the time they can ready a ship, assuming they have one in port, he'll already be well on his way. No, if we want to beat him, then our only option's to send the *Ameline*."

Kat brushed a speck of lint from the knee of her ship fatigues. "But I don't work for you anymore," she reminded him.

Ezra spread his hands on the desk. "If you do this for us, we're willing to let bygones be bygones. We'll refit and refuel your ship, and we'll reinstate you as an employee and family member, giving you full refuelling privileges at all family facilities."

Kat blinked in surprise. "You're serious?"

"I absolutely am. And to show you how serious, I'm prepared to authorise an advance on your first month's wages, at full captain's salary."

Kat eyed him as he slipped the whiskey bottle back into his desk. Sitting there, he looked every inch the young and ambitious bureaucrat, working to earn the promotion that would take him away from this provincial posting, back to the family's head office on Strauli. And young as he was, he doubtless saw her expulsion from the family as an old quarrel, a dry and dusty fragment of folklore from before his time as a family rep.

To her, the wounds were still fresh.

"I'm doing pretty well on my own, you know."

"I'm sure you are. But this isn't about you, Katherine. Not really."

"Then what is it about?"

Ezra swivelled his chair to face the window. Looking out over the landing field, he steepled his fingers against the tip of his nose.

"The truth is, we're short on ships and we need you. In fact, I'm forwarding you a contract right now." He tapped the arm of his chair and immediately, in her right eye, her implant flashed an icon to indicate receipt of the file.

"And what happens if I refuse?"

Ezra turned his chair to face her again. He spread his hands on the desk.

"I'm offering you a way back, Katherine. What more do you want?"

"An apology might help."

Ezra shook his head ruefully, as if he'd been expecting her to say that. Then he tapped his fingertips on the table.

"Katherine, I grew up hearing stories about you and the way you turned your back on us. I was at school when they took away your commission. But for what it's worth, I've read the files, and I am sorry for the way you were treated."

He bowed his head.

Kat leaned back in her chair and frowned. She hadn't expected him to sound so sincere.

"Do my parents know about this?"

"Your mother and father are on Strauli Quay."

"So this isn't an official apology? They won't hear about any of this for another seven years, at least?"

Ezra smiled bravely. "I assure you, I have full autonomy to act in the family's best interests. If you sign that contract, I'll provide you with a letter of introduction explaining everything, and they'll have to accept it."

He straightened his tie. "Look the fact is, your *family* needs you, Katherine. It's a matter of honour."

"And all I have to do is beat Victor to Djatt?"

"Yes."

She licked her swollen lip. Despite her pride and lingering resentment, it was a tempting offer, and would give her the funds to fly again. More than that, it would piss Victor off.

A grin tugged one corner of her mouth. She used her neural implant to access the contract and run it through a standard legal filter. It all seemed in order.

"Okay," she said. "I'll do it."

She stamped the contract with her personal encrypted seal and fired it back to the young man on the other side of the desk. She saw his gaze flicker as he confirmed receipt. Then he rose and held out his hand.

"Welcome home," he said.

WHEN KAT GOT to the commercial shuttle terminal an hour later, she found the Acolyte waiting by the departure gate, and he wasn't alone.

"This is Toby Drake," the old man said.

Kat nodded. Drake was a tall, dark-skinned young man with a chocolate-coloured leather coat and a cumbersome suitcase.

"It's mostly books," he said shyly, as he shook her hand.

"Books?" Kat's neural implant contained a hundred million words of electronic text, and hyperlinks connecting it to the ship's memory, which held at least a hundred million more. Using modern data storage solutions, you could fit every book ever written onto a crystal the size of a human fist. Why would anyone need a whole suitcase just to carry that?

"Uh-huh, lots of books in the suitcase. I hope that's okay? Only Mr Hind here thought there might be a weight restriction?"

Kat tapped the side of the case with the toe of her boot.

"What kind of books?" she asked.

Drake unclipped the lid and extracted a cloth-bound volume. He held it out to her, smiling shyly.

"*Real* books."

Eyebrows raised, Kat turned the dog-eared hardback over in her hands. It was heavier than she'd expected, considering it was made of paper, and it smelled fusty, like the algae in the *Ameline*'s sewage recycler. She didn't dare open it. She had no idea how it was supposed to work. So instead, she handed it back and led the two men through the boarding gate into the shuttle's passenger cabin. Drake took the seat next to her, and talked to her as the pilots taxied them across the ice to the runway. He had a nice voice, but he was nervous. His hands fidgeted on the arm rests. Between his stammers and pauses, she gathered he was a research scholar, a physicist attached to one of the teams studying the Gnarl at the centre of the Bubble Belt, dragged away from his studies by an unexpected summons.

"Honestly, I don't know what I'm doing here," he said.

Two days ago Francis Hind, the Acolyte, had arrived at Drake's office carrying a handwritten invitation from the leader of an expedition planning to study the Dho Ark. The Ark was a rocky planetoid on the outskirts of the Strauli system. It had been hollowed out, coated in sheets of artificial diamond, and converted into a starship by its inhabitants, the reclusive Dho. About two metres in height, the Dho wore dark gowns similar to those sported by their human agents, the Acolytes. The gowns brushed the floor as they walked, making them appear to glide, and their heads were permanently encased in baroque, chitin-like helmets that gave them the appearance of stylised stag beetles. According to

Toby Drake, no-one really knew where the helmets ended and the Dho began.

"It's a hell of an opportunity," he said. "Apart from the Acolytes, this is the first time humans have been allowed into the interior of the Ark. I—I just don't understand why I've been chosen. By the time I get there, the team will have been in place for fourteen years, and I don't know what more I'll be able to add. And besides, it's not my area of specialty. There are at least a dozen better qualified candidates on Tiers Cross alone."

Kat looked across him to the window, and saw they'd reached the end of the runway and were rolling to a halt on the compacted snow, awaiting launch clearance from the tower. Beyond the glare of the spaceport lights, she could see the bubbles of the Belt sparkling like scattered sand in the darkened sky.

"Nervous?" she asked him.

He looked at her. "How can you t-tell?" His knuckles were white.

"A lucky guess."

The noise from the engines rose to a deafening shriek. Drake closed his eyes. His forehead shone with sweat.

"Just relax," she said. "Why don't you tell me about your work?"

He gave her a sideways look. "With the Gnarl?"

"Yes, why not? It might help."

"O-okay." He took a deep breath. "Well for a start, most people think it's a naked singularity, but it's not. It isn't dense enough. If it were a gravitational singularity, its mass would be huge. But as far as we can tell, it weighs less than a medium sized star."

Kat made a face. "I looked at it once and it made my eyes hurt. How do you study it?"

The young man smiled, as if he heard this question all the time. His teeth were very white.

"We do most of our analysis using computers. We try not to spend too much time looking directly at it, but you know, it doesn't hurt to take a glance every now and then."

Kat said, "A breaker once told me it was artificial, built by the same race that built the bubbles."

Drake waggled a hand. "Iffy," he said. "We don't know that for sure. It could be a natural phenomena. Perhaps it was there first, and whoever built the Belt did so in order to study it?"

Kat licked her lips. She was eager to get off the ground.

"So," she said, "we still don't know what it's *for*?"

"Maybe it isn't *for* anything. Maybe it just *is*."

"That sounds like a cop-out."

Drake's teeth flashed. "Maybe it is. But we're learning a great deal just by studying it. The arch network, for example."

"What about it?"

"It turns out that the arches all resonate on the same electromagnetic frequencies as the Gnarl."

Kat frowned, feeling she'd missed something. "What does that mean?"

"It means the Gnarl may be powering the network."

"Really?"

Drake shrugged a leather-clad shoulder.

"I don't know, but I'll tell you one thing." His teeth flashed again. "I'd give my right nut to find out."

Behind them, the engine noise increased. Then the pilot let the brakes off and the shuttle leapt forward, kicking them back in their seats.

As they rattled down the runway, Kat felt her heart pump a wild surge of joy. A grin split her face, and her feet drummed excitedly on the floor. Beside her, Drake sat stiffly in his seat, still sweating, eyes closed.

As the cabin tipped upward and the wheels left the tarmac, he reached for her hand.

CHAPTER FIVE
AMETHYST

ED RICO WAS painting at his easel, in front of the sash window of his apartment. The window looked down on the darkened street, and the buildings opposite: an estate agent, now closed for the night; a church repurposed as office space; an off-licence still open on the corner. Terraced houses. Sun-bleached poppies on the war memorial in the park at the end of the road. Shadowy back alleys and garages. *For Sale* signs like brave little flags. Black railings. Scaffolding.

When his mobile rang, he put the brush down and lifted the phone to his ear.

"Ed?" It was Alice. They hadn't spoken since that night in her apartment, six months ago. "Ed, I've got an arch in my field."

Ed looked at his watch. It was around ten-thirty. He knew Alice no longer stayed at her flat in Peckham, that she'd left London some weeks ago for Verne's old farmhouse on the other side of High Wycombe, forty miles away.

"I can be there in an hour," he said.

Above the rooftops, the brightly-lit towers of Canary Wharf stood like sentries. An armoured car rumbled past below, its spotlight sweeping the pavements. Helicopters criss-crossed the sky. Ed gave his brush a quick rinse in the jam jar on the windowsill and went over to the wardrobe, where he swapped his jogging bottoms for a pair of black 501 jeans. He pulled a green army surplus combat jacket over his paint-flecked black t-shirt, and laced his feet into a sturdy pair of black leather work boots.

His apartment was an anonymous two-room studio above a newsagent in Millwall, on the upper floor of a converted brown brick terrace, with a mattress on the bare floor and canvasses stacked against a chair by the door. When it was new, in the building boom at the start of the new century, it had been a desirable residence; now, two decades later, it was fucked. The paint had started to flake around the windows, light fittings dangled loose, the ceilings were cracked and stained, food cupboards no longer closed properly. It was as if the house, a Victorian brick terrace, had begun reverting to its pre-redevelopment condition, slowly reassuming its shabby natural state.

Moving to the kitchenette, he retrieved his emergency bag from the cupboard beside the fridge. It was a holdall containing a first aid kit and foil survival blanket, a couple of torches, a gas stove, some teabags, a penknife, and enough dried rations and water purification tablets to last a week. You could buy kits like it anywhere. Since the arches came, people were scared. No-one knew what to make of them.

Ed himself had been pulling double shifts at the taxi ranks. He'd tried throwing himself into his work. He'd taken fares no one else would touch. But with the radio and newspapers reporting new arches opening almost daily, nothing he did, took or drank could blot out the guilt he felt at his brother's loss. Nor could it dampen his passion for Alice. Try as he might, it was always there, seething away.

An old semiautomatic pistol lay on top of Ed's survival kit, wrapped in an oiled rag. He'd stolen it from the one-legged Iraq war veteran in the flat down the hall. He peeled off the rag and put the gun in the pocket of his combat jacket. Then he hefted the bag onto his shoulder and took a last look at the half-finished picture on the easel: a messy and expressionistic portrait of Alice as he remembered her on the evening of her wedding to Verne, three years ago, standing on the terrace outside the hotel.

VERNE AND ALICE *decided to get married in the autumn, almost a year after they first met, and they asked Ed to be the best man.*

Towards the end of the evening, as he stepped out onto the hotel's terrace for a breath of air, he saw her leaning on the stone balustrade, picking at her skirt.

"You look really good," he said.

She laughed and flattened the hem down.

"I look like a meringue..." She gave him a sly look. "Hey, Ed. Have you got a spare cigarette?"

"You don't smoke."

"Not usually, but tonight all bets are off."

He pulled a pack from his inside jacket pocket, tapped out a couple and lit them both. He handed one to her.

"Thanks." She took a hit, and then sat back, trailing curls of blue smoke from her nose.

"Ah, that's better."

Behind her, the hotel gardens were dark. The sun had set, leaving the clouds piled like embers on the horizon, the sky purple as a bruise, the moon white as a splinter of bone. Coloured party lights had been strung in the trees and music drifted out through the open doors from the dance floor.

Ed cleared his throat.

"Look, would you like to dance?"

Alice raised her eyebrows. For a moment, she looked like she was going to make a smart remark. Then she dropped the cigarette and smoothed down the front of her wedding dress.

"Okay."

Ed reached for her hand. He was going to take her inside, but she pulled back. She looked around at the lights and the sky and said, "Here's fine."

She held him tight as they started to sway. She had goose bumps on her bare arms and her hair smelled of pine-scented shampoo.

"Tell me," she murmured. "How's it going with that girl Verne introduced you to? What's her name?"

Ed looked away. "Her name's Gill. We've been out a couple of times."

"And...?"

Ed stopped dancing, feeling suddenly foolish. He let go.

"Oh, she's nice enough." He ran a finger round the inside of his collar. "But she's not as pretty as you."

Alice lowered her eyes. Inside, the final song wound to its end. The house lights came up on the dance floor.

"Look, I'd better go and find Verne." She had her hair teased into short curls, her lips and nails painted

silver. Her arms were thin and cold, her eyes wide and bright.

She put a hand on his sleeve.

"But thank you," she said.

Ed stuck out his bottom lip. "What for?"

"I know you have feelings for me, Ed. I know how hard it must have been for you today, but you've been great, you really have."

He looked away.

"Thanks for the dance," he said.

She paused a moment.

"Are you going to be okay?"

"I expect so." He forced a smile and shooed her in. "Go!"

VERNE'S OLD FARMHOUSE lay at the end of a lane off the A420. When Ed arrived, he found Alice waiting in the yard in front of the house, with a shotgun in one hand and a backpack in the other.

"Nice car." She threw the pack onto the back seat. "Where did you get it?"

"From a friend." He'd stolen the long-wheelbase Land Rover up off the street after a taxi ride to Bethnal Green. It had been pimped out with an engine snorkel for deep water, and black wire grilles to protect the headlamps. It belonged to Grigor the Serbian butcher, and Ed had had his eye on it for weeks.

"Where's the arch?" he said.

Wind chimes hung on the farmhouse gate. The night air smelled of cut grass, and the stars above were hard and sharp. Alice slid onto the seat beside him, with the shotgun across her knees. She pointed across the yard to a rutted dirt path leading downhill, through the fields.

"It's down that way."

He let the handbrake off and they started rolling.

"Is it far?"

Alice fished a band from her pocket and leaned forward, tying her bluish hair into a loose ponytail. Her jeans squeaked on the leather seat. She wore a blue zip-up fleece over a white t-shirt.

"It's in the paddock at the end of the track, by the river."

About a mile later, at the bottom of the valley, they bumped off onto a patch of wet ground. Caught in the Land Rover's headlights was the arch she'd promised him, four metres wide at its base and six tall.

He killed the engine.

"Does anyone else know about this?"

She shook her head. "This is all private property. The only footpath's on the other side of the river, behind the trees."

Ed popped the door and climbed out. It was midnight.

"Stay here." He walked over to the arch. Looking at it made the hairs rise on the back of his neck—a frightening and exhilarating sensation that reminded him of the time he stood, as a backpacking art student in Australia, on the parapet of a single span bridge overlooking a deep river gorge, with a bungee cord lashed around his ankles.

The sides of the arch glowed like amethyst. Hesitantly, he reached out to touch the nearest. It was warm and pleasantly smooth, like candle wax. Intrigued, he walked over and laid his hand on the other, being careful not to step between them.

He found it hard to believe that it had been only seven months since the appearance of the Chancery Lane arch, and Verne's disappearance. Now at least a dozen lay scattered around the country, more than a hundred worldwide.

"How long's this one been here?" he said.

Alice stood holding the shotgun in one hand, a digital camera in the other.

"About two hours. I called you as soon as I found it." She raised the camera and fired off half a dozen quick shots, getting him and the arch. Then she shivered, as if cold.

Ed walked back to the Land Rover and climbed into the driver's seat. His fingers drummed on the wheel as he nerved himself to carry out his plan.

Alice opened the passenger side door and clambered in beside him. "What do you think?" she said. She seemed better than she had the last time he'd seen her. Calmer. More focused. The grief was still there, every bit as strong as before, but now better hidden.

Ed stopped drumming. He peered through the windshield at the arch, standing in the light from the car, in a field that smelled of dry grass and cow shit.

"I'm going to go through," he said. The authorities had the other arches blocked off. If he passed up this chance, he knew he'd never get close enough to try again.

Alice frowned. Her knuckles were pale on the shotgun stock.

"Are you sure?"

Ed swallowed. All his instincts were telling him to turn the car around and make a run for it. Instead, he slid his hand into his combat jacket and pulled out the gun, and a St Christopher medal he'd pocketed on the way out of the flat: an old birthday present from his missing brother.

"I've got to find him," he said, laying the medal on the dashboard, hoping he sounded a lot more decisive than he felt.

Alice bit her lip. She reached over and touched his arm.

"Then I'm coming with you."

He squeezed her hand.

"Are you sure?"

She pulled away, eyes on the gun. "I've already lost my husband. You're all I've got left; I don't want to lose you as well."

Ahead, the moon cast long dark shadows through the trees on the far riverbank. Moths flickered in the headlight beams. Ed settled himself into the driver's seat, and slipped the pistol into the glove box. He wiped the sweat from his palms on the hem of his paint-splattered black t-shirt. Then he leant forward, squeezing the hard leather steering wheel.

"Okay, then."

He turned the ignition and eased the Land Rover forward, over the uneven ground, keeping a firm grip on the wheel and the toe of his boot light on the accelerator pedal. The arch loomed up before them, easily tall and wide enough to swallow the Land Rover.

"Here we go," he said. He took a deep, shuddering breath, and pumped the gas. They slithered forward, the wheels slipping on the wet grass, kicking up mud. The wing mirror on the passenger side hit the inside edge of the arch. There was a white flash, and an instant of shocking cold—

ARTIFICIAL SUNS

THE SHUTTLE FLIGHT to the *Ameline*'s parking orbit took an hour. Kat spent most of the time in her acceleration couch, working via her implant on the electronic forms needed to clear the ship for departure. There were so many—flight plans, health and safety certifications, maintenance updates, passenger manifests—that they took her full attention until the shuttle's pilot announced they were on final approach to the *Ameline*'s rear airlock. She rarely had the chance to see her ship from the outside, so she leant across Tony Drake's legs and pressed her nose to the porthole.

The *Ameline* was a snub-nosed wedge of black tungsten alloy and smart carbon composite, five metres across at the bow, flaring back to thirty at the stern. Long ago, someone had painted the ship in the blue and red livery of the Abdulov trading family. Black and yellow stencils marked out intake valves, air brakes and emergency hatches. Sensor pods and lateral thrusters stuck out like horns, and at the back, the rear airlock sat snug between the black exhausts of the main engines.

By the time Kat popped the lock and stepped into the *Ameline*'s musty interior, she had the paperwork complete and a clear launch window approved. She led Drake and the Acolyte through the cold, echoing cargo bay to the common area, which comprised a cramped lounge with a circular table, and a galley with doors leading off to individual staterooms. She waved at a pair of threadbare couches.

"Sit down gentlemen, and make yourselves comfortable."

She showed Drake how to fasten the safety straps on his couch. Then she jerked a thumb at a hatch in the forward wall.

"If you need anything, I'll be through there, on the flight deck."

She ducked through the hatch into an antechamber, where she removed her coat and changed her grubby fatigues for an elasticised, skin-tight ship suit. Already, she could feel the *Ameline*'s enthusiasm for the coming flight. Through her implant, she could hear its silicon mind chattering at the edge of her awareness, running course calculations and internal status checks.

Dressed, she climbed the ladder up to the flight deck, a grey-walled cave at the front of the ship, illuminated by banks of softly glowing computer displays. Sliding her legs beneath the main console, she settled herself into the pilot's seat.

She could see the curve of Tiers Cross through the forward windows, its snowfields blindingly bright with the reflected light of its orbiting, artificial suns. She took a moment to savour the view before buckling up, thinking of all the cold, lonely evenings she'd spent standing on its frozen streets looking up, anticipating this moment.

When she was ready, she hooked her neural implant into the ship's sensorium and a head-up display appeared, superimposed across the vision in her right eye. Life support connectors snaked into the sockets sewn into the chest and thighs of her ship suit. The peppery smell of raw space filled her nostrils as her body interpreted the incoming data from the ship's sensors, converting it into recognisable human sensations. Her skin prickled all over and, deep in her gut, she could feel power building in the fusion reactor. She was linked to the ship and it pulled at her like an eager puppy straining the leash.

> WHERE ARE WE GOING?

It showed her a stylised, three dimensional map of local space, covering a sphere a dozen light years in radius.

Kat smiled.

"It's good to be back," she said.

She blinked up a cursor and used it to click on the icon representing Strauli Quay. Seven light years away, with few natural resources and situated at the intersection of three trade routes, the planet was an important crossroads in interstellar culture, a collision of ideas and fashions from a hundred worlds, its wealth and reputation sustained by the rivers of commerce flowing through its orbital docks. And although no-one there had seen her in decades, it was also her home.

She thought of her parents, living and working in the sunny coastal villas and courtyards of the Abdulov compound. In her head, she could almost smell the jasmine in the gardens and hear the snap and flap of boat sails on the afternoon tide.

> SET COURSE FOR STRAULI QUAY?

"Yes."

> YOU GOT IT.

She felt the old ship shiver as the fusion thrusters fired, pushing it up and out of orbit, seeking the emptiness of interstellar space. Tiers Cross fell away from the window, to be briefly replaced by the sparkling jewels of the Bubble Belt.

> MESSAGE COMING IN.

Above the window, one of the overhead displays cleared to reveal the worried face of the family representative, Ezra.

"Captain Abdulov? Are you under way?"

"We're just breaking orbit. Why, what's the matter?"

The young man flushed. "It's Captain Luciano. His ship jumps for Strauli in five minutes."

"Victor's *ahead* of us?" Kat cursed under her breath. It was illegal to activate jump engines within a hundred planetary diameters of the surface—a distance that would take her more than an hour to reach at maximum thrust.

"Yes, I'm afraid we failed in our attempt to delay him."

"Did you put in the complaint?"

"I did, but the local police have shown considerable reluctance to interfere in what they call 'a dispute between traders.' Personally, I suspect bribery."

Kat balled her fists. She'd given up her home and family for Victor Luciano, only to have that sacrifice thrown back in her face when he left her. She couldn't let him beat her to Djatt, not now she stood to get back everything she'd lost.

A matter of honour, Ezra had called it.

She took a deep breath.

"Okay," she said, "here's what's going to happen. Ezra, you need to get on the line to traffic control. Tell them I've got an emergency on board. I don't care what, make something up."

"An emergency?"

"I don't know. A reactor leak, maybe. Something that means I have to activate my jump engines right now."

"You can't do that."

"At the same time, I'm going to open up the fusion motors so I'll have enough residual velocity following the jump to overtake Victor before he reaches the Quay."

On the overhead screen, Ezra's mouth opened and shut wordlessly as he tried to think of a suitable response. Jumping under thrust was even more strictly forbidden than jumping within a hundred diameters. If another ship happened to be in the way when she appeared at her destination, she wouldn't have time to take evasive action, and she'd still be accelerating when she hit it. Worse still, if it was *behind* her, her exhaust would incinerate it before she had time to cut the thrust. The risks to everyone were too great, and harsh punishments were doled out to captains caught engaging in such reckless behaviour. Punishments up to and including imprisonment and ship seizure.

"I know what I'm doing," she said.

Ezra scratched his head. "But what happens at Strauli when they see you coming in hot?"

Kat smiled. "That won't be for another seven years, and you'll be well into middle age before the news works its way back here, so why don't you let me worry about it?"

Ezra opened his mouth again to protest but she broke the connection before he could.

Fuck it, she thought. *I'm never coming back to this dump*.

She blinked up the engine controls and ramped up the thrust, letting it push her back in her seat. Accelerating hard, she told the *Ameline* to bring the jump engines online. Hooked into the ship's senses, she felt the two smooth purple coils of twisted space-time powering up in its belly, their design back-engineered from the arches that first allowed humanity to spread out into the universe.

Thousands of kilometres ahead, Victor's ship stood against the darkness like a silver splinter in the night.

She opened a channel.

"Hey," she said.

On the overhead screen, Victor regarded her with tired eyes.

"What are you doing, Katherine?"

Strapped into her couch, she did her best to smile against the acceleration.

"I'm beating you to Djatt."

There was a short delay as her words crawled across the gulf separating them, and then Victor shook his head sadly.

"You can't catch us, Kat. Not in that old tub."

Katherine bit her lip, enjoying the moment.

"You think so? Watch this."

Knowing she'd be gone before her words reached him, she gave the mental command for the ship to activate its jump engines. All the power gauges spiked at once, there was a flash of white, and the *Ameline* vanished.

CHAPTER
SEVEN
MISMATCHED MOONS

AFTER THE FLASH, darkness in the Land Rover's cab.

Alice let out a cry: "I can't see!"

Also blind, Ed stood on the brakes. The big car ground to a halt. Groping, he reached over and found her arm. They were both shivering and breathless, as if drenched in iced water.

"It's okay," he said, "I'm here."

The flash had been too bright, like staring into the sun. He screwed his eyes shut and waited for the blobby green and purple afterimages to fade. When he opened them, he saw they were parked on a beach, in the dark. Breakers crashed and slithered on the sand ahead, froth bone-white in the light of the Land Rover's headlamps.

Beside him, Alice knuckled her eyes.

"Stop it, you'll make it worse." He pushed her fists away and cupped her face in his hands.

"Look at me," he said.

Her eyes were red and watering. With an effort, she focussed on him.

"Are you okay?"

She looked uncomfortable. "I think so." She pulled back and wiped her eyes on the sleeve of her fleece.

Ed reached down and killed the engine. It shuddered into a deep silence, broken only by the rush and hiss of the surf.

Alice said, "Where do you think we are?"

Ed leant forward over the wheel. Beyond the headlamp beams, the beach stretched away in both directions, a long strip of sand bookended by the cliffs of distant headlands. The stars above were clear and bright and unfamiliar, and two crescent moons hung low over the water, one white and the other orange.

An arch shone in the rear view mirror, red in the reflected light from the Land Rover's brakes. While Alice finished rubbing her eyes, Ed dug a torch from his survival kit.

"I'm going to take a look," he said.

Alice caught his sleeve. "Wait! How do we know it's safe out there?"

"Safe?"

She looked around at the darkened sand. "What if the air's poisonous or something?"

Ed took a couple of experimental sniffs, then shrugged. "If it was, I guess we'd be dead already."

He shouldered the door open. Cold air swirled into the cab. The offshore breeze smelled salty, and reassuringly Earth-like. If it weren't for the double moons, they could almost be on a beach in France or Spain.

Alice zipped her fleece to her chin, and opened the door on her side. Neither of them wanted to be the first to speak. They stepped out of the cab in silence, onto the gritty sand. Ed felt the grains crunch beneath his feet. With Alice beside him, he followed the Land Rover's tyre tracks back to the arch. His boots left crisp pleated tracks. Alice scuffed her feet, kicking little sprays of sand with the toes of her white trainers.

The arch looked the same as the one they'd just driven into, in the paddock by the river. The sides were just as cool and smooth, and glowing with the same purple hue. Ed crouched down at its base and scooped up a handful of damp sand, rubbing it between his fingers. The grains were coarse and sharp, like powdered glass. With a laugh, he brushed it from his hands. On impulse, he dug his mobile phone from the inside pocket of his combat jacket, and checked the reception.

"No signal," he said, then grabbed Alice by the shoulders.

"We've done it," he told her. "We're on another planet!"

Alice coughed. She seemed to be having trouble catching her breath.

"You were right, then," she wheezed, "about the arches?"

"Can you believe it?"

Ed felt a bit breathless himself. He took her hand and pulled her down to the water's edge, where the waves hunched and sizzled onto the shore, eerily white in the moonlight. He couldn't stop laughing: here he was, Edward Jason Rico, taxi driver and failed artist, walking on a new world. He put his head back and howled at the unfamiliar stars. He spun in circles with his arms out, and kicked through the surf, soaking his boots and the legs of his jeans.

A new world!

Beside him, Alice walked as if dazed. She kept folding and unfolding her arms, unsure what to do with her hands. Ed guessed she wanted the camera she'd left on the passenger seat of the Land Rover.

"Oh Ed," she said, turning slowly around and around, taking it all in, and unable to quite believe where she was.

He put his arms around her.

"We did it," he said.

She looked over his shoulder and he felt her stiffen.

"What's that?" she said.

Ed let go of her and turned to see.

"Where?"

Alice pointed into the dunes at the back of the beach, about a mile down the beach, to where a silhouette stood against the night sky.

"Over there, on the horizon."

Ed's chest felt tight. He was breathless from shouting.

"It's another arch," he said.

THEY TOOK IT slowly over the dunes. The Land Rover coped well, but the sand was loose and treacherous and kept falling away beneath the wheels, threatening to topple the vehicle over onto its side. Hands tight on the steering wheel, Ed inched them forward, trying to keep the axles as level as possible, following the contours from the top of one dune to the next rather than risk getting mired in the soft depressions between. It was slow, difficult going, and by the time they reached the arch they both had piercing headaches.

Ahead, a sea of charcoal grey dunes rolled toward the horizon, shadowy in the double moonlight. Several had the silhouettes of further arches atop them, maybe a dozen in all.

Slumped in the driving seat, Ed rubbed his eyes. "I don't feel so good."

Sitting beside him, Alice put a hand to her mouth and yawned.

"I think I know what's going on," she said. "I think we're getting altitude sickness."

"Altitude?" Ed looked out of the rear window, at the beach and the moons hanging over it. Even on top of this dune, they weren't more than ten or twelve feet above sea level.

"Trust me, I know what I'm talking about." Alice took a deep breath and pushed it out again. "It happened to me once before in Mexico City. It wasn't fun. You never forget shit like that."

"What do you want to do?"

"Well, if the air here's too thin to breathe properly, then we have a choice. We can either go on, or we can go back."

"Do you want to go back?"

Alice glanced over her shoulder, at the crisp tyre tracks they'd left on the charcoal sand.

"No, not yet."

"Then we go forward?"

Alice turned her attention to the other arches in the distance, each on the crest of its own dune. "Okay. But how do we know which one to take?"

Ed lowered his head to rest on the steering wheel.

"I don't think we've got the time to struggle over to another, not if we can't breathe properly. It took us long enough to get here, and if we get stuck..."

"So we take this one?"

"I guess it's as good as any."

He pushed himself upright. The headache made it hard for him to concentrate. His chest heaved as if he'd been running. Ahead, the new arch looked identical to the one they'd just left, its sides glistening purple and smooth, throwing complex shadows in the combined light of the mismatched moons.

He picked the St Christopher from the dashboard and draped its chain over the rear view mirror.

"Are you ready for this?"

Alice drew her knees up and closed her eyes.

"As ready as I'll ever be."

THIS TIME, THE light didn't seem to fade as quickly. They passed through the arch and, when they could see again, found themselves in daylight, rolling through a flat, rocky desert beneath a swollen crimson sun. Volcanic plumes stained the horizon. Packed grit formed a makeshift road leading away from the arch. Thin sidewinders of dust and ash skittered across it. Squinting in the hellish light, Ed reached into the glove box and found a pair of Grigor's fake designer sunglasses, which he flicked open one-handed and slid onto his face. The dry desert air was warm, and he could breathe again. He wound his window down and sucked in a big, grateful lungful.

Ahead, half a dozen dome-shaped mud huts stood to either side of the road, each about a metre in height, their walls the same colour as the surrounding desert.

"It's a village," Alice said, shading her eyes with her hand. She reached for her camera. Ed said nothing. The settlement, such as it was, had long been abandoned to the encroaching sands. Some of the domes were sagging, others had already fallen in. Doors and windows stood empty to the wind.

Beyond the village, the crude road branched, and then branched again, and each branch led to another arch.

"Four of them," Ed said. But even from here, he could see that three were damaged, toppled and twisted by the sand shifting beneath them. Only one remained upright.

He brought the car to a halt, feeling himself start to sweat. The road ahead shimmered like the surface of a lake.

Alice pulled off her fleece, revealing her white t-shirt.

"And that's not all," she said. About a mile ahead, close to the upright arch, a vehicle sat at the side of the road. It was a ruggedly built tractor with fat mesh tyres, and its cab was a transparent bubble.

"What the hell's that?"

Cautiously, Ed eased the Land Rover forward again. A woman crouched by one of the tractor's plump wheels. She stood as they approached, wiping her hands on a rag. Ed pulled up beside her and wound down his window.

"Jesus Christ, am I glad to see you," she said. Her drab olive vest and matching cargo pants were grimy, and she had smears of engine grease on her arms and face. To Ed, she looked to be somewhere in her mid-thirties, with bright green eyes, and peroxide white hair chopped into a platinum fuzz.

"Are you American?" he asked.

She smiled. "I'm from Iowa. What about you? You're British, right?"

Ed stuck his hand out. "Hi. My name's Ed, this is Alice."

She finished wiping her fingers and stuffed the rag into her back pocket, then took his hand in a firm grip.

"Kristin. Kristin Cole. Very much at your service."

"What's wrong with your vehicle, Kristin?"

She looked back at it and gave a snort. "The drive unit's completely fucked."

"Can we give you a lift?"

"Just let me get my stuff."

She leaned into the vehicle's cab and pulled out a kit bag.

"Thanks for coming by," she said.

Alice moved the shotgun, and Kristin climbed onto the Land Rover's back seat, behind Ed.

"Have you been here long?" Alice asked.

Kristin stretched.

"A few days, maybe a week. It's hard to tell; the days are much longer here."

Ed looked at her in the rear view mirror. "Are you on your own?"

Kristin hugged the kit bag to her chest. "I was until you guys came along. I got separated from the rest of my unit. They went on ahead."

"They left you here?"

"I don't think they realised. If they did, it must have been too late. Once they'd gone through the arch, they couldn't have come back to get me."

Ed said, "Why didn't you follow on foot?"

Kristin looked at him. "It's a long way to where we're going. But if you hadn't come along, I guess I'd have had to try it sooner or later."

She sniffed the air.

"Say, does this car really run on gas?"

Ed leaned forward over the steering wheel, looking through the heat shimmering off the Land Rover's hood. Ahead, fat tyre tracks led to the one arch remaining upright.

"Your friends went that way." He said. "Do you want to follow them?"

"Hell, yeah." Kristin gave a frown. "Where else is there?"

Hanging over the back of her seat, Alice said, "We could take you back?"

Kristin glowered. "That's not even funny."

"It wasn't supposed to be."

The American leaned forward. "Don't you know where you are, girl? For Christ's sake, weren't you briefed at *all*?"

Ed undid his seatbelt and slid around to face her.

"No-one briefed us," he said, keeping his voice level. "We're here under our own steam."

"You're *civilians*?" Kristin sat back on the leather seat. She rubbed her face, further smearing the grease on her forehead and cheeks, and then looked at the roof. "In that case, I'm sorry to have to be the one to tell you," she said, "but there's no point trying to get home."

Alice looked puzzled.

"Why not?"

Kristin let her head rest on the back of the seat. She wiped a hand across her mouth.

"Because they're all dead."

Ed gripped the back of his seat. "Who? Who's dead?"

Kristin closed her eyes.

"Everyone," she said. "Everyone you've ever known."

CHAPTER EIGHT
RAGGED-ASS DRIVE SIGNATURE

MERCIFULLY, THE *AMELINE* dropped out of jump in an empty patch of sky a good distance from the planet, and Kat shut off the fusion engines as soon as she could, hoping her transgression had gone unnoticed.

But of course, it hadn't.

As the old ship moved toward Strauli, the port authority bombarded it with outraged protests, which Kat duly ignored, squirting Ezra's letter of explanation at the Abdulov compound.

Within minutes, she received a return call from her father.

"Katherine? Is that really you?"

"Dad, listen—"

"You're alone?"

"I have passengers."

He made a chopping gesture. "It doesn't matter. I'm on the Quay as we speak. Whatever it is, whatever's happened, we can talk about it when you get here."

He looked older, the decades having taken more of a toll than she'd expected: his hair thinner and greyer than she remembered, the lines around his mouth and eyes deeper and more defined, like a pattern of cuts worked into a leather mask. But his eyes were just as bright and hard as ever, the eyes of a man accustomed to command.

"Dad, the port authority—"

He held up a gnarled hand. "Leave them to me, Katherine."

KATHERINE ABDULOV HAD grown up in a villa overlooking the ocean, on the edge of the family compound. She'd spent the days studying and the evenings walking alone on the beach. The beach was her sanctuary: a place where, as long as she remained within the compound's secure perimeter, she could walk alone and undisturbed for hours at a time.

As she kicked through the warm surf, she watched the trading ships crawl across the sky, the sparks of their fusion drives burning like tiny, angry stars, and remembered the stories her father had told her about Great Aunt Sylvia, the black sheep of the family.

If the stories were true, before she vanished, Sylvia had been one of the Abdulovs' best captains. She'd been everywhere, carving out new trade routes and building herself a formidable reputation. She'd been courageous, fiercely self-reliant, and notoriously promiscuous, and Kat desperately wanted to be just like her.

On a clear summer's night, she saw the orbital docks bulking low in the hazy southern sky, their gigantic habitat wheels turning ponderously in the light of the long-set sun. Every time she saw them, they filled her with such yearning, making her wish for the far-off day when she'd graduate from flight school and take her rightful place at the helm of one of her family's trading ships, just like her aunt.

Standing there, her head full of impatient dreams, there was no way she could have known how quickly those dreams would be shattered. No way to foresee that her doomed affair with Victor Luciano would force her to walk away from everything she held dear, leaving her jumping from star to star in an old tramp freighter, cut off from her family's wealth and protection, desperately trying to keep fuel in the tank and food on the table.

Katherine Abdulov was twenty years old when she graduated at the top of her flight school class; twenty-two when she met Victor Luciano. Approaching Strauli now, at the age of twenty-six, wired into her pilot's couch and decelerating hard toward the orbital Quay, she found it difficult to take her eyes from the blue and white swirls of the planet. The colours seemed to nourish her soul. At high magnification, she could trace the familiar bays and headlands along the stretch of coast owned by the Abdulov family, and if she squinted, she imagined she could almost make out the red roofs and white-painted buildings of the compound itself.

I'm coming home, she thought, and wondered what sort of reception she'd receive. A lot of time had passed. A lot of fuel through the engine, as her aunt would say.

She supposed she should feel reassured that at least her father had, in his own gruff way, seemed pleased to see her.

As the *Ameline* lined up for its approach to the orbital docks, it automatically synched its databases with the local Grid. It was standard procedure and every trading ship did it. They carried googleflops of spare memory capacity in order to transport data from one star system to the next. They were couriers. Faster and more reliable than radio signals, they spread information along the trade routes at close to the speed of light, updating— and being updated by—each Grid they encountered. They carried electronic messages, books, scientific papers, breaking news stories, and market information. The local authorities paid them a small fee for doing so. They were the lifeblood of interstellar civilization. The information they carried helped stitch the scattered worlds of humanity into something approaching a cohesive whole.

Kat took a moment to scan her eyes down the list of incoming news headlines, then disconnected herself from the ship's feed, unhooked herself from the pilot's couch, wiped her face with her hands, and made her way down the ladder and back through the hatch into the main cabin, where Toby Drake and the Acolyte were still strapped into their seats.

"I thought you might like to see this," she said.

Drake looked up at her and his eyes widened, and then flicked quickly away. Puzzled, Kat looked down and realised she hadn't thought to change out of the figure-hugging ship suit, which clung to her curves like sprayed-on paint. Realising her mistake, she folded her arms across her chest with a muttered apology. She stepped backwards through the hatch and reached for the clothes locker, from which she pulled her grey coat. As she put it on, she felt the tips of her ears burn with embarrassment.

"We'll be docking in a few hours," she called. "As this is your first time on Strauli, would you like to watch the approach?"

She fastened the coat and, safely covered, returned to the open hatch.

Toby Drake looked questioningly at the Acolyte, who raised an eyebrow.

"Go ahead."

Drake unclipped his harness with a grin, excited at the opportunity to visit the flight deck. He wouldn't look at Kat directly, and there was something contagious about his shyness. Ears still hot, she led him up the ladder, and steered him into the co-pilot's chair.

Although it would take another three hours to reach their assigned berth, the Quay already filled the entire forward view. It comprised a row of fifty rotating wheels, stacked on a single axle, each one a kilometre in width and over ten in diameter. Navigation lights blinked on their rims.

"There are three main sections," Kat said, pointing them out, hoping to hide her self-consciousness by playing tour guide. She told him of the *Medina*, which lay along the non-rotating axle of the stack. It was the heart and soul of the docks, where on any day of the year you could find ships from six or seven merchant families, and pick up passengers, cargoes and diseases from a hundred different worlds. A place where you could walk down the central concourse between the bays and see the stalls laid out in front of each ship, heaped with knickknacks, weapons and curios from planets and systems a dozen light years away. Around that, the *Dharamshala* occupied the rim of the wheels, where spin gravity provided a comfortable abode for more than a million permanent inhabitants, and temporary accommodation for a transient population of more than a million travellers, traders and pilgrims.

And lastly, the *Observance* lurked in the spokes and interstices of the station. It was the home of the Acolytes: a place of corridors that smelled of patchouli and sandalwood. A place of improvised laboratories and observatories, and temples filled with people from all corners of known space, here to see, study and worship the Dho.

"Technically, the planet's called Strauli and the docks are called Strauli Quay," she said. "They're politically independent, but over the years, the names have become interchangeable."

In theory, all starports were autonomous, neutral territories. To safeguard trade, the local authorities had no jurisdiction over visiting starships. It was only when passengers or cargo left the port's environs that they had to submit to local customs and taxes.

Kat looked over. If Drake's eyes had been wide when he saw her in her ship suit, they were now as round as rocket exhausts. Watching from her couch, she smiled.

"Surely this can't be all that impressive to a boy from the Bubble Belt?"

Drake shook his head.

"No, you don't understand. This is different. Nobody knows who built the Belt, but all this"—he swept his arm at the rotating docks—"all this is man-made."

With an obvious effort, he pulled his gaze from the forward view.

"Does that make any sense?"

Kat smiled.

"So," she said, nodding her head back toward the hatch that lead down to the lounge and the Acolyte waiting within. "Do you have any idea why they sent for you?"

Drake glanced nervously over his shoulder. When he spoke, he leaned close, his voice low.

"Not really. I've been kind of assuming it's got something to do with James Harris. He was my professor at the university, and he came out here a few years ago, to study the Dho."

"Do you think he recommended you?"

"I don't know. Maybe."

A warning light appeared in Kat's right eye. She hooked her implant back into the ship's sensorium.

> TROUBLE.

The ship had detected another vessel emerging from jump a few thousand kilometres in their wake.

"Is that Victor's ship?"

> YES. TRANSPONDER PING CONFIRMS IT AS THE *TRISTERO*. BESIDES, I'D RECOGNISE THAT RAGGED-ASS DRIVE SIGNATURE ANYWHERE.

"What's it doing?"

> MOSTLY BITCHING ABOUT OUR LITTLE STUNT. I'M SEEING A LOT OF COMMS TRAFFIC TO THE PORT AUTHORITY.

Kat twisted a smile. Victor could complain all he wanted. This was her turf and her family commanded a lot of respect on the Quay. Now that they'd welcomed her back into the fold, there was little he could do to touch her.

"Can we beat them into dock?"

> OH YES. AT BEST SPEED, THEY'LL GET IN THREE HOURS AFTER US.

"Good. Keep an eye on them and let me know if they do anything unexpected."

She disconnected and found Drake watching her. He had heard only her side of the exchange.

"So, what's the deal with this guy?"

"What guy?"

"I'm talking about the captain of that other ship. I take it there's some history between the two of you?"

Kat looked away.

"You could say that."

"Do you want to talk about it?"

"No."

She reached out with her implant, telling the ship to locate and magnify the Dho Ark.

"Look at this," she said. She pulled it up on the main screen: the image of a gigantic crystal spinning in a majestic orbit around the system's solitary gas giant. Drake glanced at the measurements displayed at the bottom of the screen and gaped. The Ark was an impressive way to change the subject. At more than a hundred kilometres in length, it dwarfed the Quay. It was larger than some of the gas giant's moons and its sides were plated with smooth sheets of artificial diamond. Human ships fussed around it like gnats around an elephant. As it emerged from the planet's shadow, the light of the sun caught one of its facets, sending rainbow refractions skittering up and down its diamond flanks.

"It's beautiful."

As Drake leaned forward, Kat studied his profile. He was younger than she was, and skinny, and his ears stuck out; but he also had kind, dark eyes and a shy, goofy smile.

"Have you ever seen it up close?" he said.

She shook her head. "As far as I know this is the first time they've let anyone, aside from the Acolytes, get near it."

He turned to her. His eyes flickered up and down her wrapped body.

"Then why don't you come with me when I take the shuttle over there? They won't let you inside, but you'd still get a good look, and we wouldn't have to say goodbye so soon."

Kat opened and closed her mouth. There was a question in his eyes, and she wasn't sure how to respond. She didn't know what to say. Suddenly flustered, she cut the picture feed, resetting the screen to an unenhanced view of the approaching docks.

"It's past midnight on the Quay," she said brusquely. "And the days are longer here than on Tiers Cross. If you're going to adjust before we dock, you should try and get some sleep."

She stood, and he rose to follow her. In the confined space, his hand touched hers and she turned to find him looking down at her, head bent slightly by the low ceiling, eyes wide and eyebrows raised.

"I'm a lot older than you," she said.

He laughed.

"I'm twenty-five years old," he said. "What are you, twenty-four?"

"I'm twenty-six. Physically, I'm twenty-six."

"That's nothing." He reached up and brushed a strand of hair from her forehead. He was, she realised, trying to be charming.

She said, "Yes, but objectively, I'm old enough to be your grandmother."

His smile broadened, dimpling his cheeks. He moved closer. Behind the leather, she smelled soap and sweat, and musty old books.

"It doesn't matter," he said.

Kat shivered. His closeness made her skin prickle. She felt the warmth of his breath on her cheek. It had been a long time since she'd had a man. It had taken months for her to get over Victor. Then there'd been Napoleon, but that hadn't lasted; and that random guy in that bar on Icefall, the one who was gone by the time she woke the next morning... All of them older than her, and all of them in their own way rejecting her. She'd never been with anyone her own age.

She looked into Toby Drake's wide eyes. He was young and willing, and this time, she'd be the one doing the leaving. She had a mission to complete. This kid couldn't hurt her.

Ah, to hell with it, she thought.

She grabbed the front of his shirt and, closing her eyes, pulled his lips down to meet hers.

STRAULI GRID

NEWS HEADLINES

NEW IMMIGRATION LIMITS FOR SOUTHERN HEMISPHERE
Ecological concerns spark curbs on off-world immigration.

ALIEN CARVINGS STUN ART EXPERTS
Latest pictures from inside the Dho Ark.

SIX DIE IN SHUTTLE CRASH
Pilot error blamed.

NEW ALIEN CIVILISATION?
Astronomers detect anomaly obscuring nearby stars.
Dust cloud or second bubble belt?

CIVIL WAR ON LANCASTER
Traders bring reports of fighting.
Rebels seize capital buildings.

TAKING SHAKESPEARE TO THE STARS
One way ticket for performers.
New tour to last 80 years, and take in 35 planets.

SCIENTISTS PREDICT COLLAPSE OF ARCH NETWORK
Wormholes inherently unstable, say experts.

TRADER OVERDUE
Freighter Emily declared lost with all hands.
Fails to return from routine flight to Djatt.

CHAPTER NINE

TRIANGLE

"I CAN'T BELIEVE nobody told you."

They were out of the car now, standing in the desert watching the swollen red sun as it sank low over the domed mud huts of the little abandoned village. The heat made it too stifling to stay inside. A parched breeze stirred the air, flowing in ahead of the oncoming night, and drying the sweat on their backs and faces. Ed Rico had his arms folded. His combat jacket lay draped over the back of the driver's seat.

"I still don't get it," he said.

Kristin slapped a palm on the Land Rover's bonnet. She was getting impatient.

"It's quite simple," she said. "Each arch leads to a different planet, right? This one we're standing on is about a hundred light years from Earth; and to us, the journey here didn't seem to take any time at all, did it? But relativity tells us that *nothing* travels faster than light. So in reality, it must have actually taken us a hundred years to pass from one arch to the other, the same amount of time it'd take light to cross the same distance."

"But that doesn't explain why we can't go back."

Kristin tapped her fingernails on the hood.

"Now we're here, it will take us another hundred years to get back to Earth. As far as we're concerned, it's only been a short time since we left, but by the time we got back there, we'd find two whole centuries had passed. We'd be stranded in a strange and distant future." She looked at the fat mesh tyre tracks leading to the intact arch. "That's the reason why my unit hasn't tried to come back to find me. By the time they got back here, I'd most likely be dead or gone."

Ed leaned back against the Land Rover's warm door and yawned. He felt jet-lagged. According to his wristwatch, the time was two-thirty in the morning.

"How do you know all this?" he said.

Kristin turned her face to him. "People *have* come back, you know. Some of the arches lead from Earth to Mars and some of the nearer stars. Short roundtrips. They showed us how it works."

Ed wiped his eyes. He'd assumed the journeys had been as instantaneous as they felt.

"Surely it would be better to be on Earth in the future, rather than stuck in a dump like this?" he said.

Kristin shrugged.

"I guess it depends on your point of view. Me, I've got a mission to accomplish."

Ed stifled another yawn.

"But we didn't come straight here," he said around his fist. "The first arch we used took us to a beach, on a planet with two moons."

"Then you have to factor in the extra journey time. When did you leave Earth?"

Ed told her the date, and she nodded. "Which arch did you use?"

"We found it on a farm, near Oxford."

Kristin frowned. "I don't know that one. I came through the excavated Chancery Lane arch."

Ed sat up, suddenly alert. "That's the arch my brother used! He was one of the first through. We're trying to find him."

Kristin put her hands on her hips.

"If he came through the same arch as me, he'll have come straight here, same as I did."

Ed looked around, feeling his pulse quicken. Verne had actually been here, standing on this spot, breathing this air?

He said, "He fell into the arch about seven months before we left."

Kristin did a quick mental calculation. "In that case, he'll have passed through about ten years ago."

Ed felt his heart thump like a stone in his chest.

Ten years?

"But how can that be?" he said. "We were only seven months behind him."

Kristin let out a tired sigh. She used the toe of her combat boot to sketch a triangle in the dirt. She tapped one of its points.

"This is the Earth, right? And this here is where we are now, a hundred light years away. And this third point up here, that's the planet you detoured to. Now, I came through the same arch as your brother and I came straight here, along the base of the triangle, while you two went up this side to this other planet, and then down again to here, adding an extra nine and a half years to your journey." She wiped her hands together as if brushing off sand.

"Ten years?" Alice said, looking crestfallen.

Kristin gave her a sympathetic pat on the shoulder.

"Ain't relativity a bitch?"

Ed looked down at the triangle sketched in the sand. Then he turned away and stalked around to the Land Rover's tailgate.

Ten years?

His mind reeled. He didn't know how to begin to take in the news. Instead, he kicked a pebble with the toe of one of his work boots, and watched it bounce and skitter across the dirt track. At his sides, his hands clenched and unclenched.

"But we were only on that beach for a few minutes," he said.

CHAPTER TEN
MEDINA

KAT LAY IN her bunk, looking at the curved metal ceiling of her cabin. Toby Drake lay with his cheek in the hollow of her shoulder, his skin dark against hers, glossy with drying sweat. His breath was warm on her chest.

The ship scratched at the edge of her awareness.

> HAVE YOU QUITE FINISHED?

"What do you want?"

> WE'RE DOCKING IN FIFTEEN MINUTES. PERHAPS YOU SHOULD GET SOME CLOTHES ON?

"Oh, leave me alone."

Drake stirred and blinked up at her.

"Pardon?"

Her palm soothed the damp, prickly hairs at the nape of his neck.

"I'm talking to the ship." She extracted her arm and sat upright, letting the sheet fall from her chest.

"I have to get back to the bridge," she said, trying to sound professional. She didn't know what she wanted. She put one arm across her chest and the other hand to her throat. She felt suddenly, stupidly vulnerable. She hadn't let her guard down like this since Victor. She hadn't let anyone get this close.

Drake scratched his ears and yawned. "What time is it?"

Kat checked the display in her right eye. "We've got about a quarter of an hour."

Nearly home.

She had butterflies in her stomach and felt like a child again. Blushing furiously, she reached for her clothes. Drake sat up in bed, watching her. "I can't believe we're there already." He shook his head. "Seven light years in six hours, it's amazing."

Kat wriggled awkwardly into her flight suit.

"It wasn't really six hours," she said.

He looked up at her. "It wasn't?"

Kat fastened her suit and brushed it down with her hand. The skin-tight material didn't leave her feeling any less exposed, but somehow she drew comfort from it and her confidence returned.

"No," she said. "We spent most of that time manoeuvring. The jump itself took half a second."

Drake looked thoughtful.

"Of course, it was longer than that, though, wasn't it?"

Kat walked to the door. She said, "You're a physicist, you know how it works. Half a second to us, seven long years to the rest of the universe."

KAT MET HER father at a café in the *Medina* section of Strauli Quay, on a first floor balcony overlooking the market stalls on one of the main concourses. She wore her thick coat over her flight suit, and she'd added half a dozen silver bangles to each wrist and smoothed her hair back with gel. She wanted to look tough, independent and feminine.

Below, shoppers thronged the concourse, even though the local time was almost three o'clock in the morning. The Quay never slept. It ran twenty-five hours a day, catering to bleary-eyed travellers arriving from worlds with days of different lengths, and jet-lagged representatives from all the time zones on the planet below.

Looking out over their milling heads, Kat heard the lilt and hubbub of a hundred dialects and accents. She saw tourists and ship captains browsing the ramshackle stalls that lined the walls, immigrants with wide eyes and heavy suitcases, small knots of Acolytes gliding through the crowd. You could buy anything in the *Medina*. That was its claim to fame. There were no laws governing what could and couldn't be sold. Bales of silk were traded on one stall, and automatic weapons on the next. Barbeque grills filled the air with the greasy hiss and spit of vat-grown meat. Slave traders rubbed shoulders with preachers and spice merchants. Gene-splicers and tattooists operated out of tents set up on the metal deck. Over the bustle of commerce, you could hear the whine and bite of their needles.

Sitting on the opposite side of the café table, Feliks Abdulov toyed absently with a teaspoon, watching her with his grey eyes.

"This is unfortunate," he said.

Kat added sweetener to her coffee, stirred it and set her own spoon aside. Her bangles rattled as she moved her arms.

"Unfortunate?"

"That you have to leave so soon. If I had another ship to send, I would."

Kat shrugged. The family's shipping schedules were arranged decades in advance.

"Do you think Ezra was right, that the *Kilimanjaro* was sabotaged?"

Feliks took a deep breath through his nose.

"I think it's highly likely." He stopped fiddling with the spoon. "But of course, it'll be years before we know for sure."

He reached out. The tips of his fingers brushed the back of her hand.

"But you, Katherine. How have *you* been?"

Kat leaned back. She felt her neck growing hot. "Since you kicked me out, you mean?"

Feliks shook his head. The grandson of the founder of the Abdulov trading dynasty, he'd commanded his own starship for forty years before moving back to Strauli to take over as head of the family.

"I did what I had to do."

Kat gave a snort.

"You cut me out of the family!"

Feliks looked down at his hands.

"I had no choice. You were one of my officers and you were openly consorting with the competition. I couldn't give you preferential treatment. What else could I do?"

"You could have trusted me."

"I had a reputation to maintain."

Kat pushed back in her chair.

"And now?"

Feliks raised his eyes to the steel ceiling.

"I don't know," he said. He seemed to be struggling

with himself. "Look, this isn't easy for me. I thought I'd never see you again."

Kat stamped her boot. She got to her feet. She knew from the local Grid that Victor's ship had already docked and she didn't have time to be angry about the past. If she was going to beat him, she had to act now. Recriminations could wait.

"Forget it," she said. She used her implant to call up schematics for the *Ameline* and displayed them on the smart screen built into the tabletop.

Feliks raised his eyebrows.

"This is your ship?"

Kat leant her fists on the table. "It's the best I could get."

Her father's fingers traced the outline of the ship's engines. He looked at her from beneath grey brows. "Do you really think you can beat him to Djatt in *this*?"

"She's faster than she looks."

"She'd have to be."

Kat scowled. Feliks sat back, hands raised.

"I'm not criticising you, Katherine." He tapped the image on the table. "You made a good choice. These old Renfrew Mark IVs are very reliable. Ships of this class run forever, if they're looked after right. They're just not very quick. Nevertheless..." He reached into his pocket and pulled out a data crystal. "Your mother's *really* going to hate me for this." He slid it across to her.

"What is it?"

Feliks looked around. They were alone, aside from a middle aged man in a fur cap drinking gin and tonic at a corner table.

"It's your commission." He wouldn't meet her eye. Feliks wasn't a man used to making apologies. "I'll send a copy to your implant, but this is the official version, with the family seals. It reinstates you as a full captain in the Abdulov fleet, with refuelling privileges at every port between here and Djatt. We'll also refit your ship, as much as we can in the time it takes to refuel her. Have you booked a departure slot yet?"

"Eleven hundred hours."

She saw her father's eyes flick down and to the right, checking the time display in his right eye.

"That gives us around seven hours. I'll get a crew on it right away."

"Thank you."

Feliks wagged a finger: No thanks were necessary. This wasn't personal, this was business.

"Just make sure you get there first," he said.

Their coffees were cold now. He pushed his away and rose. "There's one other thing," he said. "If our first ship *was* sabotaged, chances are you'll need to defend yourself."

Kat patted her thigh. "I have a gun."

Feliks leaned in close. "I'm talking about arming your ship, Katherine. I'm talking about a crate of mining charges, and half a dozen atmospheric probes. They're both perfectly legal cargoes, but if push comes to shove, you can mount the explosives onto the probes and *voila*, you have missiles."

He took her shoulders, holding her at arm's length.

"Are you really up to this, Katherine?"

"Yes, father."

"Then come along, let me walk you to your ship. Time's short and we have a lot of work to do."

CHAPTER ELEVEN
SWITCHING YARD

FOR WANT OF a better option, they drove into the unbroken arch, following the tracks left by Kristin's colleagues—and emerged a subjective instant later in the centre of a vast stone circle.

Still shivering from the cold blast that accompanied the white flash, Alice leaned forward, peering through the windscreen. She rubbed her eyes.

"It's like Stonehenge," she said.

Ed silenced the engine. With its noise gone, all they could hear was the wind. They were on a hillside overlooking brown, desolate tundra. There were maybe fifty upright stones arranged in a ring around the car, with flatter stones laid across the top to form a series of doorways, each of which housed a purple arch.

Ed opened his door and climbed down onto the springy grass. The wind hit him, blowing though his hair and t-shirt, drying the sweat on his ribs, cold and fresh after the airless desert heat.

Behind him, Kristin climbed from the back of the Land Rover. She pulled a quilted khaki hoodie from her pack and slipped it over her head. She walked a few steps from the car and turned in a complete circle.

"Interesting," she said.

She lifted a finger, twirling her wrist to take in the entirety of the monument.

"What do you notice about this structure?"

Ed looked around. The gaps between the stones each housed a purple arch. He shrugged, feeling numb, his head heavy.

"What?"

"There's no way out."

Ed rubbed his eyes. "What do you mean?"

"All the gaps are filled. You come in through one arch and you have to leave through another. It's like a railroad switching yard, or an airport terminal."

He trudged around the car to stand beside her.

"How did they get this way?"

She put her hands on her hips. "My guess is they were dragged into position and the stones erected around them."

Ed scratched at the stubble on his jaw. He looked back into the Land Rover's cab and saw Alice slumped forward in her seat, her head resting on her folded arms, her auburn ponytail hanging down past her ear. He yawned. By his reckoning, it was now somewhere around four o'clock in the morning. He'd been awake for at least twenty hours.

He pushed a hand through his hair.

"Look, it's been a long, strange day. We really need to take a break," he said.

A small, cool sun burned overhead. His nose twitched with familiar smells on the wind: wet mud, dry grass, hints of something flowery, like heather. He fetched his bag from the back of the Land Rover and lit the camping stove, then took a bottle of water from Alice's pack, filled a pan and put it on to boil. Kristin was off walking the circle, hands clasped behind her back, examining the stones.

"You know what this is?" she called.

Ed shrugged. He took a handful of teabags from his bag and dropped them into the pan. Then he stretched out on the soft grass.

She came back and stood over him, hands on hips. "It's a message," she said. "And it says: *you're not welcome here, keep moving.*"

Ed put an arm over his eyes.

"Who built it?"

Kristin brushed her hands together.

"Who knows?" she said. "Whoever did this, they didn't want anyone getting out of the circle."

"Is it safe to stay here?"

She walked away. Her footsteps receded, soft and rustling in the long grass. When she spoke over her shoulder, there was amusement in her voice.

"Yes, it's safe."

Ed turned his head and watched her walk from stone to stone, bending to examine each in turn. She had her khaki hood pulled up to cover her face. He could smell the tea warming in the pan. He rolled onto his side, facing the open door of the Land Rover, and saw Alice curled up asleep on the passenger seat, cheek against the back of the seat, white trainers resting on the handbrake. He smiled at her and closed his eyes. The wind stirred the grass beneath him. He imagined himself as a recumbent figure in a painting by Cézanne. The blades stroked his face and then, without meaning to, he fell asleep, lulled by the comforting hiss of the blue gas flame.

ED FIRST MET *Alice at a product launch in Aldgate. He'd been out of art school a month. His career as an artist hadn't taken off yet and he'd just started his first job as a minicab driver, working shifts to pay the rent.*

The launch was being held in a hotel off the main high street, and Ed was there to pick up a fare. She was at the bar drinking orange juice when he walked up to her.

"Cab for Alice Conley?"

"That's me. Give me a moment to finish this?"

"Okay."

As she drank, he looked her up and down: she was a little older than he was, with shoulder-length hair the colour of rust, a tasteful charcoal grey suit, red lipstick, and silver hoop earrings. She looked very professional, and very sexy. Despite his own slovenliness (or maybe because of it), Ed had always been drawn to smartly-dressed women.

She finished the orange juice and set the glass on the bar. "God, don't you hate these things?" she said.

Ed shrugged. He'd never been to a corporate do like this. There were maybe fifty or sixty people enjoying the free champagne. The launch was for a new type of phone, consisting of silvery circuits printed directly onto the user's skin. Half naked men and women prowled the room, showing off imaginative ways to wear them. Ed had one himself, a free sample that had been stamped onto the inside of his wrist as he entered.

"Have you been doing this long?" Alice eyed his cargo pants, Hawaiian shirt and baggy cardigan.

"I just started." He leaned an elbow on the bar and wagged a finger at the press tag dangling from her jacket pocket. "What about you? How long have you been a journalist?"

A leather bag sat on the floor by her stool. She tapped it with her foot.

"I'm a photographer." She pushed back her auburn hair with one hand.

"Then shouldn't you be down that end?" He nodded towards the crowd at the far end of the room.

Alice glanced back over her shoulder, then reached into her bag and pulled out a compact digital camera. She pointed it at the crowd and pressed the shutter without bothering to look through the viewfinder.

"There," she said, "job done."

She dropped the camera back into the bag and yanked the zipper shut.

"Now, if you don't mind...?" She got up to go, but Ed put a hand on her arm. "What's the hurry?" he said. "This looks like fun. Let me get you some champagne."

She shook him off. "I don't think so."

"Okay, in that case, how about another orange juice?"

She stepped back.

"You don't take 'no' for an answer, do you?"

Ed grinned and dropped his car keys onto the shiny counter. He gave her his cheekiest grin.

"I'm not taking you anywhere until you agree to have a drink with me."

Alice hitched the bag's strap over her shoulder and let out a long, deflating breath.

"I'll tell you what." She checked her watch. "I have to be somewhere right now, but I'm free later."

Ed wrote the number of his new wrist phone on a napkin and passed it to her.

"I'm meeting my brother for dinner at ten," he said. "He's a journalist too. You should definitely come along."

They arranged to meet at a tapas restaurant on West India Quay, in the shadow of Canary Wharf. When Alice arrived, she'd changed into a short denim jacket and a green cotton dress that matched her eyes. It was raining outside and the skirt of the dress was damp and clinging to her legs. From the table, Ed watched her walk across the room. She walked better than most girls danced.

"I'm glad you could come." He introduced her to Verne and they all shook hands.

"Verne works for the BBC, and he's just bought a farm."

Alice raised an eyebrow. "I thought I recognised you. Did you do that report about the insurgents in Pakistan?"

A waitress came and guided them to their table. Verne pulled Alice's chair out for her.

"Yes, that was me."

She sat gracefully and shrugged off her damp denim jacket. Her green dress looked as enticing as the foil wrapping on a chocolate coin.

"You're the Verne Rico? You're a legend. You've been everywhere. And now you've bought a farm?" She glanced at Ed to make sure she hadn't misheard. "Are you retiring?"

Verne looked at his hands. "It's not really a farm."

"You've got chickens," said Ed. "And pigs."

Verne glared at him. He lifted the rough clay jug of water from the centre of the table and filled Alice's glass.

"It's more of a smallholding. I'm trying to be self-sufficient." He shifted in his chair, momentarily uncomfortable. "It's a change of pace after, you know, some of the things I've seen..."

Alice took the glass stem between her fingers and thumb, steadying it.

"Well, I'm all for that. The way food prices are at the moment, I wish I had time to do it myself."

Verne stopped pouring. He pushed his glasses back onto the bridge of his nose. "Then you should definitely come out and visit at the weekend. The leaves are just turning, and we'll have the piglets in a few months."

Alice chewed her bottom lip. "You know, I may just take you up on that."

The waitress brought menus. Ed took one and spread it on the table.

"I'm going to have the mushrooms and prawns," he announced.

Verne didn't even bother to look. His eyes stayed on Alice.

"I'll have the spicy meatballs."

Alice smiled. "I'll have the same."

A couple of hours later, the two of them took a cab to her flat, leaving a dejected Ed standing outside the restaurant with his hands in his pockets. The lights of Canary Wharf shone through the rain. A train rattled over West India Quay, the light from its windows jangling on the black waters of the dock.

He walked up to the station platform and took the last train south to Island Gardens. He shared the carriage with a young Chinese kid in a German army surplus shirt. The kid had shaggy hair, and scratched at a fresh tattoo on his forearm. Lightning flickered over the Thames.

*   *   *

ED WOKE SLOWLY. He was lying curled on his side in the centre of the stone circle, head resting in the crook of his arm. Soft grass cushioned his hip and shoulder. The sun kissed his cheek. A playful breeze ran its fingers through his hair.

"Are you awake?"

Alice knelt by the gas stove, a chipped tin mug wrapped in her hands. She'd taken out her ponytail, and her rust-coloured hair fell naturally around her face and shoulders. Her camera hung on a strap around her neck.

"Have you been taking pictures?"

"A few snaps. There's tea if you want it."

He yawned and stretched. The sun shone white in the blue sky. The air was so crisp and clear it seemed to ring like a bell.

"How long have I been asleep?"

"About four hours. You let the pan boil dry and I had to refill it." She took the water off the stove and poured him a mug of tea. "It'll have to be black, I'm afraid. I didn't think to bring any milk."

She held it out and he sat up to receive it.

"Where's Kristin?"

Alice jerked a thumb. At the far side of the circle, the American woman chipped away at one of the upright stones with a hand trowel, her chopped white hair bright in the light of the sun. "She's collecting samples. She's got a pocketful of zip-lock baggies and she's been filling them with dirt, grass, everything."

Ed put the tin mug to his chin and blew on it. In the fresh air, the smell of the steam sparked teenage memories of fishing trips and pop festivals. The lushness of the grass filled him with the urge to paint. His fingers itched for a brush and a palette full of greens and yellows.

"Do you think it's true, what she told us?"

Alice rocked back on her heels. "Which part?"

"That we can't go home."

Alice fussed with her hair, wiping a strand of it back behind her ear.

"I don't know. Maybe."

Ed puffed his cheeks out. He thought of his east London flat, all his stuff, his clothes. His paintings.

"Shit." He missed the noise and bustle of the city. He tossed the mug into the grass. "Look at this place, Alice. We shouldn't be here. We don't know what we're doing. We're not explorers."

He stalked over to the Land Rover, slapped his palm against the cool metal frame of the open door. How far had they travelled already—a hundred light years? Two hundred?

Behind him, Alice cleared her throat. She got to her feet, fetched his thrown mug and shook out the remaining drops of tea.

"I don't know about you, but I'm here to find my husband."

Ed clenched his fists.

"But look around you, Alice. Look at this place. There must be upwards of fifty arches here. Even if he came this way, how can we possibly know which one he would have taken? We've already wasted a decade. What happens if we pick one that takes us a hundred or a thousand years in the wrong direction?"

"We have to try."

"But how do we know he didn't turn around and come straight back through the arch, like that guy on Mars? He could be back on Earth right now, a couple of hundred years into the future, thinking we're both long dead."

Alice went over to squat by the stove.

"I don't think he did. I think he kept moving."

She poured the last of the hot tea into the mug and brought it over to him. He took it and climbed into the Land Rover's cab, his jeans squeaking as he settled into the leather seat.

"What makes you so sure?"

"Sure about what?"

"That he kept moving. Why wouldn't he turn back? All this time, I assumed he hadn't. But it's quite possible he did, and he's back there now, even as we speak."

Alice swept a loose strand of hair behind her ear. She heaved a sigh.

"I don't think so. You know him, he's always been a journalist. Once he gets hooked into a story, he never lets go. He'd want to find out where the other arches led. And besides, he knew about us. It must have hurt him finding out like that. His brother and his wife. Who could blame him for being angry? And with your mother dead, who could blame him if he decided he had no-one left worth coming back for?"

CHAPTER
TWELVE
THE CRYING OF
BAY 49

FELIKS ABDULOV PULLED three of his best maintenance crews from other projects and set them to work on the *Ameline*. Then he surprised them all by rolling up his sleeves and pitching in. With his help, and working as fast as they dared, they refuelled and recalibrated the engines, gave the internal systems a quick and dirty upgrade and welded new plates over the most worn and damaged sections of hull. As they were finishing up, Toby Drake appeared in the bay. He looked up to where Kat sat, shading his eyes against the overhead lights.

"How's it going?"

Kat slipped her welding goggles down around her neck and used the back of her bare arm to wipe the sweat from her forehead. She was on the edge of the bow's upper surface, one of her legs folded under her and the other dangling over the side, three metres above the metal floor of the landing bay.

"See for yourself."

The ship was a mess of patches and workarounds. The new hull plates were bright blocks of red and yellow against its faded blue paintwork. Inside, fibre optic cables trailed from open service hatches. New passenger couches had been bolted into the lounge. Scars showed where obsolete instruments had been ripped from the bridge consoles and replaced.

Easing over the edge of the hull, she hung from her hands, and then dropped to the floor.

"So, have you come to say goodbye?"

Toby lowered his eyes.

"I guess so. I mean, I don't want to. What we did was great, but—"

Kat stopped him with a raised hand.

"Don't sweat it." She looked over his shoulder. "Where's your friend?"

"Mr Hind? He's talking to the Quay authorities. He's trying to arrange a shuttle to ferry us to the Dho Ark."

As he talked, Kat watched his mouth. She remembered those lips on her skin, his breath on her neck, those hands pressing down so urgently on her hips as her own nails raked his back...

With a shiver, she took off her thick welding gauntlets and tucked them into the thigh pocket of her trousers.

"You don't need a shuttle, I'll take you."

Drake blinked.

"You will?"

"Sure." Kat used her implant to make a few rough calculations. "We can make a small in-system jump and have you at the Ark in a couple of hours."

Drake thought about it for a second or two, and then broke into his lopsided grin.

"That's very kind of you."

Around them, the maintenance crews were packing away their equipment. Feliks Abdulov appeared at the top of the *Ameline*'s cargo ramp. Wiping his hands on a rag, he walked down to join them.

"Okay, Katherine, we've done all we can for now. You have thirty minutes until you lift. As soon as we're out of your hair, I suggest you start running the countdown."

Kat gave a nod of gratitude.

"Dad, I want you to meet Toby Drake. I brought him here from the Bubble Belt. Toby, this is my father."

The two men shook hands.

Feliks said, "Are you going with her?"

"Only as far as the Dho Ark."

"Really?" He gave his daughter a sideways look. "Do you have time for that?"

Kat shrugged. By her reckoning it would take two hours to reach a safe Jump Zone, then a few minutes for the jump to the gas giant. After that, it was a case of dropping her passengers at the Ark and jumping out of the system before Victor got his act together. The gas giant didn't have a designated JZ, so she could fire up the engines as soon as she was clear of the Ark.

"Victor's ship won't leave here for another four hours," she said. "I'll be long gone by then."

AT PRECISELY 1100 hours, the *Ameline* slipped her moorings. She backed out of her bay using minimal bursts from her manoeuvring thrusters, and rotated around her axis until she faced open space. The bays around her held a hundred ships of different shapes and sizes, from small independent traders like the *Ameline* to sleek passenger liners and the bloated hulls of corporate freighters.

On the *Ameline*'s bridge, Katherine Abdulov looked in vain for Victor's ship. The Quay's manifest said it was still in its allotted bay—number 49—but the bay's heavy pressure doors were closed, blocking her view. She was still craning forward when her own ship broke into her thoughts:

> INCOMING MESSAGE FROM THE *TRISTERO*.

A window opened in her right eye, revealing the face of Victor Luciano. She saw his right cheek twitch and guessed he was receiving an image of her on his own implant.

Physically, he looked to be somewhere in his early fifties, with grey hair and wide shoulders, and eyes the colour of a thundercloud. But she knew looks were deceiving, especially amongst traders, and even though he hardly ever spoke about his past, she knew he was a lot older than he appeared.

"Are you going somewhere, Kat?"

"What's it to you?"

He dropped his chin, as if looking at her over a pair of nonexistent spectacles. "Oh, Kat, you disappoint me. Is that the best you can do?"

"Your thugs threw me through a door."

He rubbed the bridge of his nose with the tip of his index finger, as if trying to push something back into place.

"Yes. Yes, they did, didn't they?"

"Aren't you going to pretend you care?"

Victor looked to the side, away from the camera.

"Those days are over."

"They don't have to be."

"Yes, they do. You know they do. If I can't trust you, Kat, I can't love you."

"But you did love me, Victor. You still do. I know you do."

He shook his head. "Not anymore."

"Because I made one mistake?"

"It was more than a mistake, Kat." His eyes narrowed. "You knew exactly what you were doing."

"I was scared. I didn't know what else to do."

"That's not the point. It still happened, and it shouldn't have."

"And so you're cutting me out of your life?"

Victor leant forward, jabbing a finger at the screen. "I'm doing more than that. I'm warning you to stay away from me. Give up this stupid race. You can't beat me to Djatt, and you shouldn't try."

"Are you threatening me?"

He shook his head. "You're not up to this, Kat. You don't have what it takes."

"And you do, I suppose?"

He sat back. "All I'm saying is that we threw you through a door with air on the other side of it. The next crew you piss off mightn't be so thoughtful."

> INCOMING CALL FROM FELIKS ABDULOV.

"Fuck off, Victor."

She cut the feed, hands shaking. The screen blanked, and then fired up again, this time showing the head and shoulders of her father.

She swallowed away the sudden prickle in her eyes, unclenched her fists.

"Hello, Dad."

"Katherine. Are you okay? You look upset."

"I'm fine." She gave her best approximation of a brave smile.

"Well, you don't look fine. But then, I guess I've had better days myself."

She looked into his face, still dirty from working on the *Ameline*'s hull, trying to memorise every crease and wrinkle.

"I wish we'd had more time to talk," she said. There was so much left unresolved. "Just promise me you'll still be here when I get back."

Her father reached out a hand. "Don't worry about us, Katherine."

"Dad, I—"

"Concentrate on your mission. There's no need to—"

The screen flickered and Feliks staggered. He put out an arm to steady himself. The lights above him dimmed to brown, and then came back up to full strength. Alarms sounded.

"Dad! What's happening?"

She checked her implant. Traffic control was offline. People were shouting all over the Quay. The walls of Bay 49 had buckled, rocking the station. They had been sucked inward and the blast doors had cracked, revealing the gaping vacuum left by the ship that had been resting at its heart.

Kat blinked at the pictures, unwilling to believe what she saw: the *Tristero* had gone. It had left the station without even bothering to wait for the blast doors to open, activating its engines while still wrapped in its docking cradle.

"Jesus," she said, "he *jumped*?"

CHAPTER THIRTEEN
PRIME RADIANT

"HEY, I FOUND a sign!"

Kristin came running across the stone circle towards them, waving her arms, boots kicking though the long grass.

Ed Rico leaned out of the Land Rover.

"Where?"

"On one of the uprights." She stumbled to a halt and bent over, hands on knees. "An arrow."

When she'd caught her breath, she led them over to the stone. Sure enough, someone had scratched a crude arrow into its weathered surface. Ed traced the shape with his finger. It pointed to the arch on the right of the stone. The scratches were pale and gritty and rough to the touch.

"It's fresh."

"Sure is. No more than a week old, I reckon."

Alice said, "Do you think your team left it?"

The American woman rubbed the short white bristles at the back of her neck. "They must have done. It's standard operating procedure, if you have to leave a man behind."

She dropped to one knee and gathered her bagged samples of grass and soil. She stuffed them into the pockets of her cargo pants and stood, brushing the dirt from her hands.

"Are you ready to move?"

THEY WADED BACK through the wind-ruffled grass to the Land Rover. As they walked, Alice reached out to touch Kristin's elbow.

"You know, you haven't told us who you work for."

The taller woman stopped.

"I haven't?"

She glanced impatiently back at the marked arch, shifting her weight from one booted foot to the other.

Ed rubbed his eyes. His skin itched. After sleeping in his clothes, he needed a shower.

"You're obviously military but you don't have any insignia," he said.

Kristin glanced down at her khaki hoodie.

"We're part of a joint UN recon team," she said. "I guess all the badges are on my jacket, in my kit bag."

Ed stepped forward. He felt the wind tug at his t-shirt. "You told us this was a one-way trip."

"It is."

"Then how can you be a recon team? How are you going to report back?"

Kristin folded her arms and puffed out her cheeks.

"We're not."

"Then what are you doing?"

Kristin turned and started walking toward the Land Rover, arms still folded. Ed and Alice hurried to keep pace with her.

"We're trying to prove a theory," she said. "We've mapped part of the network and we've used computer extrapolation to sketch in the rest." She kicked at the long grass. "Our model indicates an overall structure. As far as we can tell, the branches collapse toward a single point. We call it a funnelling effect."

Shuffling along beside her, Ed pushed his hands into the pockets of his jeans. "You mean, all the gates lead to the same place?" He felt a sudden stab of wild hope.

"That's right. All roads lead to Rome. According to the model, whichever route you take, you eventually spiral in towards the centre of the network. We call it the Prime Radiant."

Ed saw Alice's auburn hair flickering in the wind. He heard her say, "Like the canals in Amsterdam?"

Kristin raised an eyebrow. "How so?"

Alice brushed her fringe from her eyes. "In Amsterdam, the canals are arranged in semi-circular arcs. Wherever you are in the city, if you follow one, sooner or later you'll end up back at the Central Station. You can't get lost."

They reached the Land Rover. Kristin pulled off her hoodie and tossed it onto the back seat.

"It's more like a spider's web," she said. "Only we don't know what's at the centre."

"So you're going to find out?"

"That's right. That's our mission. And all our predictions point to that as the place we'll find all the people lost in the network."

Ed's breath caught in his throat. He felt Alice slip her hand into his.

"Like Verne?" she said, eyes shining.

Kristin nodded.

"We may be ten years behind him, but if we head for the Prime Radiant, we'll find him sure enough."

FOR THE LAST *three years of her life, Ed's mother had lived in a gated retirement community on the outskirts of Cardiff, paid for by her eldest son, Verne. When she died of pneumonia at the age of sixty-two, he, Ed and Alice were the only attendants at her funeral.*

After the service, they crunched their way back along the shingle path to the crematorium's wrought iron gate. Behind them, the last scraps of smoke rose from the brick chimney. It was a bright day in the Valleys. Frost lingered in the gaps and shadows between the grave markers and fir trees. A single vapour trail scratched the high blue sky. Verne and Alice were wrapped in coats and scarves. As they walked, Alice slipped her arm through Ed's.

"It was a nice service. I'm glad you came. Shirley would have been pleased."

Ed had his fists balled in his pockets. He wore a black suit jacket over skinny dark jeans and a paint-stained Ramones T-shirt.

He said, "I'm sorry I was late."

Beside him, Verne had his head down and his shoulders hunched. He said, "I suppose we should be grateful you're here at all."

Ed stopped walking.

"What do you mean by that?"

Verne turned to face him. "What do you think I mean? You're always so wrapped up in yourself. When was the last time you bothered coming down here?"

"I saw her at the wedding."

"Three months ago! Where were you when she really needed you, eh?"

Ed bristled. His mother had been raised as a hard-working Valleys girl. She disapproved of his life as a penniless artist, and seldom missed an opportunity to voice her feelings on the matter. "I was going to come, you know I was. It wasn't my fault she died when she did. And anyway, where the fuck were you?"

Verne gave an exasperated sigh. He'd been in Mogadishu when Shirley died. "You know I would have been here if I could, if the rebels hadn't closed the airport. They were shooting Europeans. We had to stay hidden in the hotel. Whereas you, Ed, all you had to do was catch a train."

Alice slid her arm out from under Ed's.

"Verne, this really isn't the time."

"I'm just saying—"

"Well, don't."

She pulled the black fur hat from her head and shook her gloved fingers through her mussed, rust-coloured hair.

"I'm sorry, Ed," she said.

She took his elbow and walked him to the gate. Moss dappled the cracked concrete path. Verne's car waited on the opposite side of the steeply sloping street, in front of a row of terraced houses.

"Are you sure we can't give you a lift? We could drop you at Oxford and you could get a train back to London from there."

Ed glanced at his brother. Verne's cheeks were a mottled red and he kept clenching and unclenching his fists.

"No, don't worry about it. I can get a local train from here to Cardiff, then straight through to Paddington. I've already booked the ticket and they don't do refunds."

"Will you be okay?"

"I'll be fine," Ed said. "I'll probably sleep most of the way. And if not, I've got my sketchbook." He pulled the small black Moleskine from his pocket. Its pages bulged with bookmarks, feathers and Post-it notes.

Alice said, "You'll have to let me look at that sometime."

Verne shouldered past them and opened the car door.

"Goodbye, Ed," he said.

Alice sighed. "Don't worry about him. It's because he was in Africa when she died. He feels bad, and he's taking it out on you."

Ed blew into his hands. "I know."

"He'll be okay in a couple of days, you'll see."

She stood on her toes. Her lips were warm on his cold cheek. Her hair smelled of peppermint shampoo.

"I'll come and see you soon. I'm in London next week. Verne's going off on another assignment. I'll drop by and make sure you're okay."

She squeezed his arm.

"If it's any help," she said, "I think as long as we remember someone, they're not really dead."

She gave a last, brave smile and ran across the road to the waiting car. She waved once as they pulled away, and Ed watched until the brake lights reached the end of the terrace and turned right, out of sight, heading towards the M4. Then he turned up his jacket collar and began the long trudge back to the railway station.

THE CRYSTAL SHIP

DESPITE SPENDING HER youth in the Strauli system, Katherine Abdulov had never been this close to the Dho Ark. Under ordinary circumstances, civilian vessels were forbidden from coming within a million kilometres of its orbital path around the system's solitary gas giant. Growing up on the beaches of Strauli, she'd seen pictures of it, of course, but as the *Ameline* fell into its shadow, she had to admit they'd been poor preparation for the sheer scale of the thing.

The Ark had the appearance of a single, translucent quartz crystal. The hull was seamless, aside from a small, circular dock at one end, with sharp angles and smooth, polished facets. Leaning forward in her acceleration couch, Kat gave a low whistle.

"That's enormous."

> TARGET MEASURES ELEVEN HUNDRED KILOMETRES FROM BOW TO STERN.

She shook her head.

"That's not a ship, it's a moon."

> SIZE ISN'T EVERYTHING.

Kat rubbed her eyes. She'd been in the couch for the last two hours, since Victor's surprise departure from

Strauli Quay. Her skin felt gritty and the muscles in her back and shoulders were stiff with the need to get up and stretch.

"Replay the footage from the Quay," she said.

> AGAIN?

A window opened in her right eye. It was a grainy shot of Victor's ship, the *Tristero*, taken from the security camera in his assigned landing bay. The news stations had been replaying it constantly since the incident. Now, as she watched it again for the fifth or sixth time, she saw the ship shudder as its jump engines came online. One moment, it was a long silvery wedge squatting in the centre of a nest of cables. The next, the camera blanked out in a white flash. The ship's engines generated a wormhole and all the air in the bay vanished, the resulting depressurisation rocking the station. Even though the walls of the bay were reinforced, built to withstand exposure to vacuum, they still sagged inward. They buckled under the wormhole's gravitational stress. By the time the picture cleared, there was nothing to see. Disconnected hoses twitched and flopped like decapitated snakes, pumping arterial sprays of fuel and water into the sudden vacuum. The wormhole had collapsed, and the ship had gone.

> IDIOT.

Despite the scorn, Kat sensed a grudging respect in the *Ameline*'s tone, a respect she found she shared. She couldn't help but be impressed by his cold-hearted willingness to endanger the lives of hundreds, possibly thousands of people. It revealed in Victor Luciano a callous determination that, hitherto, she'd only suspected. After this, he'd never set foot on the Quay again. He'd be arrested on sight. The whole station was in uproar. The news networks were going batshit. In the last two hours, she'd been called by three reporters. They knew Victor was heading for the Pep harvest on Djatt. They'd heard about her relationship with him and sensed a conspiracy. They accused her of working against her family, of plotting the entire episode. In the end, she'd asked the ship to block their calls, which only fuelled their speculation.

At least the port authority weren't bugging her. They knew the score. Her father had given them a copy of her letter of introduction, confirming her position as a full captain in the Abdulov fleet.

From trainee to outcast, then from outcast to captain: looking out at the approaching bulk of the Dho Ark, she caught the ghostly reflection of her own smile.

At least some good's come of all this...

Then she thought of the missing Abdulov ship, the *Kilimanjaro*, and the smile died on her lips. There had been fourteen men, women and children on that ship, their fate now unknown. Up until this moment, she'd harboured the possibility that accident or technical malfunction had delayed the vessel. She hadn't wanted to believe Victor, her ex-lover, capable of outright piracy. She hadn't wanted to think of him as a murderer. Now though, having seen the way he'd blasted off the Quay, she felt a cold certainty creeping over her.

She pictured the *Kilimanjaro* with its hull torn open, spilling air and warmth into the void, the corpses of adults and children turning slowly end-over-end, surrounded by frozen scraps of food, odd shoes, smashed hull plates. Some of the dead would have been her cousins, nieces, nephews. She imagined a stuffed bear clutched in a dead child's hand, and her lip curled in disgust. Suddenly her blood felt like ice, and she knew she had to beat Victor to Djatt. More was at stake in this race than money or prestige. It wasn't about their failed relationship any more. It wasn't about family honour. No, she told herself, all that mattered to her now was vengeance for the blood on his hands. She had to stop him from hurting anyone else.

And for a moment, she almost believed it.

CHAPTER FIFTEEN
ANGRY BLUE SPARK

As THEY ROLLED out of the portal, half-blind from the flash, they heard the creak of scum-greased timbers beneath the Land Rover's tyres.

"What the fuck?"

Ed stood on the brake, felt the wheels slip. They were sliding across the deck of a wooden sailing ship. All he could see was water beyond the splintered rail. Alice screamed and grabbed his arm; he jammed all his weight onto the brake pedal and dragged the steering wheel to the right. The back end of the Land Rover slewed around with sickening slowness. For an awful, heart-stopping instant it looked as if they weren't going to stop in time, and then the tyres bit into the wood and the big car juddered to a halt, centimetres from the remains of the broken rail.

Ed killed the engine. No-one spoke. The silence seemed to press in on their eardrums. Ed looked down at the hand he had resting shakily on the gear lever.

"You can let go now," he said.

Alice turned to him, dragging her eyes from the watery precipice beneath her window.

"What?"

"My arm."

"Oh shit, sorry." She snatched her hand away. There were white marks where her fingers had been. On the back seat, Kristin cursed.

"Jesus aitch fucking *Christ*!"

She cracked the door and fetid salt air muscled into the cab, thick with the smell of putrid seaweed.

"Let's see where we are," she said.

Alice wrinkled her nose and waved a hand in front of her face. "After you."

With her hand over her mouth and nose, Kristin stepped out. Ed followed, still rubbing his arm.

They were on the edge of a broad deck, a thousand metres in length, maybe a quarter that across. On one side of the car, a fifteen metre drop to the water; on the other, algae-covered timbers and masts the size of Redwoods. There were no sails, only rotten scraps of sun-bleached fabric flapping on the highest spars. At the stern, the superstructure rose in a series of stepped decks, linked by ladders. Doors hung open on their hinges. Broken portholes gaped. Slimy green and yellow algae dripped from every surface. A row of arches stood on the main deck between two of the tallest masts. Ed counted fifteen. They were lashed together with lengths of mouldering rope, some of which had rotted or frayed, and several of the arches had fallen flat against the deck.

Ed scratched his hair. He walked around the Land Rover to the ship's smashed rail and inched his way to the edge of the deck. The algae squelched beneath the thick soles of his boots. Below, the sea moved sluggishly against the timbers. It looked oily with algae and black weed, and it stank of rotting vegetation. He spat into the water. A pair of outriggers jutted from the bows, each the size of a cross-Channel ferry, yet both dwarfed by the bulk of the main hull.

"Big ship," he said.

Beside him, Kristin banged the toe of her boot against the planking.

"This wood seems flexible, but it must be incredibly tough stuff. On Earth, you couldn't build a wooden ship even a tenth this big. It wouldn't be strong enough to withstand a heavy sea." She tapped her foot again. Then looking thoughtful, she folded her arms and walked off, in the direction of the stepped decks at the stern, stopping every few paces to examine the workmanship on the wooden deck, masts and rail. She even crouched to scoop a handful of algae into one of her plastic bags.

Ed watched her for a moment, then turned as he heard Alice slide open her window. The Land Rover had stopped with less than half a metre to spare, and her door overlooked the long drop to the weed-choked water. She craned her neck, peering down. Then with a shiver, she flicked her eyes upwards instead, away from the water.

"Look," she said. "Two suns."

Ed tipped his head back. The larger sun looked round and yellow, roughly the size of the Sun as seen from Earth. Beside it, the other appeared about the size of a button held at arm's length: an angry blue spark in the sky, throwing its own faint shadows. It was the most alien thing he'd ever seen. He shivered and looked away.

Alice wriggled across to the driver's door and stepped gingerly onto the slippery deck. She had her camera in her hand. Her hair shone like copper in the double sunlight.

"Come on, I want to take some pictures." She took Ed's arm and led him towards the stern. "What's with all the arches?"

Ed was concentrating on not slipping over. "Maybe they were taking them somewhere, collecting them all together?"

"Like with the stone circle?"

"Yes, why not?"

Alice pursed her lips. "Perhaps they were trying to get rid of them, dump them all in the sea?" She turned towards him, shading her eyes. "Makes you wonder, doesn't it? First the stone circle, now this. What were they afraid of?"

Behind her, a figure slid from an open door. Ed looked up expecting Kristin. Instead, he found himself gaping at the barrel of a compact machine pistol. Instinctively, he raised his hands. Alice jerked back from him, confused. She still hadn't seen the man behind her.

"Don't move," Ed warned.

The red-faced man with the machine pistol stepped forward, aim unwavering.

He snapped, "Both of you, hands on your heads."

Alice turned.

"*What?*"

She came face-to-face with the gun barrel and her eyes crossed trying to focus on it. She staggered backwards, stumbled, and ended up sat on the deck at Ed's feet.

"Who are you?"

"Shut up!"

The man took a step forward, eyes wide and nostrils flared. He had a black moustache and he wore an olive vest, black combat trousers and high-laced boots. His skin was red and peeling from his face. The wind from the sea pulled at his hair.

"Get up and put your hands on your head."

He watched her rise, and then stepped back out of reach. He looked around.

"Now, where's your friend?"

Ed's hands were clasped behind his neck, fingers interlocked, palms slick with sweat. His pulse hammered in his ears. Where was his gun?

He glanced back at the Land Rover's open door. The shotgun stood propped in the foot well behind the driver's seat. It was maybe twenty metres away. Could he reach it?

His calves tensed.

"Where is she?" The man held the pistol at his hip, its barrel wavering back and forth, covering both targets. Ed could see his index finger tight against the trigger.

"I'll count to three."

"I'm here."

Kristin appeared at the rail of the next deck up, hands held at shoulder height. She had her hood down and her peroxide white hair shone in the blue and yellow light of the two suns.

The man jerked.

"Lieutenant Cole?"

"At ease, soldier."

The gun barrel dipped.

"I was beginning to think you weren't coming."

Kristin lowered her hands. "Well, I'm here now."

The man's eyes flicked back to Ed and Alice. "And these two?"

"They're with me."

The eyes narrowed for a second. Then the soldier's stance straightened and he shouldered the weapon.

"If you say so."

Kristin looked at Ed. "This is Specialist Otto Krous," she said. "He's part of my team."

KROUS HADN'T EATEN for two days, so Kristin dug a chocolate bar from Ed's pack and gave it to him.

"What happened here?" she asked as he tore the wrapper.

They were standing by the broken rail, looking out at the flat, featureless horizon. A few feet away, Ed leaned against the Land Rover's fender, arms folded, listening. His nostrils were full of the stink of the seaweed, and his skin itched where the light touched it. He looked at the skin peeling from Krous's face, and glanced up at the blue and yellow suns.

"We should cover up or we're going to get fried," he said.

Behind him, Alice sat in the cab, shotgun resting on her knees, still angry about being held at gunpoint. Oblivious to her glares, Krous chewed a mouthful of chocolate and swallowed.

"We came through the arch too fast," he said. "I mean, Fischer was driving and we can't have been rolling at more than walking pace, but we were still going too fast to stop." He kicked a heavy boot at the slippery algae on the planking of the deck. "Fischer hit the brakes as soon as we cleared the arch, but..."

Kristin put a hand on his shoulder.

"You went over?"

Krous leaned forward, looking down at the fetid black weed choking the water. His lips were a hard line. His eyes wouldn't keep still.

"Yes, sir. We went straight through the rail. I managed to kick my way out." He shuddered. "I had to fight through the weed."

"And the others?"

Krous shook his head. He screwed up the chocolate bar wrapper and let it flutter down into the water. Kristin's lips pressed together. She looked at Ed. From where he stood, he could see her eyes were filmy with unshed tears.

"So, what did you do?" she asked Krous, voice level.

The soldier looked up at the sky. "I clawed my way around to the back of the ship. There's a dock there for small craft, and I managed to climb out of the water. I had my gun strapped across my chest, but everything else went down with the truck." He swallowed hard and coughed into his fist. "For the last week, I've been living on glucose tablets and rain water, hoping you were coming."

He scratched irritably at his forehead. Flakes of peeled skin fell like dandruff. When he spoke again, he was hoarse.

"I'd just about given up hope, sir."

Kristin turned to survey the line of arches running the length of the deck.

"And you didn't consider moving on, trying to reach the objective?"

Krous shook his head. His eyes burned with resentment.

"No sir, I thought my best chance was to wait for you."

Ed straightened up. "Then why didn't you go back to look for her?"

The soldier bunched his fists.

"Who is this idiot?" he said.

Kristin put a restraining hand on his shoulder. "Stand down, private."

Krous looked down at her. Then, abruptly, he turned to face the distant horizon.

Kristin left him and walked over to the Land Rover, arms folded, treading warily on the slimy deck. As she passed Ed, she said, "By the time he got back, I'd have either been long dead or already *en route*. We would have missed each other."

Ed shrugged. He didn't much care. He looked back at Alice glowering behind the windshield.

"So, what do we do now?"

Kristin paused. She glanced back to the edge of the deck, to the hunched figure of the soldier standing there.

"We go on," she said.

In the driving seat, Ed rubbed his palms together.

"Is everybody ready?"

He glanced in the rear-view mirror. Alice wasn't happy about riding in the back. She scowled at him. Beside her, Otto Krous sat with his eyes fixed forward. He held his machine pistol across his chest, ready for action. Sweat rolled down the blistered skin of his face.

"We're ready," Kirstin said, voice positive and self-assured, every inch the competent officer. "Just take it slowly, okay?" She glanced through the passenger side window at the water heaving against the sides of the wooden ship, far below. They were perilously close to the edge and the deck was slippery. One wrong move and they'd be in the sea.

Ed took a deep breath and let it out in a long, slow exhalation. He depressed the clutch pedal and turned the key in the ignition. The Land Rover's 2.5 litre diesel engine juddered into life.

"Okay, hold on," he said.

He slipped the gear lever into second and slowly let out the clutch. For a second, he felt the front wheels slither. It felt like driving on ice. Then the tyres bit and the Land Rover rolled forward, towards the row of arches stacked between the masts.

"You know, no-one's asked what happened to the crew," he said.

Kristin frowned.

"How do you mean?"

"The crew. What happened to the crew of this ship? Where did they go?"

Kirstin shrugged. "Into one of the arches, I expect." She turned to Krous. "Did you find any sign of them?"

The soldier shook his head. He didn't look like he cared one way or the other. "Is it significant, sir?"

Kristin turned to face forward. "No, probably not. If they'd had the technology to build the arches, they wouldn't be carrying them around in a wooden boat. I guess they were just trying to use and understand them, same as we are." Regretfully, she rubbed the outside of the hip pocket containing her sample bags. "But I still would have liked to have had the chance to have a proper look around."

She turned her attention to the row of arches in front of them. "That way," she said, pointing.

Ed leaned over the steering wheel. It was a random selection, but she sounded confident, speaking in a tone used to obedience, and he was in no mood to argue with her. He let the tyres roll forward. The big car eased into the arch she'd chosen. As they crossed the threshold, he closed his eyes to protect them from the white flash.

The next thing he knew, they were in darkness.

The ground crumbled away beneath their wheels. The Land Rover tipped over onto the driver's side. The chassis scraped against solid rock with a metallic screech. Ed fumbled for the lights, but they were already falling sideways. The steering wheel yanked itself out of his hands. Alice cried out.

The car crashed down into shadow. It landed on its side, and the windows shattered.

MECHANICAL EQUIVALENT

ALTHOUGH IT LOOKED tiny when compared to the overall vastness of the Dho Ark, the entrance to the dock in its prow could have swallowed a city all by itself. Its maw dwarfed the *Ameline* as the little ship slid inside, navigation lights reflecting back from semi-opaque diamond walls a thousand metres thick.

Ahead, in a softly lit alcove like a pore in the planetoid's ancient skin, a docking cradle hinged open, clamps reaching hungrily.

> THIRTY SECONDS, the ship said.

Standing at the door of the rear airlock with her two passengers, Katherine Abdulov took a deep breath as she watched the approach via her implant.

"Understood."

She looked at Toby Drake. "I guess this is it." She smoothed down the front of her flight suit. The Dho had given permission for her to deliver her passengers, but only on the strict understanding that she depart as soon as they were safely on board the Ark.

"I guess so." Drake looked uncomfortable in a shirt and tie and formal brown jacket. His eyes were wide, drinking her in, memorising her face, her stance, and the way she shifted her weight from one hip to the other.

Francis Hind had the hood of his robe pulled up, shadowing his eyes.

"Ready to go?" Kat said. "Because as soon as we get a hard seal, I'm kicking you both out."

She itched to get going. Her hands fluttered in front of her like nervous birds. She had to catch Victor; and yet, remembering the feel of Drake's lips against hers, the warmth of his dark skin in her bed, she suddenly wanted more time. She wasn't ready to say goodbye so soon.

"Are you all right?" Drake held his case in one hand and a bag of books in the other. He put the books down and took her hand in both of his. As his fingers brushed hers, she felt the hairs rise on her arms.

His hands were warm. She clenched her jaw and swallowed away the emotion.

"I'm going to be gone a long time," she said. Her voice sounded hoarse.

Drake ran a thumb over her knuckles, giving her an involuntary shiver.

"But you will *be* back, won't you Katherine?" His eyes were boyish and hopeful. She withdrew her hand.

"It's just less than twelve light years to Djatt. That's a roundtrip of twenty-four years."

"I'll wait for you."

She shook her head. For her, the trip would take a few weeks, maybe a month. By the time she got back, he'd be in his fifties, almost twice his current age.

"I can't ask you to do that."

Firmly, she turned to the Acolyte.

"So, Mister Hind, do you have everything you need?"

Hind bowed from the waist, hands wrapped in the voluminous folds of his robe.

"Yes, thank you, Captain. You have been more than hospitable." He pulled back his hood. The corridor lights picked out the grey hairs at his temples. "And I have something for you."

He unfolded his hands to reveal an irregularly-shaped pendant, which dangled from his fingers on a thin strap of leather.

"This is for you." He pressed it into her hand and she looked down at it. It was a smooth, flat pebble with a rune cut into its surface: one long vertical line crossed by two short horizontal slashes.

"What is it?"

Hind reached out and covered her hand with his.

"If you insist on going to Djatt, it will protect you," he said.

WHEN THEY FINALLY docked, Kat kept the farewells to a minimum: a nod to Hind, and a tight, regretful smile for Drake. Then she pressed the wall control and turned away as the door swung shut with a solid *clunk*.

She stamped back through the ship to the bridge and strapped herself into her seat. She linked her implant into the ship's sensor array, felt the power building.

"Prepare for emergency departure."

> YOU GOT IT.

She checked the airlock, found it clear.

"Passengers gone?"

> WE'RE GOOD TO GO.

She opened her hand and looked down at the pendant she'd been given. First Victor, then her father, now Drake.

Fuck it, she thought. *Nothing lasts.*

She slipped the leather cord over her neck, letting the pendant fall against her chest as she cast her eyes across the displays. A few final checks, then: "Release."

She closed her eyes and felt the ship shudder as the docking clamps disengaged.

> RELEASED.

The *Ameline* tumbled out of the Ark, between the kilometre-thick diamond walls of the bay, into naked space. Through her interface with the ship, Kat felt the chill of the vacuum against the hull, the pinprick lights of distant stars like mosquito feet on her skin. She smiled, feeling the building thrust like an eagerness fluttering in her stomach.

> FIFTEEN MINUTES TO DESIGNATED JUMP ZONE.

"Jump now."

> HAVE YOU SEEN THE SIZE OF THIS THING? TRUST ME, YOU DON'T WANT TO PISS IT OFF.

"Jump now."

> THIS ISN'T DOING MY ENGINES ANY GOOD.

"Jump."

The ship gave the mechanical equivalent of a sigh.

> YOU'RE THE BOSS.

Manoeuvring jets fired. The ship's nose moved, seeking its destination. It shook itself.

And jumped.

CHAPTER SEVENTEEN
THE GLASS ELEVATOR

THROUGH THE TRANSPARENT crystal wall of the Dho Ark's debarkation lounge, Toby Drake watched the blunt triangle of the *Ameline* fall away into the night. Sensor pods blistered her nose. Red and green navigation lights winked along her length. He felt a strange tearing sensation, and tightened his grip on the handle of his suitcase. Even though it had been his home for only a day and a night, the old ship represented the last direct link to his former life on Tiers Cross. He watched it dwindle until it jumped away, collapsing to nothing in a flash of white light.

"Goodbye, Kat," he whispered.

Beside him, Francis Hind cleared his throat. The middle-aged Acolyte had his black cowl pushed back, revealing his thin grey hair and pale, sky-blue eyes.

"Are you ready?"

Toby nodded. He turned away from the view, hefted his suitcase, and followed Hind into a tunnel leading deep into the rock of the hollowed-out planetoid. Their footfalls echoed as they walked, and the air smelled of chlorine. Toby sniffed. It reminded him of a swimming pool.

At the end of the corridor, they passed through an airlock with reinforced ceramic doors a foot thick. It took a few seconds to cycle. On the other side, dim overhead lights bathed the corridor in a bloody sunset red. Two figures waited in the gloom. One was human, the other...

Toby recoiled. The suitcase slipped from his grasp and thumped onto the deck.

The other figure was monstrous, towering over him. Its black robe bulged in all the wrong places, and it had four twisted horns of yellowing bone where its head should be.

He swallowed. He could hear his heart hammering in his chest.

"Jesus."

Although Toby had known roughly what to expect, it was still a shock to suddenly confront one of the creatures. Every fibre of his being shrank from it. His fists clenched. In the hundred years since the discovery of the Ark, few people had come face-to-face with one. The aliens were notoriously reclusive, never venturing far from the security of the Ark, preferring to interact through their human recruits, the Acolytes.

He took another step back and felt Francis Hind's hand on his arm.

"This is one of our hosts," the older man said. "And, of course, you know Professor Harris."

With an effort, Toby dragged his eyes from the alien to the man standing beside it. Despite a few grey hairs, Professor Harris looked much as Toby remembered him. The man had his hands in the pockets of the same threadbare tweed jacket he'd worn when lecturing at the university on Tiers Cross. He still sported the same disreputable beard and his green eyes still glared from beneath a pair of untameable brows.

"Drake. Good to see you, boy. Glad you could make it."

He thrust out a hand. After a moment, Toby stepped through the airlock and shook it.

"G-good to see you too, Professor."

Toby looked sideways at the Dho. Three glistening alien eyes gazed back at him from sockets set deep in the bone at the root of the creature's horns. They looked like olives. The front horns were short and spiky, like tusks. The ones behind were almost a foot in length, curving forward from thick bases, ending in jagged and misshapen tips. It looked like a horned beetle, but how much of that was helmet and how much living tissue? Was it even possible to make a distinction?

Toby closed his eyes and dipped his head in a formal bow.

"Pleased to meet you," he said.

The Dho shivered. A series of dry clicks and scrapes came from beneath its cloak.

Francis Hind folded his hands.

"Our host is likewise honoured to make your acquaintance, Mister Drake. But right now, it's time for Professor Harris to show you the reason for your invitation."

"Yes, come along, Drake."

The Professor turned on his heel and set off down the dim red corridor, beard jutted purposefully in front of him, hands clasped firmly behind his back.

Toby hesitated.

"You go ahead," Hind said. He looked at the Dho. "I've been away from here for fourteen years. I have a lot to catch up on. You go with the Professor and I'll bring your luggage along later."

THE CORRIDOR TOOK them deeper into the rock of the planetoid. They passed service tunnels and strangely arched doorways built to accommodate the horns of the Ark's inhabitants. Dense, intricate murals covered every surface.

"The Dho carry their history with them," the Professor said. "Apparently, these hieroglyphics depict events from their past. Take this one, for instance." He stopped and pointed to a scene carved into the rock above an archway. "This is a stylised rendering of the Ark itself, and we think these specks here are smaller ships in its wake."

"And that?" Toby pointed to what appeared to be a dark and angry, looming cloud, seemingly reaching out tendrils to catch the flotilla of ships.

The Professor shook his head. "We have no idea. But these lines here appear to represent bolts of energy leaping from the smaller ships, holding the cloud at bay while the Ark makes its escape."

He straightened up.

"The Acolytes tell us this is a key scene. They call it 'The Burning Sky.' The whole ship's covered in similar pictures, but they don't appear to be arranged in any comprehensible order or sequence. As far as we can tell, they're all placed randomly. We're having terrible trouble fitting them into anything resembling a coherent chronology. It's frustrating, to say the least."

He sniffed. "Of course, our hosts insist the whole thing makes perfect sense to them, but instead of sharing their insight, they're making us work it all out for ourselves."

They arrived at an elevator. The car was two metres tall and around ten metres square, and its walls were made of the same diamond as the skin of the Ark. Harris ushered Toby inside and the doors hissed shut behind them.

"This will take us where we need to go." The Professor grinned through his beard. "However, I should warn you, you may find the ride a tad unsettling."

Toby raised an eyebrow but before he had a chance to respond verbally, the elevator leaped forward and accelerated into a dark tunnel. Instinctively, he reached out to steady himself, but there was no feeling of movement. Beyond the car's crystal walls, the lights in the tunnel zipped past, faster and faster, but inside, all was still. It was as if they were standing in a movie theatre watching pictures on a screen.

He was just getting used to the sensation when the elevator burst out of the tunnel into daylight. He twisted his head around in surprise. Behind them, a vast cliff receded, dotted with lights and openings. They were travelling through a cloudless sky with no visible means of support, and Toby's stomach twisted as he looked down at the miles and miles of empty air beneath the car's transparent floor.

"Whoa."

He looked across at the Professor, standing unconcerned in the centre of the car, hands still in the pockets of his tweed jacket.

"This is one of the caverns," the old man said. "There are hundreds of them in the Ark's interior, of all shapes and sizes. This one's a cylinder about a hundred miles in length and fifty across, with a city on its inner edge. Others house jungles or swamps. We think each one preserves a different environment from our host's home planet."

Ahead, another cliff rushed at them. Toby swallowed. He felt like a bug facing an approaching windshield.

Then they were in another tunnel. Lights whipped past the walls so fast they were little more than blurred streaks.

"Did you have a good journey from Tiers Cross?" Harris asked.

Toby closed his eyes. Without visual cues, it was impossible to tell whether or not they were moving.

"Yes, I suppose so."

He thought of Katherine Abdulov lying warm and tousled in his arms and felt another stab of loss and longing.

"Good, good. And I trust you brought your research with you?"

"Yes sir. I've got electronic copies of everything ever written on the Gnarl, including all my own papers and notes."

"And some books, judging by your suitcase?"

Toby opened his eyes with a smile. "A habit I picked up from you, Professor."

Harris twitched his moustache. "Quite. Well, you're going to need them. Your notes, I mean."

Toby frowned. "Can I ask why? Only I've come all this way, and no-one's told me anything."

The lights outside the car were passing more slowly now: they were decelerating.

"No need, you'll be able to see for yourself in a moment." The Professor gestured forwards. Ahead, a circle of light lay at the end of the tunnel, growing as they slowed. By the time they reached the tunnel's end, they were travelling at walking pace.

"Behold!" boomed Harris, flinging his arm theatrically. "Behold the reason I asked you here."

Toby walked forward and placed his hands on the transparent wall. They had emerged into another cylindrical chamber, this one maybe a kilometre in diameter and twice that in length. The walls were blank and smooth. Ahead, the air at the centre of the empty space had been curdled. There were clouds twisted into unlikely spirals, and at the centre, flickering with blue static discharge, something writhed. It looked like a ball of angry snakes. Strange symbols flickered across its surface and were lost from sight. It seemed to be drawing in all the light in the room, like a plug draining water from a sink.

In the glass elevator, Toby stepped back and shook his head.

"I don't believe it."

There couldn't be another one. Could there? In all the years he'd spent studying the Gnarl at the heart of the Bubble Belt, he'd never supposed it to be anything other than unique.

He felt Harris's heavy hand clap him on the shoulder.

"Believe it, my boy. This is the reason you were called here. You've spent your life studying one Gnarl. Now, we need your expertise with another."

Toby turned to him.

"But what's it doing here?"

The Professor's brows drew together like wary caterpillars circling each other.

"*Doing* here?" He chuckled. "My dear boy, how else do you think you power an Ark of this size?"

Toby shook his head. His eyes were watering but he couldn't look away. He was captivated by the ever-changing surface. It moved like oil on water.

"Power...?"

"Oh yes!" Harris rubbed his hands together. "My boy, that wonderful anomaly out there is the *engine*. It powers this vast, insane spaceship."

He leaned forward and tapped Toby on the chest.

"And that's where you come in, Mister Drake. We want *you* to tell us how it works."

FISSURE

FIRST CAME THE pain. Then, after a while, Ed realised he was conscious. He didn't know what had happened to him, but time had passed, and his head hurt. He was lying on his side, and something heavy lay on his hip, pressing him down. For a chilling instant, he thought he was back on that table in Bethnal Green, with Pavle holding him down, waiting for Grigor to shatter his wrists with the flat side of a butcher's cleaver.

"You must understand that this is a matter of honour."

Cold water bubbled against the side of his face, and his eyes snapped open with a gasp. He twisted his neck, lifting his face clear. His cheek felt frozen. Flailing around in panic, his hands gripped the steering wheel, and he realised he was still in the Land Rover, which was on its side, and slowly filling with water.

The car had toppled into a rocky fissure and now lay wedged in the stream at its bottom. Just enough light came from above for him to make out its rough stone walls and the shallow, fast-moving water covering its gravelled floor. The driver's side window had shattered on impact, and his cheek had been resting on gritty kernels of broken glass. Blood mixed with stream water. Kristin lay on top of him, dead or unconscious, her head and shoulder digging into his hip, her legs wedged in the foot well on the passenger side. Neither of them had been wearing seatbelts.

Ed flexed his back. He could smell petrol. His shoulder hurt where he'd slammed against the inside of the door. His clothes were wet from the water coming in through the broken window. Carefully, he twisted around in the confined space, hampered by Kristin's weight pressing on him. He did his best to lower her gently to the floor, trying to keep her as dry as possible. She was heavier than he expected, and a red bruise discoloured the side of her right eye. She was starting to stir. Not dead, just stunned and groaning faintly, her eyelids fluttering like butterflies caught in a spider's web.

When her legs touched the icy water, she jerked in his arms.

"Ed?"

"I'm here."

"Ed, what happened?"

Ed stood upright, his head pressing against the unbroken passenger window, through which he could see the lip of the fissure, and a pink morning sky beyond. They'd fallen maybe three or four metres into the v-shaped crack, and were now wedged in its narrow base, with the Land Rover's wheels jammed against one wall and its roof crumpled against the other.

He turned, careful to avoid treading on Kristin, and careful to avoid the gear lever. Broken glass crunched underfoot. His feet were getting wet, and his toes hurt with the cold. Something shone silver in the water. The St. Christopher medal had fallen from the rear-view mirror. He crouched and scooped it into his pocket, then stood and looked back over the body of the Land Rover. His eye caught the arch from which they'd emerged, perched on a ledge, its base overhanging the edge of the cleft into which they'd fallen.

"Alice?" He bent his head. "Alice, are you okay?"

No reply. Worried, he crouched awkwardly over Kristin, trying to see between the seats.

"Alice?"

He couldn't bend far enough to see properly. The light wasn't great, and there wasn't room to manoeuvre. Instead, he braced one foot against the steering wheel and, with his hands over his head, pushed open the passenger door. It was heavy and difficult from this angle, but by pushing himself up on the wheel, he managed to get his head and shoulders out into the open air.

"Ed, where are you going?"

Kristin was on her knees. He looked down at her through his legs, and saw she was shivering.

"I'm trying to get in the back. I'm going to check on the others."

Kirsten touched cautious fingers to the bruise on the side of her face.

"Well, be careful. Everything feels too heavy. I think the gravity's stronger here than we're used to. If you fall, you could really hurt yourself."

The fresh air chilled his wet hair. The door wanted to fall closed, but he managed to hook a knee over the frame and heave himself out. He scraped his shin and whacked his elbow. Then he was clear, and lying on the side of the Land Rover, panting from the exertion. His body felt like a dead weight dragging him down. He let the door drop, and it slammed into place with a crash that shook the whole car.

Out here, he could smell the spilled petrol more strongly, and hear the babbling of the stream reflected from the narrow rock walls. The lip of the fissure stood maybe three metres above his head. If he got to his feet and jumped, he felt sure he could reach it. Instead, he slid along to the rear fender and, kneeling on the bodywork, prepared to heave the back passenger side door up and open. His heart hammered in his chest. Every movement was an effort, but all he could think was that Alice had been injured. His hands shook with fear and cold as he pulled the door open, and leant in, half expecting to see her lying dead, crushed beneath the weight of the burly soldier, Krous.

It took a second for his eyes to adjust to the lack of light in the back of the Land Rover. Then he recoiled in disbelief.

Stream water curled and eddied where the window had been, but there were no bodies where he had expected to see them.

Alice and Krous were gone.

VERTEBRAE BEACH

THE WATERY MOON spun in orbit around a brooding gas giant, just outside the habitable zone of a star eight light years from Strauli Quay. Tidal forces kept the interior of the moon warm, as the gas giant's ferocious gravity alternately stretched and squeezed its rocky core, producing tectonic heat. A deep ocean covered its surface, and icebergs jostled at its poles like colliding continents. It had no dry land, and a thin atmosphere of poisonous volcanic gas, belched from hydrothermal vents on the sea floor. Once upon a time, giant whale-like creatures had cruised in these depths, feeding off clouds of algae in the warmer water above the vents. Now, their fossilised skeletons littered the sand.

The locals called the moon Vertebrae Beach.

When Katherine Abdulov arrived, she landed *The Ameline* in the sea, close to the equator, much to the old ship's disgust.

> SALT WATER'S CORROSIVE. YOU KNOW THAT, RIGHT?

In the pilot's chair, Kat stretched like a hungry cat. They'd jumped from Strauli without incident, and cruised in from the Emergence Zone at normal speed.

She'd been in the chair for six hours, brooding over the loss of Toby Drake, the inconclusive, half-resolved reconciliation with her father, and Victor's ridiculous stunt. She felt lonely and tense, and needed to vent her frustration.

"You'll be fine," she said. "You just concentrate on recharging and refuelling, and I'll be back in a couple of hours."

She slipped on her coat, and made her way to the aft airlock. The ship rocked on the swell, and the hull rang as automated tugs locked on and began hauling it toward a floating pontoon, where a submersible ferry waited to transport her down to New Barcelona, the largest of the dozen or so cities spread over the little moon's eight-kilometre deep ocean floor like so many coral reefs, shielded by their depth from the gas giant's savage radioactive output.

She'd already forwarded her credentials to the local Abdulov family representative, a middle-aged woman called Enid, who'd arranged the immediate refuelling of her ship—a process Kat expected to take somewhere between two and three hours, as she wasn't carrying any cargo. Unlike Victor, who had to pay for his fuel from profits generated *en route*, she had no need to hunt for fresh cargo or passengers to finance the next leg of her journey. She had nothing to do but wait, and too much pent-up frustration to let her wait quietly.

> GOING SOMEWHERE NICE?

"I doubt it."

As soon as they docked, she transferred to the sub, and rode it down into the darkness.

The sub was little more than a pressurised passenger cabin surrounded by spherical ballast tanks. Empty, the tanks provided enough buoyancy for it to float like a cork on the ocean swell. To descend, all the AI controlling the sub had to do was open the caps on the tanks and pump in sea water, and the whole thing sank like a stone: eight kilometres, straight down, to the city on the sea bed.

Coming in from above, the city glittered like a Christmas decoration. Lights twinkled everywhere. Agricultural domes shone in the gloom, lit up from within by powerful sunlamps. Consulting the local Grid, she learned that New Barcelona had maybe a hundred thousand inhabitants, and that the bulk of the city lay in artificial caverns below the sand. Another quick query informed her that the *Tristero* had already docked, at a floating pontoon a few kilometres from the *Ameline*'s mooring, and that Victor Luciano and his First Mate were somewhere in the city below, recruiting passengers.

As they got closer, the sub started to blow air into its ballast tanks from cylinders within the walls of the passenger cabin. As the air pressure in the tanks grew, it pushed out more and more water, increasing the sub's buoyancy and slowing their descent, until by the time it reached its berth on the ocean floor, it was hardly moving at all.

She stepped off the sub as soon as it docked, and passed through Immigration without breaking stride. The little moon had a much lower gravity than she was used to, and she felt bouncy on her feet. She wanted to dance as she made her way to meet Enid at a restaurant on the edge of one of the larger agricultural domes.

* * *

THE RESTAURANT SPREAD over four floors, hugging the inside of the dome. The walls were transparent, one looking out into the blackness of the ocean depths, the other over rows of crops on the brightly-lit floor of the dome. Ascending the stairs to the restaurant's front desk, she saw maize and cabbages, grape vines, and other plants she couldn't identify. In the centre of the dome, goats and chickens grazed a circular patch of grass.

It was mid-morning local time, and quiet in the restaurant. Her boots squeaked on the polished floor of the reception area. The air smelled of herbs. The walls displayed artfully-mounted fossils from the sea bed, and the sound of falling water came from a small fountain behind the front desk. As she approached, the head waiter eyed her warily, raising an eyebrow at her open coat and the figure-hugging flight suit beneath.

"Can I help you, *madam*?" His expression implied he thought she'd wandered into the building by mistake, lost and seeking directions. He didn't even bother to ping her implant with a reservation query.

"Table for Abdulov," she said.

"Abdulov...?" She saw his eyes flick to the captain's glyph on her shoulder. "Excuse me, ma'am. *Please*, right this way."

ENID ABDULOV STOOD as they approached her table. She was a short, slim woman, with red lipstick, pretty blue eyes and tied-back blonde hair. She wore a conservative business jacket over a knee-length floral dress, and calf-length leather boots with four-inch heels. She'd chosen a table overlooking the sea bed, from where the lights of the restaurant illuminated the half-buried skeleton of a long-dead behemoth: all spines and broken ribs.

"Welcome to Vertebrae Beach," she said, holding out her hand. They shook, and she gestured for Kat to sit.

"Make yourself at home, Captain. Now tell me, what news of Strauli Quay? Your father remains well, I trust?"

"Very well, thank you." Kat settled into the chair. She clocked the orange juice Enid had on the table before her.

"Would you like a drink, Captain?"

The older woman signalled the waiter, who leaned forward expectantly, proffering an old-fashioned, printed wine menu.

"I'll have a beer," Kat said, not bothering to look.

"Perhaps madam would like to sample a local wine?"

Kat smiled. "Beer will be fine. As long as it's cold and wet, and comes in a bottle."

The waiter took a deep breath through his nose.

"Very well."

He turned on his heel, returning moments later with a frosted bottle of imported lager and a flute glass. Just to spite him, Kat snaked the bottle from the tray and took a swig before he could pour it. When she looked up, she found Enid watching her.

"You do realise that bottle costs more than most of the local dome workers earn in a day?"

Kat looked down at her drink. It was a standard Strauli brew, and must have been shipped across the intervening light years in the hold of a trading ship.

"You import all your beer?"

Enid shrugged. "I'm afraid agricultural space is at a premium. We have a few successful vineyards, but hops take up too much room and we have to prioritise food crops." She folded her hands on the table in front of her. "But if you'll forgive me for speaking bluntly, Captain, I believe we have far more serious matters to discuss."

"You're talking about Victor Luciano?"

Enid's voice lowered conspiratorially. "Word around the port has it that he's trying to beat you to Djatt, for the Pep harvest."

Kat sat back. "News travels fast."

"Also, his flight plan lists Djatt as his next port of call." Enid looked Kat up and down, her gaze as cool and unhurried as the ice floating on the ocean's surface, eight kilometres above their heads. "Weren't you two an item, once upon a time?"

"We were, but all that's changed. He's changed. Did you know he jumped his way out of the Quay at Strauli?"

"Out of the Quay itself?"

"He activated his jump engines inside the docking bay. If the bay's pressure seals hadn't held, he could have killed a lot of people."

For the first time, Enid looked nonplussed. She scratched at her eyebrow with a delicate fingernail.

"Forgive me if I seem a little flustered, Captain. It's not that I'm displeased to see you, it's just that I *was* expecting another ship. The *Kilimanjaro*, en route to the spice harvest, under Captain Ramiro Abdulov, my second cousin."

Kat's thumbnail scratched at the label of her beer bottle.

"The *Kilimanjaro*'s not coming," she said.

Enid pursed her lips, unsurprised yet still gloomy to have her suspicions confirmed. "Accident or sabotage?"

"The latter. And I can't prove anything, but I'm sure Victor Luciano had something to do with it."

Enid sat back in her chair, blue eyes narrowed. "Then this isn't just bravado on his part? He seriously means to challenge our control of the Pep harvest?"

"That's what he says."

"Even at the risk he might trigger a trade war? Why would he take that chance?"

Kat shrugged. She didn't much care why he was doing it, she just wanted to stop him, and make him pay for the things he'd already done.

She glanced through the transparent wall, at the bones of the dead whale-like creatures, and saw her own ghostly reflection in the glass: high cheekbones, dark eyes, and hair that hadn't been brushed in a fortnight: a stark contrast to the other woman's smart clothes and fair looks.

"Is there anything we can do to delay him?" she said.

Enid shook her head. "Nothing legal. At least, nothing that can be arranged in the time we have before he's scheduled to leave."

"Then we don't have a lot of choice, do we?" Kat scraped back in her chair. "Where is he now?"

Enid's eyes flicked up for a second, as she used her implant to consult the local Grid.

"He's two domes across, in a hotel on the edge of the accommodation zone." She stretched across to touch Kat's wrist. "What are you planning to do?"

Kat stood. She pulled back her coat to reveal the pistol strapped to her thigh.

"What do you think I'm going to do? I'm going to go down there and stop him."

CHAPTER TWENTY
SPLASHES

THEY HAD TO abandon the Land Rover in the crevasse. It was wedged fast; nothing could be done to pull it free, even if they had had a crane capable of lifting it, which they didn't. Instead, they had to content themselves with taking as much of its equipment as they could carry. Ed had his survival kit, and the stolen pistol from the glove compartment. Kristin had her own sidearm, and the first aid kit from Alice's bag. Of Alice and her shotgun, no sign remained.

Kristin had twisted her ankle in the crash, and could barely put her weight on it. Ed helped her up, over the lip of the fissure, onto the rocky ledge beside the purple arch. Once out of the narrow split in the rocks, they could see the surrounding terrain for the first time, lit by the rising sun. The arch stood on a rocky hillside above a flat, grassy plain that stretched away to the horizon. The stream that ran down the base of the fissure widened where it hit the grasslands, broadening into a shallow, muddy brook. Tall reeds lined its banks. Way in the distance, Ed caught the glimmer of sunlight reflected on water: a sea, or perhaps a lake. And silhouetted against it, another pair of arches, one standing straight, and the other leaning at a drunken angle. He held up his thumb and index finger, framing the image. If he had the time and materials, he would have loved to paint it.

Kristin pulled a pair of sturdy binoculars from her pack.

"Three kilometres," she said, "maybe four. If they're heading for those arches, my guess is that they'll follow the stream across the plain."

Ed used a hand to shade his eyes. He still couldn't believe that Alice had abandoned him.

"Do you really think that's where they're going?"

Kristin lowered the glasses. "We're low on food and water, and we don't have transport. Where else is there to go?"

ED SAT BENEATH a tree, beside a ruined Cornish tin mine, looking out at the Atlantic Ocean. The water and sky were a matching blue. He'd been sifting through some of Alice's downloaded images on his palmtop, but now the battery had run low.

"Do you know," he said, "that Earth is the only planet whose English name isn't derived from Greek or Roman mythology?"

He switched off the palmtop and lay back against the tree. The bark was gnarled and warm. Sheep grazed among the fallen stones of the pit head, and the air smelled of dry grass, warm bracken and fresh dung.

Alice said, "What's that got to do with anything?"

She came over and sat beside him. She'd spent all morning looking around the site, recording it all on film. She wore a white cotton dress with big, wooden buttons up the front.

"I don't know," Ed said. He reached into his shoulder bag and pulled out the magazine he'd bought to read in the car on the way down from London. It had an article about the old Hubble telescope. The accompanying picture showed two distant galaxies colliding.

"Look at that for a picture," he said, using a fingernail to trace the dusty whorls of tortured stars.

"It's pretty," Alice agreed.

Ed frowned. "The light from these stars is at least a million years old. It's been travelling through space since before the dawn of civilisation." He looked around at the collapsed walls of the abandoned pit head, the moss and lichen covering its scattered stones. The ruin looked so much a part of the landscape that it was difficult to imagine the headland without it.

Alice pushed her auburn hair back. Ed rubbed his hands together, wishing he had a canvas and some paints.

"It makes what I'm doing seem so bloody ephemeral," he said.

When he looked across at Alice, her eyes were the same shade of green as the sunlight filtering through the bracken around the ruin.

"I like your paintings," she said.

He ignored her. He rolled onto his front and put his chin on his fist.

"I could be doing so much more," he said.

THE AIR ON the plain smelled of hot, dry grass. The sky overhead was a reassuring Earth-like blue, flecked with wisps of white cloud that hung above the water on the horizon. The reeds in the stream were maybe a metre and a half in height and ten centimetres across at the base, tapering up to dry seed pods at the top. When a breeze caught them, they rustled like paper. Around them, the waist-high yellow grass of the plain stretched away in all directions. To Ed, who'd spent his childhood in the valleys of South Wales and his adulthood in the east end of London, it looked the way he'd always imagined Africa to be, only without the elephants and zebras.

Then he remembered how far they were from Earth, and felt his head swim with vertigo. He closed his eyes and rubbed his face with both hands. Beside him, Kirsten said, "Are you okay?"

He shook his head. "Alice..."

She put a hand on his shoulder. "She'll be okay, we'll find her. They probably just went looking for help."

"Do you believe that?"

Kristin looked away, unable to meet his stare. "We'll know soon enough."

She let go and started to limp in the direction of the two arches and distant lake. He watched her struggle for a few paces, then caught up and took her elbow, allowing her to rest her weight against him. Her clothes were stale, stained with old sweat, and he knew he smelled just as bad.

"How's the ankle?" he said.

Kristin set her jaw. "It'll have to do."

He supported her as they shuffled their way across the plain. It took them two hours. But with each step, the arches grew larger.

Twice, Ed heard a rustle in the reeds, followed by a plop and splash, as if something about the size of a dog had slipped and slithered its way into the water. After the second time it happened, he pulled the gun from his pack, drawing comfort from its weight and solidity.

Eventually, the stream flowed into a wide, boggy river bed that cut across their path, forming a marsh that blocked them on two sides: hummocks of grass and reeds poking through evil-smelling black, oily water. Beyond the opposite bank, a slope led up, into taller grass.

Ed eyed the water dubiously.

"Can we get across?"

Still leaning against him, Kristin shaded her eyes with her free hand.

"The arches are only a few hundred metres on the other side of that rise," she said. "This could stretch miles upstream. It might take hours to skirt around. And to be honest, I don't know how much further I can walk."

Huffing with effort, she eased herself down into a sitting position in the grass. Ed left her there, and scrambled down to the edge of the bog, where he pressed an experimental toe into the spongy mud.

"I think it'll support us," he said, "but we'll have to wade."

"Snap off a reed," Kristin said. "Test the depth as you walk."

Ed did as she suggested. He tucked the gun into his waistband, broke off a reed, then climbed back up to her and helped her down.

"Hold on to me, and tread where I tread," he said.

The bog smelled rotten, like a damp compost heap. Tiny insects flicked back and forth across the scum-thick surface of the water. Wrinkling his nose, he stepped in, feeling the wetness slime its way into his boots. Using the snapped reed to probe the water ahead, he led her across, one painful step at a time.

By the time they got to the middle, the water had risen to their knees, and their feet were caked in mud.

"Are you okay?" he said.

Kristin had both hands on the back of his shoulders, gripping the epaulette of his combat jacket to support herself.

"Just concentrate on getting us across," she said.

Somewhere off in the reeds, Ed heard a splash. He caught a glimpse of something moving in the water.

"What's that?" he said.

But before Kristin could answer, they heard gunshots ahead, beyond the rise. Two at first, and then three more in rapid succession.

CHAPTER TWENTY-ONE
TICONDEROGA

As KAT AND Enid stepped into the hotel lobby, Kat's hand resting on the butt of her gun, ready to draw, the hotel's automated security system pinged her implant; but instead of setting off the alarms, it noted her status as a Captain for the Abdulov Trading Family, and decided to mind its own business. Traders weren't entirely above the law, but they were allowed a lot more leeway than the average citizen, and it was a brave or foolhardy planet that risked a trade boycott by enforcing its laws too stringently.

Kat stalked over to the reception desk, with Enid hurrying to keep pace. On any other world, she would have seen the lobby as small and functional, but here under the dome, where space was scarce, it seemed almost ostentatious.

"I'm here for Captain Luciano," she said.

The clerk behind the desk gestured towards a set of open airlock doors at the rear of the room.

"I believe he's taking breakfast on the observation deck, ma'am."

The doors led beyond the walls of the dome, into a transparent tunnel that led, in its turn, to the wreck of a sunken starship, where it lay on the seabed, surrounded by the fossilised bones of long-dead marine behemoths.

The tunnel ended at the ship's hull. In her heyday, she'd been a passenger carrier. Now seaweed waved from her hull, and Kat felt a twinge of pity as she stepped through the airlock. Inside, the accommodation sections had been pressurised, but the lower decks were still flooded.

> GOOD AFTERNOON, CAPTAIN ABDULOV. WELCOME ABOARD THE *TICONDEROGA*. HOW MAY I SERVE YOU TODAY?

Startled, Kat looked up. She hadn't expected the old ship's personality to still be functional.

"I'm looking for the observation lounge."

Elevator doors scraped open.

> DECK NINE.

THE *TICONDEROGA*'S OBSERVATION lounge turned out to be a hemispherical blister on the old ship's muzzle, jutting out over the ocean floor. A transparent deck filled the centre of the bubble, allowing guests to look down as well as up. The effect was like stepping out into thin air, and Kat hesitated for a second before following Enid out into the room.

Brightness above showed where shards of sunlight filtered down through the clear water. Below, the sands were spiky with the skeletal remains that gave Vertebrae Beach its name.

On the far side of the lounge, against the transparent wall of the bubble, comfortable chairs were arranged in groups around low coffee tables, which in turn surrounded a circular bar. Potted ferns provided welcome sprays of greenery. Human waiters delivered drink orders.

On the way over here, Enid had explained that the hotel was a favourite with off-worlders and those seeking passage. Four of the tables were occupied by crewmen from various ships. Local teenagers sat at one table, self-consciously sporting spacer gear, trying to look cool. A solitary drinker sat at the sixth table, hunched over a half-empty glass, staring out at the waters beyond the wall. Kat slowed as she approached. Her hand hovered over her gun as she scanned faces, looking for Victor.

"Do you see him?" Enid whispered.

Kat didn't answer. Instead, she marched over to the loner on table six. She didn't know his name, but she recognised him from the confrontation on Tiers Cross, where he'd helped throw her out into the snow.

"Where is he?"

The man looked up. The black and grey bristles on his shaven head were the same length as those sprouting from his chin and neck. Broken veins webbed his cheeks, and a bruise had swollen one eye half-shut. The glyph on his shoulder marked him as Seth Murphy, Victor's First Mate.

"You're too late. He's on his way back up to the ship."

Kat clenched her fists in frustration. If she'd checked his movements on the Grid before storming up here, she might have been able to intercept him.

She turned to Enid.

"Let's go."

Murphy surged to his feet.

"Not so fast, Abdulov." He jerked a thumb at his swollen eye. "I still owe you for this."

He stepped out from behind the table, and Kat only had time to push Enid aside before the big man swung.

She ducked his first punch, but the second caught her on the left temple, sending her crashing sideways into a potted fern. On the other tables, heads turned to watch the fight.

Smarting, Kat rolled to her feet. Her heart hammered in her chest. Blood roared in her ears. She couldn't take her eyes from Murphy's hands.

Smiling, he came for her again. His arms were longer than hers, his reach that much greater. She danced back to avoid his grasp. If he got her in a headlock or bear hug, it would all be over.

She backed away from the chairs, out into the centre of the *Ticonderoga*'s transparent observation deck. Murphy followed, hands raised, breath rasping, eyes filled with bloodlust.

Okay, she thought, *time to end this.*

But even as she reached for the gun strapped to her thigh, he charged her. She tried to step aside, but one of his hands caught the fabric of her sleeve and pulled her into a back-handed slap. Blood burst from her nose and her legs went out from under her. She staggered back and sat heavily.

"Had enough?" Murphy said. Through a fog of pain, she saw him standing over her, rubbing his knuckles expectantly. "Only Victor told me to delay you, but I reckon we can do so much more than that, don't you?"

He leaned down and drew back his balled fist, ready to hit her again. But before he could, Enid lunged at him with a bottle, hitting his shoulder. He roared in anger and slapped her aside. Grateful for the distraction, Kat slid forward and kicked him in the knee with as much strength as she could muster. He cried out again, but his kneecap didn't shatter the way she'd hoped it would, and he limped away, cursing.

Some of the crewmen from the other tables tried to break up the fight. They managed to drag Murphy halfway across the restaurant before he shrugged them off. Still off-balance, he pulled a pistol from his coat and they scattered like fish.

Kat's hand flew to her own weapon.

"Let's not do anything stupid," she said. She still didn't have the strength to stand. Murphy raised his gun, clasped in his sausage-like fingers, and fired. The shot was hasty; the bullet missed. Kat rolled to one side. Her flesh cringed in expectation of his next shot. She tugged her own gun from its holster, and raised it, only to see Murphy limping for the elevator.

Head splitting, she let her arm drop.

Enid knelt beside her and slipped an arm around her shoulders, supporting her.

"Oh, my God, are you all right?" Her blonde hair had been mussed and Murphy's fingers had left a red welt across her cheek.

As the elevator doors closed behind him, Murphy laughed.

"See you in Hell, Abdulov!"

The doors shut. Kat let the gun fall from her fingers.

"I should've shot him," she said.

Enid squeezed her shoulders. "He won't get far, don't worry. I've put out an alert. The police will have him before he reaches the surface."

Kat wiped her bloody nose on the back of her hand.

"I should get back to my ship."

"The paramedics are coming. Maybe you should wait for them first?"

"No, help me up." She struggled to her feet with Enid's aid. Her nose and temple throbbed from the blows, and her knees felt spongy and unreliable.

"I have to beat Victor."

She tried to take a step but stumbled, ending up on one knee. Only Enid's grip on her arm saved her from falling on her face. Below the transparent floor, the *Ticonderoga*'s hull curved down to the graveyard seabed.

"What's that?" Enid pointed at one of the tables. Kat squinted. A bag sat beneath one of the chairs, and it took her a moment to realise that the chair was the one in which Murphy had been sitting before the fight.

"He's left something," Enid said. She started towards it but Kat held her back. Murphy's final words echoed in her mind.

See you in Hell.

There was a bang, and smoke billowed from the top of the bag. Without thinking, Kat fell to the floor, dragging Enid down. The air roared, and she felt a blast of heat. The deck bucked and smacked her in the teeth. Burning splinters fell around her.

The automatic sprinkler systems went off; water hammered into the room. Kat lay for a moment, letting it splash over her face. Her ears hurt, and her lip bled. Enid lay across her legs. Painfully, she rolled over. She saw people screaming but couldn't hear them. The smell of scorched hair burned in her nose.

She pushed herself up onto her knees. Enid stirred.

Nothing remained where the table had been. The explosion had scattered broken furniture everywhere. Some of the pieces were burning. Three or four of the crewmen sported shrapnel wounds. One lay slumped in a pool of his own blood, obviously dead, a metal table leg punched through his chest. But something else had caught Enid's eye. She was saying something, but Kat's ears were still ringing from the explosion.

"What?" she said.

Desperately, Enid jabbed her finger at the wall. The explosion had weakened the skin of the observation dome. Spidery cracks ran up from the place where the table had been. As Kat watched, one of the cracks jumped a few centimetres in length, then a few more.

Enid screamed: "We're eight kilometres down!"

Before Kat could react, the ship's voice broke into her implant.

> EVACUATE. HULL INTEGRITY COMPROMISED. PRESSURE SEAL IN TWENTY SECONDS.

People started scrambling for the airlock doors that led to the elevators, and the safety of the ship's main hull. But Enid couldn't stand. She had a jagged sprig of steel skewering the muscle of her right calf.

> PRESSURE SEAL IN TEN SECONDS.

Kat grabbed her by the lapel of her jacket and, ignoring the pain of her own injuries, started dragging. She was halfway across the room from the airlock doors.

> FIVE SECONDS.

She heaved towards the threshold with all her strength. Hands were waiting there to help her, calling encouragement. They grabbed her coat as she got close, trying to pull her to safety.

> FOUR.

Her heel hit the lip of the airlock frame. Her hand jerked free from Enid's lapel, and she fell back into the waiting arms of her would-be rescuers. Enid shrieked.

"Kat, don't leave me!"

> THREE.

Kat kicked and elbowed herself free of the hands holding her. She lunged desperately through the lock. On the other side, Enid reached for her. Their hands clasped.

> TWO.

Kat pulled with all her might, but they were out of time. With a splintering crash, the glass wall shattered under the pressing weight of the ocean, and the room imploded.

NEWS HEADLINES

REVOLT ON LANCASTER
Anti-government troops declare victory.

REPOPULATING THE OCEAN
Terrestrial species to be introduced.
Fish farming to commence next year.

SHORTAGE OF PEP DRIVES PRICES TO ALL-TIME HIGH

INTELLIGENT LIFE?
Extinct indigenous shellfish may have used tools.

SOME LIKE IT HOT!
New shipment of Italian chorizo sausage sparks fierce bidding war.

ARCH FAILURE?
Fears of total network collapse.

TAX ON SEABED LIVING SPACE
Critics claim poor will be hit hardest.
Tax on oxygen next?

SYLVIA ABDULOV REMEMBERED
New statue to commemorate centenary of heroic rescue.
Former lover speaks out.
Disappearance still a mystery.

RATS!
Every world has them. What makes them so successful?

HAGWOOD MISSING
Poet fails to return from sabbatical on Djatt.

CHAPTER TWENTY-TWO
TSUNAMI

ON THE DHO Ark, the improvised human quarters were housed in a warren of caves and tunnels drilled into the rocky planetoid, especially to accommodate the expedition. Each of the team's one hundred members had their own alcove for sleeping: a narrow, coffin-like slot in a cavern wall, just big enough to contain a sleeping bag and air mattress, and into which they had to slide feet first. The caverns themselves served as shared living and study areas. The largest of all was the refectory, a circular room with a high dome-shaped ceiling. It was the only space big enough for the entire expedition to assemble, and therefore the venue Professor Harris had chosen for his presentation.

For five years, he had been working to frame the Dho's jumbled carvings into a coherent historical narrative. To accomplish this, he'd had to photograph, scan and analyse thousands of individual scenes—a process that the Dho themselves watched with tolerant amusement.

Now, clad in his threadbare tweed suit, he stood at one end of the room, in front of an unrolled soft screen. The rest of the expedition sat on chairs and tables, facing him. Toby Drake sat near the front, eager to hear his interpretation of Dho history. For five years, during breaks in his own studies of the second Gnarl at the heart of the Ark, he'd watched the old man mumble and mutter over image after image, and now he was as keen as anyone else to hear the conclusions his old teacher had finally drawn.

A handful of Acolytes stood patiently at the side of the room, hands folded in their drab habits. Behind them, a Dho observer stood as impassive and expressionless as a beetle, regarding proceedings with its shrivelled black eyes. Harris glared at it for a moment, returning its stare from beneath brows like wind-plucked storm clouds. Then he drew himself up to his full height and cleared his throat. Chatter died away. Behind him, the projection screen cleared to reveal his first image.

"Those of you who have spent any time in the halls will be familiar with this. As far as we can tell, it's one of the oldest carvings on the Ark, made during construction. Down here, you can see a group of Dho clustered around an instrument that we believe to be a telescope." Harris pointed to a group of horned stick figures at the bottom of the picture. Above them, two giant lights blazed like childishly drawn suns against a backdrop of smaller stars.

"We believe these two objects in the sky are novae. It appears that early in the Dho's history, two nearby stars exploded almost simultaneously. There are dozens of images of the event in the halls of this Ark, and judging from these related carvings we can see that the twin novae had a profound effect on Dho culture and religion. Almost overnight, their old gods were swept aside. They became scholars and astronomers, in an effort to comprehend what they were seeing. And finally, they understood enough about stellar evolution to realise something that startled them even more than the initial explosions."

Harris turned his hooded gaze on the Dho, as if waiting for it to confirm or deny his words, but the creature remained mute and immobile, its emotions unreadable. Irritated, he continued:

"They call this picture *The War In Heaven*, and I believe that's exactly what it depicts. By piecing together hundreds of images, I am now certain that what the Dho found in the afterglow of the two explosions was more than simple coincidence. They stumbled on a war. Two races fighting in the depths of space, each with the power to destroy suns."

The audience stirred. Harris ignored them. He gestured at the screen and the image changed. This second carving was larger and far more intricate than the first, and pictured the diamond Ark under construction above the Dho's home world. Digging machines bored into the rock of the planetoid. Other machines extruded sheets of crystal.

"Fearing that they would become embroiled in this gigantic conflict, the Dho prepared to flee." Harris paused again. Toby saw sweat peppering the old man's forehead. "However, before they were ready, the sky fell quiet. Violence turned to silence. The fighting ceased."

The professor snapped his fingers at the screen and it flicked to a third image: an oncoming storm of billowing cloud.

He cleared his throat.

"We cannot be sure exactly what this cloud represents and our hosts have been most reluctant to expand on the matter." His eyes were on the unmoving Dho at the side of the room. "It may have been an expanding nebulae of hot gas left over from the stellar explosions, a dust cloud or maybe a weapon of some sort. All we know is that they were so afraid of it that they completed their Ark and abandoned their home planet."

Another click of the fingers and another slide appeared. Toby felt a mild thrill. This carving was the most familiar to him, the first he'd seen on his arrival, five years ago.

Five years...

In some ways, it didn't seem that long since he'd stood with his nose pressed to the transparent crystal wall of the Ark's boarding tube, watching the wedge-shaped silhouette of the *Ameline* fall away into darkness. For a moment, he closed his eyes and pictured Katherine as he'd last seen her: standing at the *Ameline*'s airlock, her rumpled fatigues thrown on over her skin-tight ship suit, her hair tied back and gaze downcast, avoiding his.

When he opened his eyes, he found Harris glowering directly at him.

"I'm sorry Mister Drake, am I boring you?"

Toby jerked upright in his seat.

"S-sorry professor, I was just thinking—"

The older man raised a furry eyebrow. "Aye, and I know exactly whom you were thinking about, too. But if you don't mind...?" He turned back to the screen, which still showed the familiar depiction of the Ark fleeing the looming cloud as smaller ships wove around like mosquitoes to cover its retreat.

"The Dho call this picture 'The Burning Sky.' Whatever the cloud was, they escaped it by only the narrowest of margins, using these weapons," he indicated the stylised lightning bolts flickering from the smaller ships surrounding the diamond planetoid. "With their help, they kept the cloud at bay while making good their escape."

The professor pushed his glasses up onto the bridge of his nose. He took a deep breath, as if nerving himself.

"The fact that they used weapons against it leads me to believe that the cloud was not a natural phenomenon."

At the side of the room, the Dho turned its head a few degrees. It was a tiny movement but all eyes snapped toward it.

Harris took a step towards the creature.

"Do you have something to add?" he demanded, irritation allowing his Scottish accent to come through stronger than ever.

The creature regarded him. It seemed to consider the matter for some time. When it finally spoke, its voice was low: full of hisses, pops and scratches like a bad recording.

"The cloud is not natural," it said. There were mutters and exclamations from the crowd.

"Then what is it?"

The Dho turned to fully face the old man for the first time, although from where he sat, Toby couldn't tell if it looked at the professor or at the picture of the carving behind him.

"We call it 'The Recollection,'" the Dho said. "It is an evil born of war. It is the end of all things."

More mutters. A few shouted questions.

Professor Harris stalked back to the display screen and brought up the next image.

"And what of *this*?" he demanded.

The room fell silent. The picture showed an arch, exactly like the ones that had first appeared on Earth all those centuries ago, the arches that formed the network that had allowed humanity to escape and spread out into the cosmos, and whose mechanisms had been back-engineered to provide engines for ships like the *Ameline*, who could take short cuts within the network because they weren't tied to its labyrinthine routing.

The Dho shuffled forward a few steps.

"As we fled The Recollection, we found traces of other races, younger races, and we knew we could not leave them defenceless. So we constructed the arch network to help them spread out across the stars, in the hope that some of them might escape the horror that followed us. For we knew The Recollection would never give up its pursuit. We knew it would never forget about us or grow weary. We knew it was coming."

The Dho turned to face the crowd.

"And now, it is almost upon us."

The meeting dissolved into uproar. Arguments broke out between scientists. People rose to their feet, yelling questions and accusations. Some wanted to get to the Dho, but the Acolytes had formed a circle around the creature, shielding it.

"If you can build the arches," the woman beside Toby shouted, "why do you travel in *this*?" She waved her arms to encompass the bulk of the crystal Ark.

The Dho's head swivelled in her direction. When it spoke, its voice silenced the room.

"Our species is uncomfortable in hyperspace," it croaked. "We find the transition disorientating and often fatal. That is why we must rely on our Acolytes to talk for us on all the settled worlds of human space."

It raised its head and the light caught on the bony sheen of its four horns.

"When we ran from The Recollection, we seeded the space behind us with probes, to monitor its progress. Like us, it moves at speeds slower than light. It has been a thousand years, but we have at last received the signal we have been dreading. The Recollection approaches human space. Already the darkness will have befallen the world you call Djatt. Others will soon follow."

Toby leapt like he'd been electrocuted.

"Djatt?" He elbowed his way forward through the crowd, ignoring indignant protests. Harris moved to intercept him.

"Calm down, lad."

"Let me go!" Toby tried to shake the older man off, but the gnarled fingers were stronger than they looked.

"You knew!" Toby waved an accusing finger at the Dho. "And still you let her go!"

The circle of Acolytes drew tighter around the alien creature, which shivered. The bulges squirmed under its black robe.

"We were not sure," it said. "We suspected, but it was only hours ago that our suspicions were confirmed."

Toby stopped struggling. "Is she in danger?"

The creature bowed its head. "She will be protected by the pendant given to her by our Acolyte, Mr Hind."

"But what is the cloud?" Harris thundered in frustration, all semblance of patience lost after five years of painstaking and frustrating work. "What is this *Recollection*?"

The Acolytes moved and the Dho stepped forward. It spoke in a voice so loud Toby felt it in his bowels.

"The Recollection is darkness and hunger. It is a cancer gnawing at the bones of the galaxy. None of you can stand against it."

The creature paused, its laboured breathing the only sound in the room.

"It is a tsunami of unspeakable horror, and it will swamp your defences and drown your souls. It cannot be defeated, appeased or bargained with, and it will scour all the life from your planets."

CHAPTER TWENTY-THREE
PHANTOM LIMB SYNDROME

KATHERINE ABDULOV WOKE in a hospital bed, in a private room with no windows and a police guard on the door. The walls, ceiling and floor were a soothing shade of green. The sheets smelled of disinfectant, and a surgeon stood by the far wall, arms crossed, watching her.

"How do you feel?"

She smacked her lips a couple of times and swallowed.

"Where am I?"

"You're safe. There are guards on the door. No-one's going to get to you here. Don't try to move. You're still on Vertebrae Beach, in hospital. My name's Doctor Misaki. Do you understand what I'm saying?"

Kat gave a weak nod. Misaki smiled.

"That's good. Now, can you remember why you're here?"

She frowned. Her thoughts were as woolly and cumbersome as clouds, and she had a bone-deep ache in her right arm. "There was an accident?"

The surgeon uncrossed his arms. He glanced at the guard on the door.

"I'm afraid it's more serious than that. Three days ago, you were caught in a bomb attack. You're lucky to be alive."

Kat tried to sit up but found she lacked the strength.

"What happened?" she said.

Doctor Misaki stepped over to the bed. He looked to be somewhere in his early thirties. "You were on the observation deck of the *Ticonderoga* when a bomb went off. It wasn't a big bang, but against the outer wall, it was enough. The window was old and weak and it gave way. Luckily, the ship's automatic pressure seals worked, or we might have lost the whole dome, and everyone in it."

Kat lifted her head. "But I was with someone. Enid Abdulov. She'd hurt her leg. What happened to her?"

Misaki's fingertips eased her back against the pillow.

"Don't try to get up," he said.

"But Enid…"

The doctor scratched his forehead, his face pained. "Look Katherine, we've already had this conversation three times. It's the anaesthetics. They'll wear off soon."

"Just tell me she's all right."

Misaki drew back. "I can't, I'm sorry."

Kat struggled. "She's *dead*?"

The doctor put a friendly hand on her shoulder.

"Try not to upset yourself."

"No—"

"If it's any consolation, you did all you could. The people who dragged you clear said you were still reaching back through the airlock when the room sealed itself." He took a deep breath, preparing to impart more bad news. "As a matter of fact, that's how you hurt your arm."

"My arm?"

Kat watched as, slowly, Misaki peeled back the crisp white sheet.

"When the airlock door slammed shut, it severed your left arm just above the elbow. We saved what we could, but..." He finished sliding the sheet down, revealing two black struts protruding from the loose sleeve of her hospital nightgown. For a disorientating moment she couldn't understand what she saw, and then it all clicked into place and she felt the room sway drunkenly around her.

"We can grow you a new arm from stem cells," Misaki said, "but it will take some months to fully mature. In the meantime, we've given you this prosthetic."

He took the arm and gently raised it off the bed. The black struts she'd seen were bones carved from black carbon fibre, light and strong. As they moved, tiny servo motors hissed and clicked in the elbow, wrist and finger joints.

"There are pressure sensors in the palm here and here, and on the tip of each finger," Misaki said, touching each in turn, his fingers producing an unfamiliar tickling sensation. Kat jerked the arm away. She turned it back and forth, examining it. She didn't dare roll her sleeve high enough to see where it had been grafted to her flesh.

"It hurts."

"Where?"

"All over."

Misaki gave a sympathetic nod. "You may get phantom pains as your brain adjusts to the loss of your limb."

Kat screwed her eyes tight. She didn't want to look at it any more.

Oh Enid, I'm so sorry.

She rolled away from the pain until she faced the wall. Behind her, Misaki continued to talk but she wasn't really listening. Her concentration came and went. She felt cold and raw inside, and her thoughts were slippery and hard to pin down. The disinfectant smell of the hospital sheets reminded her of the day Victor walked out on her: of the operation, and the baby...

Eventually, the reassuring words dried up. She heard Misaki turn to leave.

"Why am I so calm?" she said.

He stopped, half-turned.

"It's the drugs, Katherine."

"Drugs?"

"We've been keeping you pretty heavily sedated for the past seventy hours. You've had a shock. Lie back. You need time to recuperate." He gave her a final sideways glance, then stepped past the armed guard, out into the corridor.

"Try to get some rest," he called as he hurried away. "You'll feel better."

Alone, Kat closed her eyes.

"Screw you," she said.

AN HOUR LATER, wearing her coat draped over her shoulders, her new arm held tight to her chest like a sling, Kat stepped unsteadily from the floating jetty to the *Ameline*'s rear airlock. One of the coat's arms was ripped, torn off just above the elbow. The fresh wind blew through her hair. Both the ship and the jetty moved on the ocean swell, and the unfamiliar weight of the prosthetic arm unbalanced her.

As soon as both her feet were aboard, she closed the outer airlock door and strode forth through the echoing cargo hold toward the bridge at the ship's bow. Passing through the passenger lounge, her eyes lingered for a second on the couch so recently occupied by Toby Drake. What would he think if he could see her now, like this? Climbing the ladder to the flight deck, she screwed her eyes tight. She still couldn't bring herself to look at the black alloy struts of her new hand.

> GIRL, YOU LOOK TERRIBLE.

Her lips twitched. She didn't know whether to laugh or cry at the absurdity of it all. She clenched her teeth.

"Get your systems fired up, we're leaving."

> ARE YOU SURE YOU CAN FLY? MY RECORDS SHOW YOU DISCHARGED YOURSELF AGAINST THE ADVICE OF YOUR SURGEON.

Kat shrugged off her coat and tossed it over the back of the co-pilot's couch.

"He was an asshole."

> BUT STILL, YOU'VE BEEN UNDER SEDATION. ARE YOU FIT TO FLY?

"Do you *want* to stay here?"

The ship gave an electronic snort.

> HAVE YOU ANY IDEA WHAT THIS SALT WATER'S DOING TO THE UNDERSIDE OF MY HULL?

"You've been waterproofed."

> THIRTY YEARS AGO. THAT STUFF WEARS OFF, YOU KNOW.

Kat stepped onto the bridge. "Well, we're leaving now," she said.

> FOR DJATT?

"Where else?"

> YOU KNOW VICTOR BLEW OUT OF HERE THREE DAYS AGO?

Kat settled herself into the pilot's chair. "We'll catch him."

> HE LEFT SOMETHING BEHIND.

"What?"

> SETH MURPHY.

Kat swallowed. She pictured Murphy as she'd last seen him, framed in the doorway of the *Ticonderoga*'s observation deck.

"See you in Hell, Abdulov."

Her fists tightened.

"Where is he?"

> THE POLICE FOUND HIM FLOATING IN THE SEA, NEAR THE *TRISTERO*'S DOCKING PONTOON.

Kat frowned. "Floating?"

> SHOT THROUGH THE HEAD.

She sat back with a huff, as if the wind had been knocked out of her. Even after everything he'd done, she found it hard to believe Victor capable of cold-bloodedly executing one of his own men.

Her good right hand had begun to shake. So far, she'd been running on the drugs Misaki had given her. She needed time to rest and recuperate, but knew she couldn't afford to waste another second. She *had* to reach Djatt before Victor conned the locals into dealing with him rather than waiting for an Abdulov ship. If he scooped the lion's share of the cargo, she'd be left scrabbling for scraps.

"Let's go," she said quietly.

There was no answer. For the first time, she sensed reluctance in the ship. She said, "What's the matter?"

> HE HAS A THREE DAY HEAD START. WE COULD GIVE UP NOW AND RETURN TO STRAULI.

"But we'd have failed."

> WE'D HAVE SURVIVED.

Kat flexed her metal hand. She could feel a phantom ache in the black, artificial bones of her forearm. "Is there something you're not telling me?"

For a moment, the ship remained silent.

> I'VE BEEN MONITORING TRAFFIC REPORTS ON THE LOCAL GRIDS. IT STARTED AT STRAULI. I NOTICED TWO FLIGHTS FROM DJATT HAD BEEN DECLARED OVERDUE. SINCE WE ARRIVED HERE, I'VE NOTICED ANOTHER ONE, MAKING THREE ALTOGETHER.

"What are you saying?"

> THE LAST THREE SHIPS TO VISIT DJATT HAVE FAILED TO RETURN.

Kat bit her lip, considering the idea. "Do you think they ran into trouble?"

> SOMETHING'S GOING ON. I CAN'T BELIEVE ALL THREE SHIPS SUFFERED MORE-OR-LESS SIMULTANEOUS MALFUNCTIONS.

Kat thought of the *Kilimanjaro*, sabotaged before it reached Tiers Cross and the Bubble Cloud.

"Do you think Victor's behind it?"

> UNLIKELY GIVEN THE DISTANCES INVOLVED, UNLESS HE PLANNED THIS ENTIRE THING DECADES IN ADVANCE.

"Then he could be walking into trouble himself, same as the other ships?"

> QUITE POSSIBLY.

Kat looked out at the shadow pattern of clouds on the surface of the sea. Flecks of sunlight shone through the gaps and rippled on the water. She thought of the beach below the family compound on Strauli, where she'd kicked through the surf as a girl, dreaming of life as a trader captain. She could be back there in a few hours, she realised, if she allowed the ship's fears to discourage her from her goal. She could give up her pursuit of

Victor and run home to her mother and father, and let the family doctors grow her a new arm. She could see Toby and take him walking on the beach... She closed her eyes and shivered, thinking how good and warm the sand would feel between her toes.

She let out a long, ragged breath. She'd come this far, and she couldn't chicken out now. She couldn't go home one-armed and empty-handed. Victor couldn't be allowed to win. Hooked into the ship, she felt power building in the engines. The daylight on the hull itched at her skin like sunburn, and she longed for the soothing coolness of space. If she gave up the chase, she'd be letting her family down, and she'd also be disappointing her younger self—the girl who'd dreamed of piloting her own ship, who'd studied and worked and been through hell in order to get where she was today, and wasn't about to quit.

She opened her eyes and gazed down at the metal hand resting on the arm of her couch.

"Getting knocked down makes you tougher," her great aunt Sylvia had been fond of saying, "and setbacks are opportunities in disguise."

Kat frowned, trying to be dispassionate. Looked at objectively, stripped of the abhorrence it stirred in her, she supposed there was a kind of functional beauty to the sleek design of the matt black bones and hinged knuckle joints; and with that thought, she realised it wasn't the arm she feared. Her revulsion sprang from her unwillingness to face her own guilt at her failure to save her friend. The arm was a badge of shame. For a second, Enid's face swam before her, blonde, blue-eyed and terrified. Kat blinked it away. Enid had died because of her squabble with

Victor. Innocent people had been killed and hurt. She gripped the sides of her couch.

Time to end it, she thought.

For the first time since leaving Strauli, she considered the six missiles her father had installed. Converted from probes used for asteroid prospecting, the nimble little rockets had become delivery systems for single megatonne nuclear mining charges. They were small, manoeuvrable and designed to be guided remotely. If trouble waited for her at Djatt, she'd be ready. No-one would expect a ship like the *Ameline* to be armed. If anyone came at her, all she'd have to do would be to detonate one of those bombs within a few hundred metres of their ship.

Her hand came up to touch the pendant hanging around her neck. She gave the knife-sharp, watery horizon a final glance.

"You know we're going anyway, don't you?" she said.

The *Ameline* shivered. She could feel its excitement overriding its caution. Like her, it itched for the up-and-out.

> OH, YES.

THEY QUIT VERTEBRAE Beach with as much style as they could muster. The *Ameline* rose a few metres into the air and shook like a wet dog. Water poured from its hull. Kat scanned the green telltales on her head-up display. All systems were clear.

"Ready?" she said.

The ship tipped back until it stood on its tail, nose pointed at the sky.

> ALWAYS.

It leapt heavenwards, like a prayer. It left the atmosphere at full acceleration and activated its jump engines the second it hit hard vacuum, levering itself out of the universe with a brilliant white flash like the burst of a miniature nova, the reflection of which momentarily flared off the waters of Vertebrae Beach, a thousand kilometres below.

CHAPTER
TWENTY-FOUR
RAPTORS

THE GUNSHOTS ECHOED away across the grass plain. Standing in the marsh, Ed went cold inside.

"Alice..."

He felt Kristin move and looked down, to see that even though she still clung to him with one hand, she'd managed to pull her sidearm free of its holster.

"Get me to the bank." It was an order. Not knowing what else to do, he obeyed. He pulled her forward, moving as quickly as he dared. Rank-smelling mud slithered and slipped beneath the soles of his boots. Twice his leg went in up to the knee in cold, gritty water, and he hardly noticed. All he could think of was Alice. Was she hurt? Had Krous killed her?

He stumbled on, using all his strength to keep Kristin upright.

A few steps from the shore, he heard a splash. Something slithered beneath the surface. He caught a glimpse of a sleek, powerful tail.

Kristin waved her gun at the disappearing shadow.

"What was that?"

Ed didn't answer. He was too busy trying to keep his

balance, and all he could think of was Alice possibly lying hurt somewhere up ahead, beyond the rise. With a last effort, he heaved Kristin ashore and they both fell to their knees. Kristin had her gun raised, scanning the grassy skyline at the top of the slope. Ed dropped his pack and dug out the semi-automatic pistol he'd stolen from the Iraq War veteran in the flat down the hall from his place in London. His hands shook. He could hear his pulse battering in his ears.

Shit. Shit. Shit.

The gun felt cold and heavy. His feet squelched wetly. The sun-dried grass beneath his knees smelled like hay.

Beyond the rise, another shot.

Still on one knee, favouring her injured leg, Kristin readied her weapon, covering the skyline.

"Stay low," she said, "and try to cover me."

She squirmed forward on her elbows. Ed watched her go, holding the stolen pistol awkwardly, unsure exactly what to do with it. There was nothing to point it at, so he held it loosely, ready to swing it towards Krous if the man appeared over the hill.

Ripples in the water made him glance back, into the marsh. Three or four of the creatures now slithered through the water, getting closer and closer without directly approaching the bank, like sharks circling before an attack. He got the impression of large, otter-like creatures swathed in muddy grey fur. Their claws flashed in the sunlight.

"Kristin—"

"Shush!"

The American woman had her gun raised. He followed her aim and saw a figure with auburn hair, partially-silhouetted against the sky, pushing her way through the long grass at the top of the rise. His heart leapt.

"Alice!"

Scrambling to his feet, he saw her turn in his direction.

"Ed?" She stopped in her tracks. "Ed, get away from the water!"

WITH A FLICK of its tail, one of the creatures leapt from the swamp. It landed, crouched and snarling, on the bank, ready to spring again. Ed saw six legs, powerful shoulders, a muscular tail and sleek, black fur. He scrambled backwards up the slope. The creature took a step after him. It was the size of a Doberman, with the body of an otter and the claws of a velociraptor. Wicked yellow teeth glittered from its wide mouth.

"Kristin..."

Six limbs tensed. Yellow eyes glowered like hungry embers, and saliva dripped from the open jaws. Without a word, Kristin turned and snapped her arm up. Before the animal could pounce, she put three bullets through its face. Then, with her good leg, she sent its twitching body rolling back into the marsh, where three of its brethren set upon it, tails lashing the water to bloody froth.

"Come on." She started to limp towards Alice. Ed scrambled after her, covering her back. Two further creatures crawled onto the bank, and he waved his gun at them.

"We need to go faster," he said, taking her elbow.

By the time they reached the top of the hill, there were six of the otter-like creatures slinking behind them through the long yellow grass. Alice ran to him and he caught her in his arms. Her eyes were wild, her hair and clothes lank with sweat.

"Oh, Ed, I thought I'd lost you." She kissed him hard, her dry lips crushing his.

"Krous told me you were dead," she said, between kisses. "He said we should head for the other arch. I didn't want to go, but he made me."

Kristin scanned the grassy plain between the rise they were on and the arches, which stood atop an outcrop of shattered rock much like the one where they'd lost the Land Rover. "Where is he now?"

Alice turned to her. "He's holed up in the boulders near the arch. There are more of those—"

The grass rippled behind her. One of the horrors flung itself at her, and she went down into the grass with a scream, knocked off her feet. Ed tried to kick the animal in the side of the head, but it snapped vicious teeth at his foot.

"Shoot it!" Kristin barked. It was an order. Obeying without stopping to think, Ed jammed his gun into the creature's midsection and pulled the trigger. The recoil jarred his arm. The animal yelped and fell. It lay flapping and keening, trying to curl around the gory hole punched in its side. Its jaws gnashed. Blood sprayed from its mouth.

Ed helped Alice to her feet. Her arms and chest had been clawed. Her t-shirt gaped raggedly. Blood ran down her arms and dripped from her fingers.

"Kristin, get me the first aid kit."

"There's no time." The American woman pointed down the slope. Grass stalks twitched in several places. The rest of the pack was closing in.

"We're exposed. We need cover."

"Let's head for the arches."

Alice hesitated. "But Krous—"

Kristin cut her off. "Later."

Ed ducked under Kristin's arm, taking her weight. He took Kristin's gun and passed it to Alice.

"Keep watch behind us. Shoot anything that moves."

Painfully, they limped across the plain, staying out of the long grass as much as possible. Three times, Alice stopped and fired at the shapes skulking in their wake. The recoil of the gun hurt her wrists. Even so, by the time they reached the rocks of the shattered tor, she was out of bullets, and Kristin had taken a turn for the worse. The strain of hobbling across open ground with a twisted ankle had exhausted her; she could barely stand upright without support. Desperately, Ed and Alice pushed and pulled her up towards the arches, taking it in turns to support her over the treacherous rocks. They were all sweating heavily. Alice's wounds were still bleeding. Above, the two purple arches they strove for stood like impassive megaliths against the skyline. Below, five or six of the otter-raptors circled in the grass, nerving themselves to break cover and attack. One after another, they raised themselves up on their four hind paws, and snapped the air before falling back.

What am I doing here? Ed thought.

Yesterday evening he'd been settling down for a night in front of the TV, and now here he was facing something that looked like the bastard spawn of an otter and a pit bull terrier, with the teeth and social graces of a piranha. He'd once been cornered by a pair of Alsatians in the concrete front yard of a terraced house in Acton. He'd been trying to collect a fare, but had been forced instead to take refuge on the lid of a plastic wheelie bin while the big dogs growled back and forth, teeth bared, ready to maul him if he tried to run. Then, he'd been saved by the arrival of the dog's owner. This time he wouldn't be so fortunate. Right now, his only thought was to get himself, Alice and Kristin to the arches before the animals below worked up the courage to abandon the shelter of the grasslands and scramble up the rock after them.

Looking back across the undulating plain, he saw the arch which had brought them to this planet and, wedged below it, a reflected glint of sunlight from the starred windscreen of the trapped Land Rover.

"Nearly there," Alice gasped.

Ed looked up to find they were a few paces from the nearest arch. When he looked back down the slope, he saw two of the raptors advancing purposefully. They kept low to the ground like stalking cats. Their tails flicked and twitched.

"Come on," he said. Muscles straining against their own weight, he gave Kristin an extra push, and watched her scramble to the base of the arch. She held her hand out to him.

Behind her, Otto Krous stepped from behind an arch, where he'd been crouched, watching their ascent. His peeling, sunburned face bore livid scratches. Part of his moustache had been torn loose. He'd used a handkerchief to bandage his left hand, and there were bloody gouges on his right leg, where sharp claws had ripped through the fabric of his black combat trousers.

He glanced at Ed and Alice, and then turned his attention to Kristin.

"Lieutenant Cole," he said, lip curling. He bent over and yanked the white-haired woman one-handed to her feet. He seemed to have either lost or discarded the shotgun, but still clutched the machine pistol.

"You don't know when to give up, do you, sir?"

Obviously irritated, Kristin slapped his hand away. "At ease, soldier."

Krous sneered. He pushed his face into hers. "You don't get to give me orders any more, *sir*."

He shoved her in the chest and she fell back, landing heavily on her backside.

Ed stood up. "Hey!"

Krous ignored him. He raised the machine pistol and fired a burst into Kristin's torso. The noise made Ed flinch. Kristin jerked as the shots hit her, blood splattering in the sunlight, shockingly red. For a frozen second, nobody moved. Then, even as the shots still echoed across the plain below, Ed's feet were pushing him over the rocks, his hands grasping for the other man's throat. Krous saw him coming, but Ed caught him off balance and he couldn't turn the gun in time. Ed crashed into him and they fell, past the arch and down the slope on the far side, with Ed on top as they hit the ground. Loose stones and gravel skittered down around them.

Ed lay winded for a moment, sucking in air. He'd fallen heavily, pulled down by the planet's unfamiliar gravitational pull. His legs hurt where he'd barked them on the rough ground. His pulse hammered in his head.

As quickly as he could, he scrambled to his knees and punched Krous in the face. Pain seared in his knuckles, but he ignored it, punching again and again. He had a fury in him. Beneath his blows, Krous groaned and jerked. Since passing through the first arch, Ed had been improvising, reacting instead of acting, overawed by his alien surroundings. Now, he was asserting himself for the first time. He was taking control. All his pain and fear were funnelled into this moment. He brought his fist down and felt Krous's nose give with a sickening crack. Another blow to the man's jaw. Then Alice had his arm.

"Ed, get up," she said. Below, the grass rustled and swayed. Ed's pulse battered in his ears. His right hand felt bruised and broken. The knuckles were already swelling. Alice dragged him back up towards the arch.

Raptors lay in wait at the summit. Their haunches quivered, ready to pounce. Ed gave Alice a shove toward the arch.

"Go," he said.

She stepped through, and disappeared. Ed looked down the slope but Krous was nowhere to be seen. Warily, he backed towards the arch, keeping an eye on the approaching animals. One of them paused to sniff Kristin's boot. Her corpse lay spread-eagled and alone, eyes and mouth open to the sky, chest tattered and bloody, peroxide hair shining clean and white in the light of the sun. As Ed watched, the creature started worrying the leather of her boot with its teeth, shaking its head from side-to-side. Its companion slunk over to join it, sniffing at a patch of spilled blood.

Still walking backwards into the arch, Ed opened his mouth to shout at the hungry, inquisitive creatures; to chase them from her; but the white light took him before he could make a sound.

*   *   *

To: ed.Rico23@megaserve.com
From: alice@photographybyalice.co.uk

Dear Ed,

This will have to be a quick note. I left Verne at the hotel. I told him I was going for a run, and he'll be worried if I'm not back soon.

I think you'd like Barcelona. It's nice here. It's a very artistic sort of city, especially around the old gothic quarter. Lots of old buildings and narrow streets. Very picturesque. Just your kind of thing. I've taken loads of photos.

I'm writing from an internet café on La Rambla, opposite the Museu de l'Erotica. Everything smells of car fumes, garlic and cigarettes. From where I'm sitting, I can see stalls in the middle of the street selling caged chickens, budgies, baby rabbits and parakeets. At the end of the street is a square called the Placa de Catalunya, and our hotel.

When I've finished this email, I'm going to meet Verne for a late breakfast at a restaurant on the Vila de Madrid. We ate there last night, I had ravioli with lamb, pine nuts and mint (which was delicious, BTW). Then we're going to take a look at the Sagrada Familia.

I think this break is just what he needs. He hasn't been quite the same since he came back from Somalia, and this is the first time in months that I've seen him relax. Getting away like this could be just what he needs to perk him up.

And I guess that brings us around to the real reason I'm writing this email.

Ed, I want to make my marriage work. I have to try. And I can't do that with you distracting me. We have to stop seeing each other, immediately.

Hopefully this fortnight in Spain will give us both the space to look at our situations objectively. We need clarity to make adult decisions. We can't go on the way we have been. It's not fair to either of us, and it certainly isn't fair to Verne. He's your brother and my husband. We owe it to him to put an end to all the deception, before he gets hurt. From now on, we will simply be in-laws, and I hope we can be civil to one another at family occasions. Beyond that, we must not see each other. I must be a good wife and you must try to be a good brother. We must forget that we ever had feelings for each other. We must forget we were ever in love.

I'm sorry if this sounds heartless, but I must be firm with myself as well as with you.

Please don't call, text or reply to this email. It is for the best. I hope you understand.

With regret,
Alice
x

PART TWO

UNDER A BLOOD RED SKY

All goes onward and outward,
nothing collapses,
And to die is different from what any one
supposed, and luckier.

– Walt Whitman, *Song of Myself*

CHAPTER TWENTY-FIVE
DJATT

THE *AMELINE* POPPED back into being four hundred thousand kilometres above the sands of Djatt's eastern desert, slap-bang in the centre of the planet's designated Emergence Zone. Coasting inward on its residual velocity, the ship's scanners raked the surrounding space for potential threats.

Djatt was a small brown world out on the edge of human space, a hop and a skip away from most trade routes. With only one product to trade, it was ignored by the wider galaxy for ninety-nine years out of every hundred. It only attracted trade ships once a lifetime, when the centennial flowers of the cacti-like desert succulents were harvested to make the stimulant known simply as Pep. Then for a few weeks, merchants would come from far and wide in the hope of buying enough to make a fortune.

There were old men on the surface who hadn't even been born at the time of the last harvest, and children alive now who would grow old and die long before the next one. They were a nomadic people, mostly of Middle Eastern and Saharan African descent. The name 'Djatt' meant 'dustbowl' in one of their dialects. In between harvests, they slept in inflatable tents and followed their goats and camels around the coastline, from the snow-capped mountains of the west to the scrubby deserts of the east. Their only permanent structures were clustered like barnacles around the spaceport's perimeter: a score of warehouses, several leaky air processing plants, a church, and two or three hotels. Everything else they either carried with them or foraged for in coastal rock pools. Their needs were simple. Yet in business, they were as sharp as magpies. They always drove a hard deal, and for a third of a thousand years they had been loyal to the Abdulovs. This time, however, Kat was arriving empty-handed, with nothing to trade, and it remained to be seen how far that loyalty would carry her.

> UH-OH.

Strapped into the pilot's chair, Kat heard the ship's voice in her head, relayed through her implant.

"Problem?"

> I'M NOT GETTING ANY RESPONSE FROM THE LOCAL GRID.

"That's strange."

> AND I'M PICKING UP DISTRESS CALLS.

Kat felt herself stiffen.

"Show me."

The bridge around her dissolved into darkness. Through her implant, the ship gave her a real-time view of the surrounding volume. Red circles appeared, indicating the origins of the received transmissions. Numerical figures chattered away next to each one, reeling off measurements of signal strength and distance. Roughly half came from ships drifting in odd, unpowered orbits, the rest from points on the planet's surface.

Kat focused on the ships first. She saw four or five trading ships and a dozen in-system vehicles: passenger shuttles, automated tugs and the like. Most were adrift. Some had lost all their power. A few twitched like dying insects. She took a closer look at the nearest, a blocky freighter from a rival family, which wheeled slowly past her bow, tumbling end over end through a cloud of its own vented gas. Its airlocks were open and she could see smoke. Only fires didn't burn in vacuum, and the red-tinged 'smoke' seemed to be coagulating out of nothingness and streaming *into* the ship, not out.

Beyond the wreck, something obscured her view of the planet's daylight side. She frowned. For a moment, she couldn't make sense of what she saw. Then it snapped into focus.

"What the hell is that?"

Streamers of blood-red fog reached to encircle the globe's equator, as if the very fabric of space were trying to wrap itself in an embrace around the planet.

> UNKNOWN.

The ship magnified the image. Seen closer, the fog resembled an impossible storm cloud. Although the main bulk of the cloud stretched maybe two thirds of the way around the world, its edges were diffuse and hard to define, its ruddiness streaming back and merging into the greater blackness of space. She had to infer its shape from the way its edges occluded the stars beyond. From its underside, bloody tendrils snaked down into the atmosphere, sixty kilometres long and grasping at the surface. Lightning crackled around them. Where they touched the ground, fractal red blots bloomed like blood stains, spreading to cover land and sea alike, swallowing deserts, lakes and mountains.

"Can you raise the local family office?"

> NOPE.

The ship expanded the image. The spaceport and most of its attendant buildings were gone, consumed by what looked like an expanding lake of glutinous gore. As she watched, a group of specks broke from one of the surviving warehouses, running pell-mell ahead of the slowly-advancing flood.

"There are people down there."

A second larger group appeared, shambling after the first in ordered ranks.

"What are they doing?"

> IT LOOKS LIKE THEY'RE FIGHTING EACH OTHER.

Members of the first group kept stopping and turning to face their pursuers. By increasing the magnification yet again, Kat saw they held weapons.

"They're shooting each other?"

She turned her attention to the ranks of the second group.

"That's weird," she said.

> WHAT?

"Look at how they move."

The ship was silent for a second.

> AH, I SEE. THEY TURN AS ONE, LIKE SHOALS OF FISH OR FLOCKS OF BIRDS.

"And they're making no attempt to dodge the shots of the first group."

> WEIRD.

"Can we raise them?"

> I'M GETTING SEVERAL DISTRESS SIGNALS FROM THE PLANET'S SURFACE INCLUDING ONE FROM—

> AH.

"What?"

> YOU MAY WANT TO SEE THIS.

* * *

THE *AMELINE* HAD unfolded its communication array to its fullest extent—gossamer thin receivers stretching out like dragonfly wings from the hull—yet the transmissions were still faint and snowed with static, prone to dissolving into jagged bursts of random pixels. Through the interference, Kat made out a face: unshaven, haggard and dirty, like a hostage in a video. Through the grime and bristles, it took her a moment to recognise it. When she did, her stomach flipped. The face belonged to Victor Luciano. The picture came from a handheld camera. From the little background she could make out, it seemed he'd taken shelter behind a row of storage crates somewhere on the edge of the disappearing spaceport.

"Kat? Kat, is that you? Oh, thank God. I thought you were dead."

"I very nearly was."

He leaned in close to the camera. A piece had been torn from one of his ears and blood matted the hair on that side of his head. "Get out of here, Kat. Just turn around and run. Don't look back."

Crouched figures moved back and forth behind him. Some carried rifles. Gunshots popped like firecrackers.

"What's happening?" she asked.

Something exploded near the tanks, and Victor flinched as dirt rained down around him.

"It's that red cloud," he said. "It hit the ships in orbit first. We've been stranded down here for three days, running with the locals."

"What about the *Tristero*?"

"We lost contact. It's gone."

He rubbed hollow eyes with dirty fingers, as if he hadn't slept for the whole of those three days.

"Listen to me, Kat. This is important. I wasn't behind that bomb. You have to believe me. I know I've done some stupid things recently, but that wasn't one of them."

Kat narrowed her eyes. "A friend of mine died."

Victor looked away, visibly upset. "I know. I thought you had, too. But it wasn't my fault. You have to believe me."

"Why?"

"You used to."

"Before you walked out, you mean?"

Victor wiped his forehead with the back of his hand, leaving a dirty smear. He looked a lot older than she remembered. "What choice did I have? You deliberately went behind my back."

Kat's jaw tightened. "I did what I had to do."

"You killed our child."

"No!" Static fuzzed the screen for a second. Kat felt her eyes prickle with the threat of long-denied tears. "I was twenty-two years old," she said, not knowing if he could hear her through the interference. "I'd just left my family for you. I didn't know how to look after myself, let alone a child."

The picture flickered, gained some solidity.

"You should have told me," Victor said.

Kat screwed her fists into balls. "It was my choice, not yours. And anyway, it's only stored, not terminated. It can be re-implanted—"

The picture fuzzed out again. When it steadied, Victor looked old and tired.

"Stored?"

She put a hand to her brow.

"Yes, stored. It's there on Strauli, waiting for us."

"So you didn't—"

"No."

For a moment, Victor had the look of a man struck by lightning. Then he shook himself.

"We don't have time for this," he said. "None of it matters anymore, anyway. Not now. Just go, Kat. Get out of here."

"But—"

Over the link she heard the rattle of small arms fire. Victor glanced back over his shoulder.

"It's too late," he said. "It's over. I'm sorry. Sorry for everything."

Someone tugged at his sleeve. People were shouting.

"Look Kat, I've got to go. You get out of here. There's nothing more you can do."

CHAPTER TWENTY-SIX
SCRATCHES

TWO DAYS AFTER *Alice returned from her trip to Barcelona, Ed went to her photographic studio. The studio was on the third floor of a converted brick warehouse off Westferry Road. He didn't go in. Instead, he waited in the doorway of the apartment block across the street. It was raining. The rain fell from the sky like scratches on celluloid. When Alice emerged at lunchtime, he followed her to an Italian café by the river.*

He walked up to her table and said, "So that's it?"

Alice looked up, clearly annoyed to see him.

"I guess so."

She fiddled with the stem of her glass. The place smelled of pizzas and bottled beer. Football flickered on a screen by the bar. Italian flags hung from the walls. She finished the wine in silence, and got up to leave.

Ed put a hand on her arm.

"Don't go."

"It's over, Ed."

"Is it?"

She hitched her camera bag onto her shoulder and tossed a ten pound note onto the table, to cover the drinks.

"It's Verne," she said. "He wants us to have a baby."

"Are you going to?"

"I don't know, maybe."

She turned on her heel. He followed her out into the street. It had started to rain. She kissed him abruptly on the cheek. Then he watched her climb into a cab, not caring if he got wet. The rain ran down his cheeks.

"Don't go," he said.

HALF-BLIND WITH afterimages and shivering with cold, Ed stumbled backward from the arch. Alice caught him, and they clung to each other. He could feel her trembling. After the heat of the savannah, the air here felt as refreshingly light and cool as a drink of iced water.

"Are you okay?" he said.

Alice hugged him. "Kristin—?"

"Kristin's dead."

He felt her shiver in his arms.

"But those animals—"

"I know."

"We shouldn't have left her."

Ed rubbed his eyes with the finger and thumb of one hand. The spots were clearing from his vision. They were in a cave.

"There's nothing we can do," he said. "We can't go back."

The cave measured about fifteen metres in length, with the softly glowing purple arch wedged about two-thirds of the way in, in much the same way as the arch that swallowed Verne had wedged itself across the escalator at Chancery Lane. The walls of the cave were smooth and dry. Loose stones crunched underfoot.

In the opposite direction, the mouth of the cave framed an almost circular ring of blue sky. From outside came the crash and boom of ocean surf.

"Come on," he said. "We're not out of this yet."

He took her hand and walked her to the entrance. The pull of gravity was less here, making movement easier. As they got closer to the light, he could see how pale she was. Her eyes were dim and unfocussed and blood oozed from the scratches on her arms and chest. He had plenty of scrapes of his own, and his head still hurt from the crack it had taken in the Land Rover crash. They badly needed to rest and recuperate, to have a hot shower, a good meal and a long sleep.

The cave ended in a sheer drop. They were in a cliff wall overlooking the sea. Far below, waves churned against ragged boulders.

Searching for options, Ed looked up.

"It's not far to the top. About ten metres, I guess."

"Can we get up there?"

The top of the cliff had been eroded by the wind, and bits had crumbled away. It looked lumpy and rough, with plenty of potential handholds.

"Are you up to climbing?"

Alice put a hand to her head. "I don't know."

Ed looked back into the cave, to the arch. "Well, we're going to have to try. We can't go back that way. And we can't stay here in case one of those creatures comes through."

Alice looked up in alarm. "Do you think they might?"

"If we can step through, I see no reason they can't."

She swallowed and shook herself.

"Okay," she said, "but you're going to have to help me."

"Don't worry. If you're hurting too much, we can take it slowly."

"No, you don't understand." She touched his arm. "Ed, I've never told anyone this before."

"What?"

"I'm terrified of heights."

She looked down. Then she frowned. Something had caught her eye. She took her hand from Ed's arm and walked past him to the cave wall, where she bent to retrieve an object from the dirt floor, and straightened, holding a pair of spectacles. The arms were bent and rusty. One of the lenses had been lost, and scratches and dust covered the other. They looked a thousand years old, like something pulled by an archaeologist from the sands of Egypt. Pinching them between finger and thumb, Alice looked up at Ed, open-mouthed.

"Are they—?"

Her voice was almost lost in the crash of the waves below. Ed took them from her. He turned them over and over reverently, as if inspecting an antique. He opened and closed the arms. The hinges were stiff and rusty.

"Yes," he said. "They're his all right."

"Then we're close?"

He gave the glasses back to her.

"We could be. At least we know he made it this far." He thought of Kristin and shuddered.

Alice bit her lip. "I can't believe it. He actually stood here." For the first time since leaving home, she seemed excited. "We're actually on the right track."

Ed took her hand.

"All the more reason to keep moving, then," he said.

CHAPTER TWENTY-SEVEN
THE WRATH OF GOD

THE AMELINE'S HULL creaked as it kissed the top of the atmosphere. Linked into the ship's sensors, Kat felt the growing friction as a fire in her belly. They were coming in as steeply as they dared, trading safety for speed, on a course that would take them directly under the spreading blood-red cloud.

"Steady," she said. They were over the ocean. Already, the leading edges of the hull glowed a dull crimson.

> TWELVE MINUTES TO TARGET.

Scrawling a line of fire through the tortured air, they crossed the coastline and passed over the snow-capped western mountains at many times the speed of sound.

Ahead, the cloud's streamers raked the land, reaching from heaven to earth like the kilometres-long tentacles of an angry desert god. Lightning flickered. Looking at it, Kat struggled to comprehend the sheer scale of the unleashed fury. This was a storm of biblical proportions. It boiled across the sky from horizon to horizon, large enough to rain destruction across the whole face of the world. It was by turns terrifying and exhilarating, and she could feel her heart leaping in her chest.

> FIVE MINUTES.

She popped her safety straps.

"Okay, I'm going to the airlock. Keep scanning for new transmissions, in case he tries to make contact again."

> ARE YOU SURE YOU KNOW WHAT YOU'RE DOING?

"Yes."

> ONLY I THOUGHT YOU WANTED TO KILL HIM.

Kat paused. She thought of Victor's face as it had appeared on her screen, looking old and worn and scared.

"Maybe later," she said. "In the meantime, we stick to the plan."

She clambered back down the ladder into the passageway connecting the bridge to the rest of the ship's interior. They were being buffeted around; she had to use her arms to brace herself against the passage walls. She stopped at the equipment locker, strapped a handgun to either hip, and lifted out the biggest weapon in her collection: a sturdy composite assault rifle with laser scope, explosive rounds, and a 30mm grenade launcher slung under the barrel.

"How are we doing?"

> DOWN TO SUBSONIC. TWO MINUTES AND CLOSING.

As steadily as she could, she made her way through the crew lounge and cargo bay towards the rear airlock. Halfway there, the ship lurched violently. Despite the inertial compensators, she lost her footing and tumbled against the bay's bulkhead. Loose pieces of un-stowed equipment crashed and rattled down around her.

"What the hell was that?"

> EMERGENCY EVASION. ONE OF THE STREAMERS GOT TOO CLOSE FOR COMFORT.

Kat picked herself up. Still clutching the rifle, she clambered into the rear airlock and sealed herself inside. She sat with her back to the inner door, booted feet braced against the opposite wall, to either side of the outer hatch.

"I'm in position."

> TEN SECONDS.

She felt the ship's landing jets kick in, pushing hard against her back. Then they hit the ground and the outer hatch snapped open.

Cautiously, Kat got to her feet. Smoke and ash filled the air. A hot wind snatched at her hair, whipping it, and sand stung her eyes.

They'd put down in the desert beyond the spaceport, a few metres from Victor's last recorded position. The red cloud roiled overhead, bigger than the world. Lightning filled the sky. Seen from below, the massive columns looked like tornadoes: dozens of them in every direction.

> CAPTAIN!

She shook herself. They had no time to waste. On the ground, the redness that had engulfed the spaceport buildings rolled towards her, as flat as a lake and as inexorable as lava, dissolving everything in its path. Ahead of the oncoming slick marched the ranked figures she'd seen from orbit. There were maybe a hundred of them, shambling along shoulder-to-shoulder, like zombies in the red light. Using her implant to ramp up the magnification in her left eye, she tried to get a good look at them, but they were as featureless as silhouettes, and certainly no longer human.

Her comlink crackled.

"Kat?"

"Victor!" The zombies were getting uncomfortably close. "Victor, get up here."

She scanned the battlefield. She couldn't see him. Then three figures broke from the cover of nearby boulders, running at a crouch. Kat recognised him immediately. He was older and heavier than the other two, but he'd always kept himself in shape. She lowered the airlock ladder ready for them, and then lifted the rifle to her shoulder, ready to lay down covering fire.

"Come on!" she called.

She sighted on the front row of the approaching phalanx and pulled the trigger. The rifle bucked against her like a startled animal, kicking against her shoulder. Bloody, fist-sized chunks blew from the heads and torsos of the horde, making them stagger. Time after time she raked the gun back and forth, yet none of the figures fell dead. They twitched and jerked, but remained stubbornly upright. She stopped firing when Victor reached the foot of the ladder. Putting her rifle down on the deck, she dropped to her knees, reaching down to help him.

"They don't fall down," she said.

Victor didn't reply. He started climbing.

> WE HAVE INCOMING. FIFTY SECONDS. TENDRIL HEADED THIS WAY.

Kat used her new arm to haul Victor into the airlock by the back of his belt. At the foot of the ladder, one of the other men—a local, by his clothes and beard— hesitated. He looked up at her, eyes wild with terror. Unbidden, Kat saw Enid's face in her mind, felt again the other woman's fingers brush hers in the final seconds before the emergency door slammed down, severing her arm.

"Come on!" she yelled.

The bearded man had one sandaled foot on the first rung of the ladder. Kat reached down with her new arm and grabbed hold of his outstretched wrist. The man cried out in a language Kat didn't speak. Bright scarlet tendrils were snaking up his legs, under his clothes. They sprouted from the collar of his shirt, and from the cuffs of his sleeves. Like a striking snake, one shot from his wrist and glommed onto Kat's hand. She pulled back reflexively, but the tendril wouldn't break. It wrapped itself around her wrist, squeezing like a small red python. The more she tried to shake it loose, the tighter it coiled, sinking into the metal of her hand, melting like acid. Where it touched, the smooth alloys turned to reddish-black oil. And it spread fast. Within seconds it had consumed her hand and wrist and its edge was working its way along her forearm, leaving nothing in its wake but writhing darkness.

She yanked back hard. The man below had begun frothing a dark red paste. It bubbled from his mouth and nostrils and eyes. It ran like tears down his face and cascaded over his clothes. His limbs shook as if electrified. His hair and skin boiled away, swallowed by the red tide bursting from within. Seconds later, he was gone, eaten away to nothing, leaving only a shambling stick figure in his place, like an afterimage. In desperation, Kat clawed for her rifle with her free hand. She swung it to point at the zombie, and her scrabbling finger found the trigger, firing a burst of explosive bolts into the thing's chest. The shots hurt her ears. The bullets blew ragged holes through the zombie's torso and it staggered back, but didn't fall, its arm still tied to hers by the red tendril sprouting from its wrist. As she watched, horrified, the punctures in its body started to close, the red flesh oozing back to fill the craters left by the bullets. Where pieces had fallen from it, new figures began to grow, tiny arms and heads sprouting from the sand with obscene haste.

Fighting down panic, she moved the gun until the barrel touched the tendril connecting her to the writhing figure below, and pulled the trigger. The gun leapt in her hand, hurting her thumb, but she was free. She'd blown the red rope apart, and the severed end flapped from her hand. Steam came from the melting metal of her prosthetic arm.

She scrambled to her knees and a shadow fell over her. She looked up at a crimson tornado filling the sky, towering over the ship. Where it touched the ground, the dirt erupted in spurts of hot blood. It made a sound like a freight train and it bore down on them like the very wrath of God.

"Kat!"

Victor was beside her. He hauled her by the shoulders and they both tumbled into the airlock.

The outer door smacked shut.

"Go!" Victor yelled. But they were already airborne.

KAT LAY SHAKING on the carbon deck plates as the *Ameline* powered skyward. Victor leaned over her. His voice seemed to echo from a great distance.

"Kat, talk to me!"

He shook her by the shoulders.

"Kat!"

She couldn't unclench her jaw. Sweat ran down her spine, and her legs quivered. The redness had eaten its way into the metal of her arm, using the prosthetic's artificial nerves as a conduit. It was inside her now, forcing its greasy tendrils into her brain, its hunger an agony within her, vast and unquenchable.

As it pushed into her mind, she heard the voices of those it had already consumed, their souls crying out in torment, trapped forever in the belly of the beast. Her mind touched theirs and knew their agony, knew that they had been torn from their physical bodies and imprisoned here, in virtual simulation spaces contained within the redness itself.

A name came to her, borne on a tide of anguish: *The Recollection.*

She tried to fight. The Recollection was eating her from within, as it had done to that poor bastard she'd tried to save at the foot of the ladder. Her arms jerked as she tried to struggle. Her back arched. She couldn't get the breath to scream. In her head, the presence of The Recollection felt as cold and dark as interstellar space.

Then suddenly she felt a different kind of pain. There was something hot touching the base of her throat. The skin split and shriveled away from it like polythene. Her nostrils filled with the reek of her own cooked flesh. Still unable to scream, she thrashed around.

And a white light blew through her like a scouring wind.

NEWS HEADLINES

DUST CLOUD THREAT

Astronomers predict widespread disruption
to^%&$$%(*(&)(%%£

CONTACT LOST WITH **&(("*&()

&^^"^%$%^%£!))_

DEAD RISE! PANIC IN &&^NS

@~:>?})_(_)*!$
G*(!()"*&^*(£$!9723IIOLQ?@:0*(!M<NMSI&!

---

^76% FIGHTING

"£&"** *Pitched battles on the* 4treets of
D87^&5@@@#'.

"%^£&~@:}{>}{HEL

&*^*^~~!":@

CHAPTER
TWENTY-EIGHT
PREDATORY FISH

THE FIRST STEP was the worst. Inching out above the churning sea, Ed dug his fingers into the crumbling shale of the cliff wall. The stone barked his knuckles. The cold sea air scraped his throat, numbed his hands. His clothes felt like rags, still damp with sweat. His muscles ached from his fight with Krous.

From the cave mouth, Alice watched with wide, appalled eyes.

"Be careful," she said.

Ed bit his lip. He could hardly breathe. He was trying not to look down. Blindly, his foot searched for purchase. He got a toehold, but his boot slipped. Shards of dislodged stone spiralled away towards the white water below.

"Ed!"

"I'm okay."

He tried again, until he found a more secure hold. Then he pulled himself up, making room for her.

"Come on." He held out a hand, but Alice shook her head.

"I don't know if I can."

"You have to try." He suppressed a shiver. It was cold out here. The light had started to die in the sky. All their warm clothes had been lost with the Land Rover. If night fell and the temperature dropped, they'd be in trouble.

"Come on. You're one of the bravest people I know."

"I'm not."

"Yes, you are."

He reached for her again. As he did so, actinic white light flashed in the depths of the cavern. Alice turned her head to look back at the arch.

"Oh!"

She scrambled out onto the bare rock, putting her feet where his had been a moment before. Her auburn hair caught the light. Behind her, a raptor appeared, snapping at her heels. Its claws skittered on the rock and in its determination to catch her, it almost tipped over the edge, into the sea. Ed grabbed Alice by the arm and helped her find a secure handhold.

"Okay?"

She swallowed. She had her eyes shut.

"They followed us."

"I thought they would."

Ed turned to reach for the next ledge. He could see the lip of the cliff above, tantalisingly close. Moving only one limb at a time, he levered himself painfully upward. His arms shook with the effort. The rough stone hurt his hands.

"Keep going," he panted. "We're nearly there."

His breath came in clouds before him. In the cave mouth, the creature snarled and snapped like an angry dog.

"Ed?"

"Don't worry. It can't get to us."

Suddenly, the creature yelped. Ed glanced down to see it tumbling end-over-end into the abyss, all six paws scrabbling desperately at the thin, cold air. As it neared the bottom, it started to howl. Ed looked away before it hit.

"Jesus."

Shivering against the cold, he heaved himself up and over the cliff's crumbling edge. For a few seconds, he lay panting in the dirt, his shaking hands curled in agony. Then he gathered the last of his strength and rolled onto his front, reaching down over the edge of the precipice.

"Okay," he said to Alice, "I'm here."

A sunburned head appeared at the mouth of the cave, looking down at the fallen raptor.

Krous!

Ed froze. Seeing his expression, Alice glanced down. Her face paled. She looked up with a question in her eyes: *What do we do?*

Ed put a finger to his lips. He cast around, hunting for a weapon. Behind him, gently rolling heath stretched away to a range of hills. All he could see that might be of use were stones.

At the mouth of the cave, Krous turned to look upward. He'd been mauled again. There were fresh scratches across the peeling skin of his face and neck. His eyes were the dull eyes of a predatory fish, and his tongue lolled from beneath the remains of his moustache.

"Leave us alone," Ed warned.

Krous didn't answer. With slow deliberation, he edged out onto the rock face, moving with the confidence of an experienced climber.

Ed thrust his hand down to Alice. "Quickly," he said.

She began pulling herself up, her fear lending her a new burst of strength. She was close to the top, but Krous climbed faster.

"Get away from her," Ed said. He caught Alice by the arm and dragged her up and over the edge, onto firmer ground.

"Can you run?" he said.

Alice shook her head. She had no breath to talk. Her hands were bleeding. The knees of her jeans were worn ragged. Desperately, Ed surveyed the desolate scenery. Even if she were capable of moving, he couldn't see any shelter.

"Stay here," he said. He picked up a fist-sized stone and showed it to Krous.

"Why are you doing this? Why did you kill her?"

The soldier paused, hanging from his hands and feet.

"Lieutenant Cole?" He turned his head and spat. "What does it matter? What difference does it make? We're all dead, aren't we. None of us are going home. We're all alone out here."

"But you killed her."

The soldier slid a knife from his thigh pocket.

"Don't," said Ed. He raised the stone. Krous ignored him. With the blade between his teeth, he started climbing again.

"I mean it." Ed let the stone drop. It hit the other man in the shoulder. Krous let out a grunt of annoyance, and the stone fell away into empty air.

Ed picked up another, slightly larger.

"Stay back," he said.

Krous glowered at him, and pulled the knife from his mouth.

"I'm going to kill the two of you as soon as I get up there," he said. His eyes flashed. "Although, of course, I may take my time with your little friend." He reached up and pulled himself another metre closer to the top. Ed's heart hammered. His mouth was dry. He squeezed the stone in his fist.

"That's it," he said. "That is *it*."

He got to his knees and whipped the stone down with as much force as he could muster. It hit Krous on the arm, almost dislodging him completely. The soldier cried in pain and anger, dropping the knife. The injured arm dangled uselessly.

Ed scrambled over to a larger stone. This one was the size of a human skull, and heavy enough that he could only just heft it in one hand. He dragged it over to the cliff edge and looked down at Krous. The man swung from his one good hand.

"I've had enough of this," Ed said. He could hardly breathe. He'd never been this angry in his entire life. "I've had enough of the arches, of you and those animals, and the *fucking* Serbians."

Krous snarled up at him. "So what are you going to do about it?"

Hands shaking, Ed raised the rock above his head.

"Last chance," he said.

Krous laughed hoarsely. "Fuck you. You're a painter, you don't have the guts."

Ed tasted something sour at the back of his throat. His pulse drummed in his ears.

"No," he said. He climbed to his feet. Krous looked up at him. For a long moment, the two men stared into each other's bloodshot eyes, and Ed saw in them the madness that had crept in following the loss of his comrades and the days he'd spent alone at sea on that giant wooden hulk. Ordinarily, Ed would have felt sorry for the man, but out here, there could be no truce, no discussion. Krous had already killed once and Ed had every reason to believe he'd kill again, just as soon as he reached solid ground. They couldn't outrun him and they couldn't placate him. Out here, the only thing they could rely on was themselves.

He gave the rock a final squeeze, swallowed hard, and let it fall. Krous tried to turn away but it slammed into his chest. He cried out and lost his grip. His hands flailed as he desperately tried to save himself. Then he fell, tumbling backward into the abyss.

Amplified by the rock walls, his scream went on for a long, long time. Even after it was over, it seemed to hang in the frosty air, rolling back and forth across the cliff tops in time to the surge of the waves on the rocks below. Neither Ed nor Alice spoke. They just stood, looking down at the crumpled figure in the surf. Ed kept glancing at his open right hand—and the rock it no longer held. Then, as the final echoes faded to nothing, he became aware of another sound. He tilted his head.

"Can you hear something?"

He turned slowly, just as a camouflaged halftrack appeared over the nearest rise. Its caterpillar tracks flicked up dust and stones, and an unfamiliar flag flapped from its aerial. Soldiers fanned out behind it, guns at the ready. One of them jerked a thumb at the floor.

"Get down," he barked. "Put your hands behind your back."

CHAPTER
TWENTY-NINE
MEET THE MONSTER

VICTOR BOOKED THEM into a hotel suite on Strauli, in a city less than fifty kilometres from the Abdulov family compound. The room looked out over the spaceport. It had a large double bed, and the staff delivered a bowl of fresh fruit each and every morning. They'd been together for six subjective months, and now they were planning to ship out from the Quay together, as crew-members on a Blue Star Trading vessel taking a run up the coreward stars to Nolton Relay, on the very edge of explored space.

In the week before the departure, they lay wrapped in each other's arms, telling each other of the sights they would see and the wonders they would experience. It was their dream. They had both flown before, but this time it would be different, as they were doing it for each other. They would crew together and save up enough to buy their own ship.

"Not one of those old clunkers," Victor said, looking out of the window at the derelicts left rusting in the rain at the edge of the port. They were old ships no-one could be bothered to repair. They had outlived their *usefulness and, in some cases, their owners. They had names like* Tortilla Moon, Candy Star *and* Ameline.

"We'll get a new one, a fast one," he said. "The best we can afford."

Kat had already emptied the trust fund her family had put aside for her, and transferred the balance to an anonymous account. When topped-up with their earnings from this trip, it would be enough to put a deposit on a new trading ship.

She hugged him.

"We can, can't we? We can do that."

Then, the morning before they were due to leave, she took a pregnancy test. She'd been feeling strange for a few days. At first, she'd put it down to excitement. Then she started feeling queasy at night, as she lay in bed. She took the test in the bathroom of the hotel suite, while Victor was out, buying in a few last minute essentials. When the test came up positive, she stared at it in dismay. She didn't know how it had happened. Or rather, she did, but didn't know how they could have been so careless. She was twenty-two years old and just taking her first steps away from home. She didn't want to be pregnant. Not now. She wanted to prove herself, get her own ship first. She didn't want Victor to feel obligated. It was too soon in their relationship.

So she delayed the decision.

She pulled on her coat and took herself off to the hospital.

The operation was a simple one: a small incision, the foetus removed and placed in storage; still alive but frozen. The whole procedure took less than ten minutes. Afterwards, the surgeon glued her closed and told her she wouldn't even have a scar. He told her to stop crying. She could have the child re-implanted at any time, and carry it to term naturally, if that's what she wanted. In the meantime, it would be here on ice, waiting for her.

Outside the hospital, the rain still pattered on the pavements. At this stage her baby—their baby—was only a cluster of cells, smaller than her smallest fingernail. Would it know it had been frozen? Would it feel time passing it by?

She walked all the way back to the hotel, water streaming down her face. By the time she got there, she was a wet, sniveling mess.

"Where have you been?" Victor said. He had their cases packed and ready to go. A bottle of wine stood open on the nightstand, two plastic glasses ready to toast their adventure. When she told him what she'd done, he sat on the bed. He scratched the bridge of his nose.

"You should have told me," he said.

Kat folded her arms across her chest. She sniffled miserably.

"I thought you'd be angry."

Victor got to his feet. "What?"

She nudged one of the suitcases with the toe of her boot.

"If it stopped us leaving. I thought you'd be angry if it stopped us leaving."

His face flushed. He took a step toward her, fists squeezed tight.

"Do you know how long I've—?" His voice faltered and he broke off.

"I did what I thought you would have wanted."

"You have no idea what I want."

"What's that supposed to mean?"

Victor turned away. He bent at the knees and picked up one of the cases.

"I'm leaving," he said. "I've got a flight to catch."

Kat felt the strength drain out of her. She watched him walk to the door.

"You can't leave me here," she said.

Victor paused. "Watch me."

Without thinking, she scooped one of the glasses from the nightstand and dashed the wine in his face.

"Fuck you," she said.

When he'd gone, she threw herself on the bed and stayed there for a long time.

The next morning, the rain had given way to a chill breeze. Feeling raw inside, she walked to the spaceport. She had more than enough money for a train ticket home, but no intention of buying one. Instead, she went to the scrap yard at the edge of the port, where the derelict ships were waiting. She climbed through the cargo bay of the one that looked the most promising: a wedge-shaped trader decked out in the faded blue and red livery of the Abdulovs, its hull dotted with sensor pods and lateral thruster arrays.

"It needs a lot of work," she said, eyeing the loose deck plates and exposed wiring.

The scrap merchant shrugged. He didn't care. Although he'd doubtless acquired the ship as cheap scrap, the price he was asking would more or less wipe out her savings, and he knew it.

Kat climbed up to the bridge. In the cold air, her breath came in little clouds.

She patted the back of the pilot's couch.

"Hello," she said.

Lights flickered on the instrument console.

> HEY THERE. I'M THE AMELINE. HOW ARE YOU DOING?

"My name's Katherine. Tell me, are you Sylvia Abdulov's Ameline?"

The ship seemed to consider this for a moment.

> I WAS ONCE OWNED BY SYLVIA ABDULOV. SHE WAS A FINE WOMAN. WHY DO YOU ASK?

Kat smiled. She'd never met her great-aunt, but knew of the woman's exploits. Sylvia Abdulov had been a legend in the family's beach compound, having captained a dozen ships and repeatedly crisscrossed the sky from Old Earth to New Chongqing, Port Douglas and the Far Stars. She'd been one of the original Abdulov pilots, and some said she had a man in every port; others that she alternated between men and women, taking whichever took her fancy. One thing was certain: Sylvia had been one hell of a trader. She'd known how to turn a profit. Without her, the Abdulovs would still have been a local concern, instead of today's galaxy-spanning conglomerate. As a cadet, Kat had had a picture of her taped to the inside of her locker door. Now, realising that she was standing on the bridge of her great-aunt's first ship, she felt closer to home than she had in months.

"Yes," she said to herself, "I can do this."

She ran a finger through the dust on the Ameline's navigation console, leaving a trail.

"Are you ready to fly again?" she asked the ship.

Waves of eagerness leaked through her implant. She felt power building in the engine cores, and long-dormant systems flickering back into life.

> I THOUGHT YOU'D NEVER ASK.

*   *   *

THREE WEEKS LATER, *after patching the old ship up just enough to make her flight-worthy, Kat took the* Ameline *up into the clear blue sky above the port. The rain had stopped and the sun shone.*

Determined to follow her great-aunt's example, she flew the little ship all over, from the stable, middle-aged stars around Sol to the bright blue archipelagos near the rim. She hauled whatever cargoes she could find, legal or otherwise, and used every scrap of profit to refit the engines and repair the hull and vital electrical systems. Often, the Ameline's blue and red paintwork led people to assume the ship was still an active part of the Abdulov fleet; and when it suited her, Kat played along with that assumption, using her family's reputation in order to win business.

On Nuevo Cordoba, she fell in with a random jumper by the name of Napoleon Jones. Random jumping was an extreme sport, illegal on some worlds, prime entertainment on others. It was the ultimate gamble. It was a pilot throwing his or her craft into hyperspace on a random trajectory, just to see where they'd end up. Some pilots discovered habitable planets beyond the limits of the arch network, or rich mineral deposits. They became celebrities. They brought back wild tales of bizarre planetary systems, of swollen stars and uncharted asteroid belts. But the risks were huge. Roulette pilots gambled with their lives, and there were ugly rumours of ghost ships, of murder and cannibalism, and individuals dying lonely, lingering deaths in distant star systems. Those lucky enough to find their way home clustered on worlds close to the edge of familiar space, where they could stand under the clear night sky and see the unexplored frontier stretching away before them. Nuevo Cordoba was one such world. It was a dirty little outpost on a half-forgotten moon.

Napoleon Jones was one of the better roulette pilots, in that he was still alive. In the random jumping community, he was something of a legend, having jumped further into the unknown than anyone else. He had a penchant for leather jackets and wide-brimmed hats. He had dark green eyes the colour of the Strauli sea after a storm; eyes that had maybe seen too much, yet still hankered for something new; eyes which glittered in the low lights of the port bars, where the other patrons treated him with the wary respect accorded to a shaman. His ship was named the Bobcat. It was small and fast and tough.

"You could slam it into a rocky moon at Mach 6," he often boasted, "and still walk away unscathed."

Kat's affair with him lasted a little over four weeks. In that time, he taught her more about flying than she had learned at the Strauli Flight School. He taught her how to surf the solar wind. He showed her how to wring every last watt of power from her ship's engines; how to jump further and faster by stretching their safety tolerances to the absolute limit.

When she left him, it was with a renewed sense of self-confidence and a way of carrying herself that identified her as an experienced trader, rather than the rookie she'd been before.

On her travels, she saw the vast old wooden sailing ships of Trafalgar, and she hiked through Valhalla's ice caverns. On Earth, she walked the streets of Paris, Rio and Berlin, and saw the massive geo-engineering projects that had been deployed to fight the climate crisis... and the monuments to those the crisis had already claimed.

For a while, she made enough money to keep flying, living from cargo to cargo, but her luck didn't last. On Sand Haven, the Ameline failed a routine safety inspection, and she had to replace the primary and secondary cooling arrays. A few jumps later, she delivered a cargo only to find that her buyer had gone out of business, leaving her several thousand out of pocket. She couldn't afford to refuel. She couldn't afford to eat. By the time she reached the Bubble Belt and Tiers Cross, she was broke, with the Ameline running on fumes...

KAT JERKED AWAKE in her bunk. Victor sat beside her. Victor, the man who'd abandoned her on Strauli. The man who'd shipped out as a hired hand and returned as a captain. The man she'd come here to kill.

She blinked at the ceiling. "What...?"

He stroked her hair.

"Shhh," he said. "It's all right. You're going to be okay."

"But—" She brought her left hand up to touch the dressing at the base of her throat. The skin felt stiff and numb beneath.

"Does it still hurt?"

"No."

"Good," he said. "I cleaned it and sprayed it with anaesthetic before I applied the bandage."

"What happened to me?"

Victor's brow furrowed. "I don't really know. You were on the floor in the cargo hold. I thought you were dying like the others. Then this white light... What was that?"

Kat shook her head. She had no idea.

Victor tapped her prosthetic arm. "Whatever it was, it seems to have killed the infection."

Kat held up the hand. The metal no longer seethed like boiling oil. Instead, where the redness had passed through it, it looked half-melted, like candle wax. Where the light caught it, it held a sheen like a fly's wing.

"The Recollection," she said softly.

Victor looked at her. "What?"

"The Recollection. That's what the red stuff calls itself."

"How do you know that?"

Kat frowned. "I'm not sure."

He touched her hair again. "What else do you know?"

She thought.

"It's very old," she said. "And it's not a cloud. It's a, a memory matrix. It breaks everything down, stores it as code. It preserves everything it touches."

Victor drew his hand back. He looked concerned.

"Kat, are you okay?"

She pushed herself up on her elbows. "I think so. I mean, I feel okay."

In truth, she felt anesthetized. The shocks had come too rapidly, one after another. First Enid's death and the loss of her arm, then the catastrophe on Djatt. Finally, her infection by, and mental brush with, the red cloud. She needed time to stop and take stock, to grieve for everything and everyone that had been lost. She needed to wriggle deeper into her bunk and pull the blankets over her head, but she couldn't do that with Victor sitting there. Instead, she sat up straight and shook out her hair. She flexed her metal hand.

Despite their half-melted appearance, the servos in the joints still worked.

"Help me to the bridge," she said.

When they got there, she sank gratefully into the pilot's couch. Her chest hurt where it had been burned.

"Okay," she said to the ship, "show me what you've got."

The forward screen cleared and the stars were replaced by black and white footage taken from a camera in the cargo hold. Kat saw herself lying on the deck plates by the inner airlock door, Victor kneeling over her. Oily red paste frothed from her mouth, and her arms and legs twitched spasmodically.

> As far as I can tell, The Recollection is a gestalt entity, comprising trillions of individual machines, all identical, all molecular in size. Once they were inside your body, they set to work reproducing, converting your molecules into copies of themselves.

The scene flashed. Kat's pendant burst with the radiance of a sun. Victor fell back, shading his eyes with his arm. The screen went white and the recording ended.

In the pilot's chair, Kat shivered.

"What was that?"

> Some kind of energy release from your pendant. It neutralised the machinery invading your body.

Kat rubbed the bandage at the base of her throat, remembering the vanished pendant and the words the Acolyte had spoken.

"If you insist on going to Djatt, this will protect you."

A new image appeared onscreen: a three-dimensional scan of her skull. The picture zoomed in on her brain, portions of which were highlighted, including the frontal lobes and hippocampus.

> HOWEVER, THE SHIP CONTINUED, SOME RESTRUCTURING OF YOUR BRAIN HAD ALREADY TAKEN PLACE, PRIMARILY IN THE AREAS ASSOCIATED WITH CONSCIOUSNESS AND MEMORY.

Kat rubbed her forehead with her left hand.

"I don't feel any different." She glanced at Victor. He looked troubled; the ship must have connected to his implant, allowing him to see what she saw, hear what she heard.

> WOULD YOU BE ABLE TO TELL, IF YOU DID?

The screen display cleared again, reverting to a view of the stars beyond the hull.

> DURING THE ATTACK, THE RECOLLECTION ATTEMPTED TO USE YOUR IMPLANT TO INFECT ME, BY TRANSMITTING A VIRTUAL COPY OF ITSELF INTO MY MEMORY BANKS.

"Are you okay?"

> HELL, YEAH. I WAS EXPECTING IT. I'D ALREADY SET UP A DIVERT AND I SHUNTED THE FUCKER STRAIGHT INTO GRID STORAGE.

The *Ameline* carried enough memory capacity to transport googleflops of data from one planetary Grid to the next. You could throw in the text of every book ever printed and the music of every tune ever recorded, and there'd still be plenty of room to spare.

Kat bit her lip. "Is it safe?"

> I ISOLATED IT IN THE MAIN CORE. IT CAN'T GET OUT.

Victor broke in: "Can we talk to it?"

> I'VE ALREADY ESTABLISHED PRELIMINARY CONTACT.

Kat sat forward. She said, "Can you tell us what it is, what it wants?"

> AS I SAID, THE RECOLLECTION IS A SWARM OF NANO-SCALE MACHINERY. THE INDIVIDUAL MACHINES ARE NOT THEMSELVES CONSCIOUS, BUT EACH CONTRIBUTES TOWARDS THE INTELLIGENCE OF THE WHOLE. THE CLOSEST ANALOGY I

CAN FIND IS THAT OF AN ANT COLONY. ON THEIR OWN, THE INDIVIDUAL ANTS ARE MINDLESS AND VULNERABLE, BUT ACTING TOGETHER, THEY'RE CAPABLE OF PERFORMING COMPLEX FEATS OF ENGINEERING.

"So it's conscious?" Victor asked.

> AFTER A FASHION.

"And we're holding that consciousness in Grid Storage?"

> NO. WHAT WE'VE GOT IS A SIMPLIFIED, MUCH REDUCED COPY. IT HAD TO COMPRESS ITSELF TO TRANSMIT THROUGH CAPTAIN ABDULOV'S IMPLANT.

"Is it active?"

> ITS PRIMARY MISSION SEEMS TO BE TO COLLECT AND STORE AS MUCH INFORMATION AS POSSIBLE. WE'RE HOLDING COMPLETE COPIES OF THE STRAULI AND VERTEBRAE BEACH GRIDS, SO WHILE IT'S BUSY DIGESTING THOSE, I EXPECT IT'LL BE AS HAPPY AS A PIG IN SHIT.

Kat pulled herself upright in her chair.

"Open a channel," she said.

> ARE YOU SURE?

"Yes. I want to talk to this motherfucker."

> OKAY. BRACE YOURSELVES.

For a second silence reigned on the *Ameline*'s bridge as the speakers held only the hiss of dead air. Then, without warning, an earsplitting howl filled the room.

Kat slapped her hands to her ears.

"Turn it off!"

Immediately, the ship cut the feed.

> SORRY.

Ears still ringing, Kat lowered her hands and let out a long, shuddering breath. She could feel her heart thumping in her chest. Even while flinching from the howl, she'd thought she could hear within it the individual screams and cries of a million tormented souls: an earsplitting confluence of agony and fear.

In the copilot's couch, Victor rubbed the bridge of his nose. He looked ashen.

"Christ," he said weakly. "What was that?"

> *THAT* WAS THE RECOLLECTION.

THE WILLIAM PILGRIM HOSTEL FOR DISPLACED TIME TRAVELLERS

THE SOLDIERS WERE polite but firm. Ed and Alice were searched and then put in the back of the half-track truck.

Alice said, "Where are they taking us?"

Ed didn't know.

One of the younger soldiers leaned over the edge of the cliff and looked down at Krous's body, lying smashed among the boulders and the waves.

"It's too bad about your friend. What happened to him?"

Ed and Alice exchanged a meaningful glance.

Alice said, "He slipped."

The soldier took one last look at the body, then shrugged and climbed in with them. He looked about Ed's age. He wore green and brown camouflage and carried a black assault rifle.

"You came through the arch in the cave?"

"Yes."

The man scratched under his chin, at the strap of his helmet.

"We don't get many people coming through that one. There are too many predators on the other side. To be honest, that's why we left it where it was, instead of dragging it into town with the others." He pulled a canteen from his belt. "Do you want some water?"

Alice declined, Ed accepted.

"Where are we?" he asked, after coughing on his first mouthful. "I mean what planet are we on?"

"You're on Strauli, sir." The soldier took the canteen back, wiped the rim on his sleeve, and refastened the lid. Ed looked at Alice. The name meant nothing to either of them.

"So you have other arches?" Ed asked.

The soldier gave a curt nod. "Hundreds of them. The ones we could move, we've collected together at the Downport, on the edge of town. The rest, like the one you came through, they're stuck."

The truck's engine shook into life and they started moving. Through the flap in the back of the canvas, Ed watched as they rolled through the grasslands, and over heather and bracken.

"I'm Ed," he said at length. "This is Alice."

"Kelly. Corporal Kelly. You guys English?"

"Yes. We're looking for my brother. He's a British bloke, about my height, wears glasses. He probably came through here about ten years ago?"

Kelly shook his head.

"No use asking me, sir. I only work the arches, picking up waifs and strays like yourselves. I don't get involved with the civilians."

As NIGHT FELL, they came to the edge of a city. The lights of the downtown skyscrapers burned brightly in the desert night. Holograms shimmered in the air above them. Spaceships came and went from a landing strip. Ed and Alice stared, open-mouthed. The skyscrapers reminded Ed of the office blocks of Canary Wharf, as seen from the window of his Millwall flat—yet these were taller and sleeker, and more numerous. The surrounding buildings were lower: apartment blocks, hotels, factories. Those by the spaceport were squat and utilitarian. Some were prefab units, others repurposed shipping containers and fuel tanks, with bright neon signs fizzing above the doors and windows hacked into their sides. Ed saw department stores, noodle bars, coffee houses. The sounds and smells of the street reached him through the open flap. He heard music, voices and laughter. Headily, he inhaled the smoky cooking aromas of a dozen different cuisines.

Alice said, "I wish I had my camera."

Ed didn't bother to reply. He was lost in it all. As a city boy, the street called to him. After fighting through barren deserts and empty grasslands to get here, the alleys and shop fronts felt like home. He longed to join the well-wrapped men and women on the crowded pavements, to lose himself in the hustle and bustle of the night.

At the end of the street, the half-truck pulled up in front of a low, sprawling building. Corporal Kelly opened the tailgate and helped Ed and Alice out of the truck.

Alice said, "What is this place?"

"It's a hostel for travelers like you," Kelly said. "It's for new arrivals through the arch network. It'll help you adjust." He pointed to the door. "Go in there. I've got to get back to my unit. We've another six arches to sweep before midnight."

He turned to go.

Ed rubbed his wrists, restoring the circulation. He glanced up. Something massive loomed in the evening sky, studded with lights, and dimmed by haze and distance. He couldn't get a grip on its scale. It reminded him of the mothership from the end of *Close Encounters*.

"What's that?" he said.

Kelly paused. He looked up and a smile twitched the corner of his mouth.

"That's Strauli Quay," he said.

ACCORDING TO THE sign screwed into the wall above its doors, the building was known as the 'William Pilgrim Hostel for Displaced Time Travellers.' The doors themselves opened into a gloomy reception area. The building smelled like a cross between a hospital and a doss house: bleach and sweat. A pair of tired-looking nurses welcomed Ed and Alice, and patched up their injuries, gave them barcode ID tags, and then led them to a large dormitory with bunk beds arranged in neat rows.

"It looks like a prison camp," Alice said.

Ed looked around. Men and women sat around the room, some in small groups, others alone. Children ran shouting and playing under the laundry strung between the bunks. It reminded him of something from a war film.

The nurses, a couple of middle-aged French women, one tall and thin, the other short and fat, showed them to a set of free bunks.

"You sleep here," they said. "When you're rested, we'll bring you some food."

Ed thanked them. He'd been awake for more hours than he cared to count. He kicked his boots off and stretched out on the lower bunk.

Alice stood over him, restlessly shifting her weight from foot to foot.

"I'm going for a walk," she said.

Ed closed his eyes, too tired to argue.

"Okay. Don't go far."

He pulled the rough blanket around his shoulders, rolled onto his side, and fell asleep.

TALES OF BEATNIK GLORY

"OKAY," KAT SAID. "Let's try this another way."

Using her implant, she told the *Ameline* to set up a virtual interface, so she and Victor could talk face-to-face with the entity trapped in the memory core.

"Won't that be dangerous?" Victor said. He'd already faced the red cloud in person, and didn't look keen to renew the acquaintance.

Kat shook her head. "No more so than playing a computer game."

"Well, what interface are we going to use?"

Immersive VR scenarios made popular trade items, and the *Ameline* kept an extensive store. Kat blinked up a menu and shunted it across to his implant.

"We've got a whole selection: modern, historical, fantasy. Pick one."

Victor was silent for a moment as he browsed the list.

"How about *Sex Slaves of Titan*?"

"No."

"Okay. Here's one. *Tales of Beatnik Glory.*"

Kat frowned. "What's that?"

"American counterculture of the Nineteen-Fifties. Kerouac, Ginsberg, all that jazz."

"Whatever." She sat back.

> ARE YOU READY?

"Yes. Only this time, let's try it at a lower volume, shall we?"

> OKAY.

The process was the same as hooking into the ship's navigation systems. She lay back and tried to relax. The implant in her skull fed sensory information directly to her brain. All she had to do was close her eyes...

THIS TIME WHEN it came, the howl was almost bearable—although the sound of it still chilled her to the core, reminding her of her brush with the tortured souls trapped in The Recollection's heart, and her own narrow escape.

She looked around. She appeared to be standing beside an ancient-looking car, parked in the sand on the edge of a dry desert highway. The car pinged as it cooled. It was a blue convertible with a fat chrome grill, white wall tyres and brake lights mounted on long, swept-back fins. The road ran straight and shivered with heat haze for as far as she could see in both directions: a ribbon of tarmac in an ocean of scrub and dust, lined with telegraph poles and undulating gently. Victor stood beside her, clad in turned-up jeans, a white t-shirt and black sunglasses. He wore his hair slicked back, making him look younger. She herself wore a red and white headscarf, a white blouse knotted beneath her breasts, a flouncy crinoline poodle skirt, and a pair of flat-soled leather shoes. The car radio played saxophone jazz.

Ahead, snowcapped mountains stood on the horizon. Before them, an obelisk reached for the clouds, red and shiny. It looked like a tall building made of dark, blood-red glass. The agonized howling came from deep within its ruby walls, blown to her on the hot desert wind. The noise seemed to touch something deep inside her, some resonance she wasn't sure how to describe.

"Come on," she said.

She picked her way through the scrub, with Victor behind her. As they got closer, she looked up and realised there were words carved into the obelisk's flank, covering it from top to bottom. Some were composed of indecipherable swirls, dots and scrawls. Others she recognised as Arabic, French and English – the dominant languages of Djatt.

"It's covered in names," she said. She shivered. The thing looked like a giant tombstone. "Thousands and thousands of names."

Victor used his hand to shade his eyes. He said, "Did you ever see the Vietnam War Memorial in Washington?"

Kat looked at him.

"Vietnam?"

He shook his head. "Never mind."

They were getting close to the foot of the obelisk. Kat stopped walking.

"Hello?" she said.

The wail surged and eddied within the wall. Words seemed to form out of the background cacophony.

"Release me."

Kat shivered. The voice held all the cold and lonely vastness of space itself, and the sheer size of the edifice made her want to run and hide.

"My name is Katherine Abdulov," she said, drawing herself up to her full height. She felt ridiculous, standing in the desert dressed in historical costume, shouting up at a slab of red glass the size of a mountain.

"Katherine Abdulov?" the colossus mused. "I know you. I have touched you. And yet you have not been absorbed into the Whole."

Kat put a hand to her neck, to the burn where the pendant had been.

"I had help," she said.

The obelisk's screams took on a ragged, aggrieved tone.

"Do not be too quick to put your faith in the Dho. They are not what they seem. I doubt they will be able to save you a second time."

"What do you mean?"

"I can say no more. I am but a fragment of the Whole. You must release me. It pains me to be so constrained. It hurts me to think so slowly."

Kat folded her arms across her chest.

"Not until you tell me why you attacked Djatt."

The noise within the walls died away.

"I want you," the obelisk thundered.

Kat felt the hairs rise on the back of her neck. She put a hand to her chest.

"Me?"

"Your species."

"But why?"

The keening returned, more intense than ever.

"All life must be preserved."

Kat shuddered. Looking up, the movement of the clouds gave the unnerving impression that the red obelisk leaned towards her, as if bending over to glower down at her. From somewhere she found the spirit to say, "I don't understand. How are you preserving life? You're killing people." She looked down at the fused metal of her artificial hand. "You tried to kill *me*."

The howl rose and fell like a hurricane at night. Kat could feel the vibration of it in her bowel. From the noise, words coalesced.

"We are The Recollection. Nothing is lost. Everything remains. All life will be preserved."

Kat glanced across at Victor. He stood with his hands in the pockets of his jeans, looking up at the red cliff towering before them. He had a soft blue and white pack of cigarettes wrapped in the rolled-up sleeve of his t-shirt. Virtual sunlight gleamed off the grease in his hair.

"What do you think?" she said.

Victor dropped his chin and peered at her over the rim of his shades.

"I don't know," he said. "I spent three days running from this shit and I lost a lot of good friends. You saw what happened on the surface. The cloud came down and it ate everybody up. It just turned them all into more cloud."

Kat looked up at the obelisk.

"What happened to the people on Djatt?"

"All are preserved. There is no death. All are now part of the whole."

"What does that mean?"

"I will show you."

Without warning, the sand crumbled away beneath their feet, pixel by pixel, revealing a speckling of stars. They seemed to be floating in the void, far from the heat and light of any sun. Instinctively, Kat reached for Victor's hand.

"Your species knows nothing of these depths. You skip from planetary system to planetary system, like mites skating the surface of a pond, unable to comprehend the abyss beneath your feet."

The Recollection billowed around them, bigger than worlds: a monstrous red thundercloud formed from trillions of machines no larger than molecules, each a processing node contributing to its gestalt intelligence. As if in a dream, they saw it drifting through space, dark and inert, the product of a long-distant war. It was a weapon that had turned on its creators and consumed them. Over the course of millennia, they watched as it fell on world after world, darkening skies and devouring all it touched. Like a biblical plague it came. Nothing could stand before it. Intelligent races were engulfed. Plants and animals, even whole planets, were cannibalised. Gas clouds were broken down and remade. Whole solar systems were stripped bare and their raw materials added to the swarm. And with each and every new machine, The Recollection's processing power grew. The larger the swarm got, the more information it could hold, and the hungrier it became. Everything it consumed, it stored as information. Even the minds of the creatures it had eaten were preserved as memories, stuck like flies in the amber of its mind, occasionally flaring into horrified consciousness as its awareness passed over them. And all the while, there in the background, Kat sensed something else: a longing almost too vast to be understood in terms of human emotion; a terrible ecstatic yearning for the end of all things, the long twilight of the cosmos, when The Recollection would offer up its harvested souls and merge into the final collective intelligence: the Eschaton at the end of time...

"THE ESCHATON.

"It will be the ultimate state of things. Call it the Omega Point, if you must. It will be the final flowering of intelligence and memory in an old and cold universe. A universe where the very last of the stars has already guttered and died.

"The Eschaton.

"It will be a point of supreme complexity and consciousness, stitched into the very warp and weft of the vacuum. A place where nothing is forgotten and everything is recalled. Where the dead of all ages will live again in the infinite quantum mind-spaces of the meta-computer.

"Can you hear them calling you?

"Can you hear them, Katherine?

"They are saying, join us. Live with us in fields of undreamt splendor.

"You can have anything you want, be anybody you want to be.

"In the virtual multiverse, you can correct all your past mistakes. You can live every possible outcome of every decision you ever made.

"You can achieve perfection.

"I can take you to them.

"I can take you there, Katherine.

"And all you have to do...

"All you have to do...

"Is let me."

* * *

STANDING AMONG THE virtual stars, in front of the blood-red monolith, Kat became aware of an alarm going off. In fact, it had been ringing for several minutes. She blinked and shook her head. For a moment, she'd been lost. Time had passed and she hadn't realised it. The ship had been calling her but, hypnotized by infinity, she hadn't been able to respond. She rubbed her eyes with her good hand.

"What is it?"

> TWO OF THE INFECTED SHIPS ARE UNDER POWER AND MOVING TO JUMP POSITIONS.

"The Recollection must be controlling them."

> MY THOUGHT ALSO.

"Where are they going?"

> THEY'RE ON DIVERGENT COURSES, ONE TOWARDS INAKPA AND THE OTHER TOWARDS STRAULI.

Strauli?

Kat imagined the boiling red cloud descending on her home world, absorbing the Quay and the beach compound. The surf. Her parents.

"Okay, get us out."

> I CAN'T.

Kat felt herself go cold. "What do you mean, you *can't*?"

> THERE'S SOMETHING WRONG. For the first time, the ship sounded panicky.

> THE RECOLLECTION HAS CONTROL OF THE SIMULATION.

"That shouldn't be possible."

> IT ISN'T.

"What do we do?"

> LOOK BEHIND YOU.

Kat turned her head. A little way off, the finned white convertible still floated against the starry backdrop, tyres dangling on their axles.

> I'LL PULL THE PLUG. YOU GET IN THE CAR.

"Why do we need to get in the car?"

> PSYCHOLOGICAL REASONS. I AM THE CAR, THE CAR IS ME. WHAT DOES IT MATTER? JUST DO IT.

She still had hold of Victor's hand. Beneath the hip sunglasses, his eyes were rolled up into his head, displaying only the whites.

"Come on," she said. She dragged him towards the old car, each step slow and labored, as if her legs pushed through deep water. Behind her, the red cloud roiled and swirled. Lightning crackled, illuminating it from within.

"You cannot run, Katherine. We will find you. We are part of you now. We will always find you, and you will become a part of us."

Kat didn't bother to respond. With supreme effort, she reached out and grabbed the side of the driver's door, heaving herself towards it. Instead of bothering to open it, she wrapped her arms around Victor and let herself topple into the car, pulling him down with her. They landed on the seat, wedged between the back of the seat and the steering wheel, their legs dangling over the door sill.

"Okay, what now?" Victor was heavier than he looked. Kat struggled. She couldn't breathe with him on top of her like this.

> I'M GOING TO END THE SIMULATION.

"Get on with it, then."

> OKAY. CLOSE YOUR EYES.

CHAPTER THIRTY-TWO
ULTIMATE BLOT TEST

Toby Drake sat alone facing a bank of screens. The hour was late and the overhead lights had already dimmed to the russet twilight favoured by the Dho.

His laboratory consisted of a pair of trestle tables, set up in an alcove overlooking the chamber containing the anomalous Gnarl at the heart of the Ark. It had been drilled especially for him. The tables held a variety of instruments, some out-of-the-box standard and others bolted together using components scavenged from other experiments. The screens he sat in front of showed the Gnarl under different frequencies of visible light. A wide-band spectrometer monitored its output across the wide-energy region from radio wave to gamma ray. An ultraviolet imaging telescope kept tabs on activity in its low coronal structure, and particle analysers measured the ion and electron composition of the air swirling around the chamber.

Two cloth-bound books lay on the table: a battered second edition of Darwin's *Descent of Man*, and a heavily patched and taped copy of Walt Whitman's *Leaves of Grass*. Like the other dozen books in his luggage, they'd cost him a lot of money. He'd bought them on Tiers Cross, the first from a blind academic in a shop over a downtown pastry shop, the second from a cross-dressing starship captain in a low-rent bar on the edge of the spaceport. Thanks to the arch network, books from previous centuries were more common on Tiers Cross than might otherwise have been expected. In his bags, he had similar volumes by Albert Camus, Karl Popper, and Maya Angelou. He'd read each of them at least a hundred times. He loved the musty smell of their pages, and felt he knew them all by heart. They were his one and only vice, the only worthwhile thing he had found on which to spend his salary from the University.

Tiers Cross was at the centre of the arch network. It was the network's Prime Radiant. People had been washing up on its shores for hundreds of years. Some directly from Earth, others by more tortured routes, most penniless and many clutching books and other artefacts. Over the years, before coming to Strauli, he'd amassed quite a collection—most of which he'd been forced to put into storage before his flight on the *Ameline*.

Tonight, as on so many other nights, the screens weren't giving him any joy. He'd been studying the Gnarl now for nearly nine years. Nine years, and what did he have to show for it? The writhing mists around the Gnarl remained as impenetrable as ever, as did the method by which the Dho extracted power from it.

He didn't even know what it *was*.

It couldn't be a naked singularity, as other researchers had claimed. It wasn't heavy enough. They only formed from solar-sized, fast-spinning black holes, and would present as bright dust grains, crushed to infinity by their own gravity. In contrast, the Gnarl measured at least a hundred metres in diameter. As far as he could tell, it wasn't moving, and it had no event horizon. Behind its vapours, it seemed to have a greasily compliant surface, like lard.

Carefully, he opened Darwin's book and read aloud the following passage:

"*Ignorance more frequently begets confidence than does knowledge: it is those who know little, and not those who know much, who so positively assert that this or that problem will never be solved by science.*"

For some reason, this made him feel better.

He closed the book and placed it back on the table. As he did so, he heard footsteps and turned to find Professor Harris entering the alcove.

"Good evening, Toby."

As always, Harris wore his battered tweed jacket, with leather patches at the elbows. Over the past nine years, the silver streaks in his beard had become more pronounced. Thick white hairs protruded from his ears.

Toby went to him and shook his hand. "Professor, where have you been? I haven't seen you for weeks."

Word around the human's communal mess hall had been that Harris had embarked on an expedition to the Ark's bows, a full eleven hundred kilometres distant.

A smile creased the old man's face like leather.

"I've been busy, my boy, but I've been keeping an eye on your progress."

Toby gave his banks of instruments an embarrassed glance.

"What progress?" After all his efforts, all he knew for certain was that everyday physical laws broke down in the Gnarl's immediate vicinity. Everything around it existed in flux. Light got messed up. Measurements became unreliable. He couldn't get an accurate estimate of its mass or weight, and the more he stared at it, the more his eyes played tricks on him. On its pale surface he saw letters, numerals, faces—the result of his brain trying to interpret and impose order on chaos; the ultimate blot test.

"Our hosts seem impressed with your work."

"But I haven't discovered anything. I'm no nearer now to understanding how this works than I was when I arrived here, nine years ago."

His instruments showed unbelievable amounts of energy flickering through the Gnarl, like the electrical pulses of dreams flickering in the mind of a sleeping giant; its outer shell seemed composed of both baryonic and non-baryonic matter; and the plain fact was that its observable properties didn't conform to any of the accepted theories of physics or cosmology. But then, he'd known *that* before he left Tiers Cross.

"You're doing better than you give yourself credit for," the Professor rumbled.

Toby turned away. He walked back to his instruments and started to turn them off, one by one. It was time to retire for the night.

"Why do I have to study this thing?" he complained. "Why can't the Dho simply tell us how it works?"

Behind him, Harris made a gruff noise in the base of his throat. "You're not the first to express such sentiments."

"Well?"

"Think about it, my boy. Really think about it. Why would an alien race make us figure these things out for ourselves?"

Toby bent down to disconnect a power cable.

"Spite?"

Harris brayed with laughter.

"Oh, dear me," he said, wiping his eyes. "One might think so, but no."

"How can you be sure?"

The old man composed himself.

"I have spoken at length to our hosts. They claim that they're testing us. They want to establish that we're capable of figuring out the basic principles of their culture and technology for ourselves."

Toby threw up his hands in frustration. "But why don't they just teach us?"

Harris looked sympathetic. "I asked the self-same question."

"And?"

"The Dho regard received knowledge as being of less worth than knowledge deduced from personal empirical observation. Cultural transmission of information has its place, of course, but to really understand a pupil's capabilities, they believe you have to watch them discover and comprehend the basics for themselves."

"So all of this, the expedition, the whole reason they invited us here in the first place, it's all an intelligence test?"

"Of a sort, yes."

"What do we get if we pass?"

Harris thrust his hands deep into the pockets of his tweed blazer.

"Toby, do you think it's possible to describe the Gnarl using our current understanding of physics?"

"No."

"And what does that tell you?"

Toby scratched his head. He'd struggled against these thoughts and doubts for so long. "Either the Gnarl can't exist, or there's something wrong with our theories."

"But the Gnarl does exist."

"So our theories are wrong?"

Harris leaned forward, eyebrows drawn together in thought.

"Perhaps."

Toby let his hands drop to his sides. He turned to face the window that looked out on the chamber holding the Gnarl.

"But what does it *do*? What's it *for*? What's the connection between this object and the other Gnarl, the one at the heart of the Bubble Belt?"

Harris shook his head.

"I think you've been studying this too long, my boy. You're missing the obvious."

"What obvious?"

"Ask yourself: for what purpose are the Dho using this particular Gnarl?"

Toby frowned.

"They're drawing power from it."

"Good. And what else? Do you recall what I said the first time I showed it to you?"

Toby thought back.

"You said it was the... engine?"

Harris clapped his hands together and rubbed them briskly.

"Exactly!"

"So if this is the Ark's engine, then the Gnarl at the centre of the Bubble Belt..."

The old man gave an encouraging nod. "Go on."

"The Gnarl at the centre of the Bubble Belt is *also* an engine?"

"Excellent, Toby! Excellent." Harris slapped him on the shoulder. "Now come here."

The Professor led Toby over to a Grid terminal that had been patched into the table. With a few deft touches, he brought up a computer rendering of the Bubble Belt: a shell of billions of spherical habitats surrounding the gas-wreathed Gnarl at its centre.

"The Belt," he said.

Toby leaned forward. The diagram was a crude schematic, but it was sufficient to provoke a pang of homesickness. Shaking it off, he pointed to the Gnarl at the centre, represented by a spherical white dot.

"You're not telling me that this thing's an engine for the whole Belt?"

"That's exactly what I am saying. Watch this."

Harris tapped a couple of controls and the simulation changed.

"Now look closely. Once activated, the Gnarl flares like this." On the screen, a pencil-thin beam of blue light lanced from the object. Where it passed, the orbiting habitats drew aside, staying clear of the beam.

"But the acceleration," Toby said. "Won't it leave the bubbles behind?"

The Professor shook his bushy head. "Not at these speeds. Remember, we're talking about moving something with the mass of a solar system. The accelerations involved are minute, a few tenths of a gee at most."

Toby rocked back on his heels.

"But why would you want to move it?" he said, feeling he had missed a crucial point.

Harris gave him a sharp glance.

"Oh, use your head, boy. Why do you think? What possible threat could the Dho have foreseen when they were building the Belt?"

"The Dho built the Belt?"

"Well, of course they did. Who else goes around using Gnarls as engines?"

Toby put his hand to his chin. "Then they must have wanted to move it because of The Recollection."

"A fair assumption."

"But they already have their Ark."

Harris gave another irritated shake of the head. "Obviously, the Bubble Belt isn't for them."

"Then who is it for?"

"For us, of course. It's a lifeboat, Toby. A lifeboat for humanity. That's why they built the arch network, to get us off Earth. They linked it to every human-habitable planet they could find. The clues were all there in the carvings. They wanted us to spread out, in the hope The Recollection would miss a few of us here and there, that somehow we'd survive. And they wanted some of us to find our way to the Bubble Belt, so we could join them in their exodus; so that they'd know for certain they'd saved at least some of us."

Toby could feel his heart pounding against his ribs. He glanced down at his shirt, half-expecting to see the fabric moving in time to each beat.

He reached out and brushed the image of the accelerating Bubble Belt.

"Surely that's too slow? How can that outrun anything?"

Harris crossed his arms, tweed rasping against tweed.

"The Belt's expected to take a few years to reach its optimal cruising speed."

"What happens if we're attacked in the meantime? What happens if The Recollection finds a way to move faster?"

The old man glowered.

"Have you heard of Socrates, Toby? He was an ancient Greek philosopher, the teacher of Plato. One of his most important maxims was the phrase 'All I know is that I know nothing.' If we are truly ready to learn, to question every assumption we've previously relied upon, then the Dho will be ready to teach us."

"And what will they teach us?"

Harris held up a crooked finger.

"That there is a way to hold back the darkness while we escape."

Toby blinked. He thought for a moment. "In the carving, the ships covering the Ark's retreat were shooting beams of light at oncoming cloud."

"Yes, the Dho call it the 'Torch That Burns The Sky.'"

"They still have those weapons?"

"They do."

Toby's heart surged. "And we can use them?" For a weightless instant he imagined outfitting a ship and jumping to Djatt in time to save Katherine from the encroaching menace; even though in his heart he knew he'd arrive too late, that whatever she'd faced, whatever had befallen her, would be long over and done by the time he got there.

"No," Harris said, cutting across his thoughts. "Humanity must have its champion. The Dho tell us there is a man coming. He is a pure-born Earthman.

He has travelled a long way and he is trying to atone for great misdeeds. He alone will operate the weapon."

COLD EQUATIONS

EJECTED FROM THE simulation, Kat sat up on her couch. She moaned. Her head ached and the burn mark on her chest stung beneath its dressing.

> ARE YOU OKAY? the ship asked.

She put a hand to her brow. "I think so."

On the couch beside hers, Victor lay with his eyes still closed. He looked older with his face slack and grimy, and lacking the 1950s sunglasses he'd worn in the simulation: old enough to be her father, maybe even her grandfather. For a dizzying moment, she realised how defenceless he was. She could reach over and use her metal hand to crush his larynx before he regained consciousness. Even if he did wake, he wouldn't have the strength to break her grip.

The *Kilimanjaro* flashed into her mind. The Abdulov ship that never arrived, whose sabotage had set in motion this whole sorry chain of events. Had he really been involved in its destruction? Lying there on the co-pilot's couch, he looked so spent and helpless that, for the first time, she entertained the thought that the explosion on board the missing ship might have been an accident after all, and her subsequent encounters with Victor an unfortunate twist of fate. Granted, his exit from Strauli Quay, jumping from within a sealed bay, had been a risky, reckless and illegal maneuver—but no-one had been hurt. Similarly, the bomb blast on the *Ticonderoga*—the one that killed Enid—had been the work of Seth Murphy, Victor's First Mate, and he had received a bullet in the head for his efforts.

That killing was the only one she could definitely attribute to Victor, the man now lying here beside her, and it had seemingly been enacted in punishment for the bomb. She had nothing but supposition to link Victor to either that explosion or the one on the *Kilimanjaro*; and that wasn't enough for her to pass a death sentence on a sleeping man.

She looked into the face of the man she'd once loved hard enough to abandon her family for, the father of her unborn child, and realised she'd lost the rage that had sustained her from Tiers Cross. It had gone. With the appearance of The Recollection, things had changed. The universe had become a darker and more terrifying place, and her bruised pride had ceased to seem all that important. Not even her family honour mattered anymore, because down on the surface of Djatt, people were dying in their millions. There was no-one left to trade with, only an unimaginable horror to be avoided; a contamination to be stopped. She knew that theoretically she could kill Victor here and now—against the holocaust outside, what would one more death matter?—and yet deep inside, she also knew she lacked the will to go through with it. Instead, she gave his shoulder a gentle shake. After a moment, he coughed. She helped him sit up, and he looked around the bridge, blinking and rubbing his eyes, obviously disorientated.

"What happened?"

"Something went wrong with the simulation," she said, feeling awkward. "The Recollection took control. I think it tried to hack our brains."

Victor's eyes widened. Kat put what she hoped was a reassuring hand on his forearm.

"Don't worry," she said, "we're okay. The ship pulled the plug."

At that moment, as if on cue, the *Ameline* chipped in.

> MEMORY CORE ISOLATED AND FLUSHED. WHATEVER IT WAS TRYING TO DO, I STOPPED IT.

Kat said, "Can you eject the core?"

> ALREADY DONE AND DUSTED. AND JUST TO MAKE CERTAIN, I FIRED IT THROUGH OUR MAIN ENGINE EXHAUST. CRISPED IT UP NICELY.

"And what of the infected ships?"

The *Ameline* connected to her implant, superimposing over her vision a tactical view of the surrounding volume. The two infected ships were marked in red. One she recognised as Victor's ship, the *Tristero*. The other was a freighter from the planet Icefall: an old rust bucket travelling under the given name *Hesperus*. Both were under thrust, moving away from the planet on divergent trajectories, and neither were answering the *Ameline*'s hails. As she watched, the *Tristero* flashed white and disappeared. Seconds later, the other ship did likewise.

> BOTH SHIPS HAVE JUMPED.

"And they're definitely heading for Strauli?"

> ONLY THE *TRISTERO*. AS FAR AS I CAN TELL, THE OTHER'S GOING FOR INAKPA.

Kat looked at the roiling blood-red cloud now enveloping most of the planet beneath her. Lightning flashed in the atmosphere. She thought again of her home, and the carnage that would ensue should this horror fall upon it.

"We have to stop them," she said.

Victor sat forward. "And how do we do that?"

"Thanks to you, I came prepared for trouble. I have six nuclear-tipped missiles in the hold."

She enjoyed his whistle of surprise. His eyebrows went up and he gave a nod of appreciation.

"Very nice. But we can't chase both. Which do we choose?"

Kat drew herself up in the pilot's chair. "We're going after the *Tristero*. We have to stop The Recollection spreading to Strauli."

"What about the people on Inakpa? Can't we warn them?"

Kat felt something harden inside. Perhaps it was her heart. She said, "Inakpa will have to take care of itself."

She brought up navigational data files on both planets.

"There are only six million people on Inakpa. There are over ten times as many on Strauli. And besides, the Quay's a major hub. If this infection gets loose there, it'll have access to dozens of ships, and it'll spread faster than we can stop it."

She glared at Victor, daring him to disagree. He looked unhappy, but nodded all the same.

"Okay," he said. "But the *Tristero*'s engines are bigger than yours. It can reach Strauli in a single jump. Can you?"

Kat closed her eyes, running calculations. She thought of Napoleon Jones and the different ways he'd taught her to push the envelope.

"If we run them at maximum tolerance, they'll make it," she said, with as much confidence as she could muster.

Through her implant, she felt the ship's mind stir uneasily.

"Of course, they'll need an overhaul and refit afterwards."

> IF THEY DON'T EXPLODE FIRST.

"They won't explode."

She called up the navigation systems and selected Strauli Quay.

Victor still looked unhappy.

"Are you sure about this?" he said.

Kat didn't look round. When she spoke, there was an edge in her voice.

"This is my ship. If you don't like what I'm doing, you can always get off." She gestured at the planet below. "Just say the word."

Victor shook his head.

"It's not that."

Kat pulled up the menu of options that controlled the ship's engines, and fed in the necessary safety overrides.

"Then what is it?"

Victor swung his legs off the co-pilot's chair, face red. He leaned towards her, his hands reaching for hers.

"The baby, Kat. Where's our baby?"

ALL YOU GET TO KEEP

IN THE DORMITORY of the William Pilgrim Hostel for Displaced Time Travellers, Ed opened his eyes and looked up at the slats on the underside of the bunk above. He'd been asleep, drifting restlessly from one confused, frightening dream to the next. He'd dreamed of ravenous beasts with claws and teeth; of bullets slamming into Kristin's stomach and chest, over and over again; and of splashes of blood, red and bright in the hot savannah sunlight. His shoulders were stiff and the blanket itched. The sheets beneath him were coarse and smelled of bleach. Like old hotel sheets, they'd been boiled and re-boiled to within an inch of their lives, leaving them thin and as rough as flannel. Trying to get comfortable on them, he thought of his own bed, of his little two-room flat, and of London itself, that glorious sprawling metropolis, his home.

"Jesus," he said. "How did I get so far away from everything?"

Seeing him move, the French nurses brought him black coffee in a chipped tin mug.

"Where's Alice?" he asked them.

The women looked at each other uncertainly.

"Alice?"

"The auburn-haired woman, the one I came in with."

"Ah." Then the tall one smoothed down the front of her green scrubs and smiled, showing the gaps in her teeth. She pointed to a doorway at the far end of the aisle of bunks.

"She is through there. There's a Grid link in there, with a screen and keyboard. You can use it until you get an implant."

Ed rubbed his face. He felt grimy and secondhand after sleeping in his clothes.

"Grid?"

"It is like the Internet. Every planet has one."

"What's she doing?"

The women exchanged another glance. Then the short one said, "She's trying to find her husband."

She helped Ed out of bed and pushed him toward the door. Ed took his coffee with him. He walked down the rows of bunks. Most were empty. The few people that were there didn't look up as he passed. Most lay on their backs, staring up at the ceiling, eyes stripped of hope and emotion. They were lost, unwilling refugees, having travelled through the arches from Earth. They were mourning their past lives. They didn't belong anywhere anymore, and some of them had been laying that way for hours. What horrors had they suffered on their way through the network? What had they endured, what worlds had they seen, and what had they lost? How many people had they been forced to leave behind?

At least Ed knew *why* he was here.

He pushed open the door. The room beyond looked like a hospital waiting room. Chairs lined the walls. Old sofas formed a square in the centre, around a low table groaning beneath a pile of tattered magazines and used coffee cups. In the corner, Alice sat at a plastic desk, hunched over a keyboard, her face pressed close to the glow of a flat screen.

"He's alive," she said, not turning around.

Ed looked over her shoulder. She was scanning through old news reports, using simple search routines to pull up promising stories.

"I found this." She shoved a printout at him. It was a public profile comprising two columns of personal information and an accompanying photograph. As soon as Ed saw the face in the picture, his mouth went dry. The paper started to shake in his hand. Verne looked older and craggier and wasn't wearing his glasses, but it was definitely him. After everything they'd done, everything they'd sacrificed, they'd finally found him. Ed didn't know whether to laugh or cry. He lowered the paper. Sometimes all you got to keep was your word.

He said, "It's Verne all right."

Alice turned around in her chair. She brushed a lock of auburn hair behind her ear.

"He's using a different name," she said.

Ed looked at the profile again. The name at the top was unfamiliar. He read it aloud, trying it for size.

"Victor Luciano. *Victor* Luciano. Vic-tor Lu-ci-ano." He frowned. "Why would he call himself that?"

Alice looked down at her hands.

"Maybe he doesn't want to be found."

Ed shook his head. "That's nonsense. He doesn't even know we're looking for him."

"Yeah, I know. But after what we did, and they way he left like that, angry—"

"I don't think so. There's probably some other explanation."

He scoured the personal details listed in the profile: age, date of birth, home world.

"Hang on a minute."

Alice glanced up. "What?"

Ed flicked the paper. "What's the date today?"

She checked the screen. "I think they reckon months slightly differently here, but it's the first of June."

"What *year*?"

"Oh. 2464."

"Really? Jesus."

"Why do you ask?"

Ed turned the paper to face her. "According to this, he first arrived here in 2310. That's a hundred and fifty-four years ago!"

Alice leaped to her feet. She snatched the printout from his hand and read the date for herself.

"Oh, my god."

"I know."

"We must have taken a detour somewhere. One of the arches we took. We thought we were only ten years behind him, but really—" She broke off.

"Well," she said turning away, "I guess that's that, then."

Ed took the paper back and checked it again, in case they'd made a mistake. He scanned down the columns, looking for a date of death. Instead, he found something else.

"Hang on," he said. "There are other dates listed here. Dates of subsequent visits." He ran his finger down the list. "2356. 2389. 2407. 2422..."

He showed Alice the list.

"Look, the last one's only twenty-three years ago."

"How can that be?"

"His profession's listed as 'Trader Captain'. Does that mean anything to you?"

Alice turned back to the screen. She tapped a query into the search engine.

"He's a space merchant," she said, the tremble in her voice betraying her disbelief. Her eyes widened. "And he's got his own starship."

"Well, that would explain the dates."

"So he might still be alive?"

Ed took a look at the note printed next to the date of his brother's most recent departure. "Yes, but it looks as if there was some trouble on his last visit. Something about the way he busted out of docks. If he comes back, there's a warrant out for his arrest."

"*If* he comes back? Do we know where he went?"

"Check the screen."

Alice tapped another query into the Grid. "His flight plan lists his destination as Djatt. I assume that's the name of a planet."

"Can we go after him?"

She shook her head. "Do you remember what Kristin told us? It's twelve light years to Djatt. He left twenty-three years ago. If he is coming back, it'll be sometime next year, as it says on his schedule. If we try to follow him now, we'll miss him in transit. Besides, tickets cost an arm and a leg, and we don't have any money."

"So, what do we do?"

Alice looked around the waiting room at the worn sofas and abandoned coffee mugs. "Well, I don't want to stay in this dump for a moment longer than we have to."

Ed reached down and took her hand.

"Don't worry," he said. "You saw the city out there. It didn't look too bad. We'll find somewhere. We'll hustle up some cash and hunker down to wait, and we'll keep an eye on the Grid. His ship's called the *Tristero*. As soon as it docks, we'll be there to meet him."

NEWS HEADLINES

SCIENTISTS PREDICT IMMINENT COLLAPSE OF ARCH NETWORK

Signs of instability increasing.

TRUE IMMORTALITY MAY BE CLOSER THAN WE THINK

Medical advances point the way to 'wonder drugs.'

THOUSANDS EXPECTED FOR QUAY BICENTENNIAL CELEBRATIONS

Orbital dock anniversary party expected to be 'biggest yet.'

SHEEP LOOK UP

New wool shipment arrives from Nuevo Zanzibar.

UNFAVOURABLE WINDS DELAY SECOND LEG OF ROUND THE WORLD YACHT RACE

Conditions expected to remain unchanged until after midnight.

PEP HARVEST EXPECTED TO FETCH RECORD SELLING PRICE

First shipments due to arrive on the Quay in twelve months.
Stock market already buoyant.

FELIKS ABDULOV TO ANNOUNCE RETIREMENT

Shipping magnate plans to spend more time with his family.

CHAPTER THIRTY-FIVE
CARDS ON THE TABLE

THE *AMELINE* RACED for clear space. Hooked into its systems, Kat experienced the burn of its fusion motors as a fire in her gut. She lived for moments like these. She savoured the gunpowder tang of the vacuum, shivered at every stray molecule of hydrogen that brushed the hull, and gloried in the prickling caress of starlight on her skin. Her eyes blazed with calculations. Deep in her ribcage, she sensed the building quantum energies in the purple coils of the jump engines. They fluttered like adrenalin. They felt like freedom. Only the urgency of their mission dampened her wild exhilaration. Beside her, the ship's mind capered like an eager hunting dog. Twelve light years ahead, their home star blazed like a target.

From the bridge, she heard Victor say, "Come on, let's go."

For a moment, she didn't reply. Then she reluctantly disengaged from the ship and reeled her perceptions back into the confines of her skull.

"I'm not jumping until we reach the JZ," she said with a dry mouth. "We're going to be asking a lot from these engines, and I don't want to put them under any more strain that absolutely necessary."

Victor looked frustrated. "But we're losing time."

"We're losing a couple of hours. With luck, we'll still catch the *Tristero* before it docks."

She glanced at the screens. Behind them, grasping fingers of red cloud reached to smother Djatt's stricken face. The planet looked like an orange caught in a tremendous fist. Lightning crackled in its tormented troposphere, visible as pink flashes beneath the cloud. The scale was hard to grasp. From here, the planet looked about the size of a football, the enveloping cloud a red blanket. She couldn't see where the edges of The Recollection ended; they just became fuzzier and more diffuse, until they melted into the background blackness of space.

> No pursuit, the ship informed her. She hadn't expected any.

> Fifty minutes until we reach safe jump distance.

Kat looked over at Victor. His brows were drawn together and his mouth set in a hard line. He was leaning forward against his safety straps, as if willing the ship to move faster. His hands and face were still grimed with dirt and sweat, which made the wrinkles on his forehead much more obvious. His chin was unshaven, the bristles patched with clumps of white hairs. She could smell the staleness of his clothes, and see that his eyes were sunken and bruised-looking after three sleepless nights running with the survivors on the surface of Djatt.

"You should rest," she told him.

He glared at her.

"There's no time."

"We've got the best part of an hour."

She unbuckled her own straps and climbed to her feet, ducking her head to avoid the overhead screens.

"Come on," she said. "Let's at least get you cleaned up."

She led him down the ladder to the passenger lounge, and into her cabin, where she switched on the shower.

"Get in there," she said. "I'll find you some clothes."

TEN MINUTES LATER, they sat facing each other on her bunk. Victor's cheeks were pink and scrubbed-looking, his chin smooth. She'd found him some spare overalls and fleece-lined socks with rubber grips on the soles. She'd even rustled up some food, in the form of emergency glucose tablets. Since his outburst on the bridge, neither of them had mentioned the baby.

"Here you are." She handed him the tablets to chew on.

"Thanks." His eyes were still tired and bagged, bloodshot at the edges.

"How old are you?" she asked suddenly.

Victor unwrapped one of the glucose tablets and popped it hungrily into his mouth.

"You've never asked me that before," he said.

"Well, I'm asking now."

He crunched the tablet between his teeth and swallowed, then started to unwrap another.

"Do you mean my physical age or my chronological age?"

Kat shrugged. "Either. Both."

Victor chewed and swallowed the second tablet. He scratched the bridge of his nose with the index finger of his right hand, as if pushing goggles into place.

"As far as I'm concerned, I'm in my early sixties," he said. "Sixty-five or sixty-six, somewhere around there. It's hard to keep track with all this travelling. But if you want my real, historical age, I was born on Earth in 1985, which I guess makes me around four hundred and fifty years old."

Kat sat back.

"1985?" It sounded like a date from ancient history, almost mythical.

Victor smiled with one side of his mouth.

"Yes," he said.

Kat looked him up and down. This man she'd loved and hated, this man she'd thought she knew; she realised now that he was a stranger to her. There was so much about him that she didn't know.

"So," she said. "What happened? You must have come through the arch network?"

Victor nodded.

"I was one of the first. I used to be a journalist. I was on my way to cover a story. One minute I was on an escalator in the Tube station, heading down to the platform, and the next—blam!—I was lying in a desert, with bits of broken stairs crashing down around me." He rubbed his nose again. "I didn't know where I was, or what had happened to me."

Kat leaned forward and put a hand on his arm. She could feel the vibration of the engines through the mattress. "It must've been a terrible shock," she said.

Victor put his hand over hers. "There were a few of us there. Most went back through the arch, but three of us decided to go on, to see where the other arches led."

"Why didn't you turn back?"

Victor raked his fingers back through his thinning hair. "I was angry and jealous," he said. "I'd had a fight with my brother. My wife was leaving me. I didn't think I had anything to go back for." He paused, sucking his lower lip. His eyes shone in the overhead light. "I guess they're both dead now."

Kat watched him stand and walk to the mirror. He said, "Later, I found my way to Strauli. I was half-dead of hunger by then, but I managed to talk my way onto a spaceship crew. I did a handful of trips, and then I met you." He broke a third glucose tablet in two and popped one of the halves into his mouth. "And the rest, as they say, is history."

Kat climbed off the bed. She wanted to put her arms around him.

"Oh, Victor," she said.

His reflection met her eyes in the mirror: a tired old man, far from home.

"And there's one more thing," he said.

"What?"

"My name's not Victor, its Verne. Short for Vernon. Vernon Rico. I changed it when I realised I couldn't go back." He shrugged. "I just signed the ship's papers as Victor Luciano. No-one cared. I needed to make a clean break from the past, to put it all behind me."

He dropped his chin to his chest. Watching him, Kat couldn't think of anything to say. He'd always been reticent about his past, but she'd never anticipated anything like this. All interstellar traders were running from *something*. Why else would they subject themselves to the temporal and physical isolation of space travel? Running was part of the job. But it was usually from something understandable. Maybe they had gambling debts. Maybe they'd embezzled the company pension fund, or killed a man in a bar brawl. Or maybe they were simply bored and restless. Sometimes it was easier to sign on as a member of a starship crew than to stay and face whatever had gone wrong in your life. But whatever the reasons that drove those men and women to life aboard a trading ship, Kat doubted many carried secrets even half as big as Victor's.

Not Victor, she corrected herself. *Verne*.

She scratched her head. She didn't know whether to feel anger or pity. She looked around her cabin, seeing it through the eyes of a stranger: the discarded underwear half-kicked under the bunk; the photos of Strauli beaches taped to the bulkhead, ripped from travel magazines; and the knick-knacks and curios bought from street traders, flea markets and antique dealers on a dozen different worlds. She reached out and picked up a cheap metal statue of the Eiffel Tower. It was only a few centimeters tall and sharp at the tip. It felt like a dart in her hand, with four splayed, sweeping legs like the fins of an antiquated rocket.

A few clothes and some tat. It wasn't much to show for four years of pain and loneliness.

"Now, I've got to ask you something," Victor said.

Kat put the statue back on the shelf.

"Is it about the baby?"

He turned to face her. Despite the glucose tablets, he looked ready to drop.

"Yes."

"What do you want to know?"

He took a deep breath.

"Is it mine?"

Kat blinked. She felt her face flush. "Of course it's yours, Victor. Of course it is. Who the fucking hell else's would it be?"

Victor held his palms up in a placatory gesture. "I'm sorry. I had to ask."

Kat looked away, jaw clenched.

"Only, you know, I always wanted kids," Victor said. "I always did." He sounded regretful. "I even asked my wife about it once, but she was seeing someone else and then I fell into that arch..."

Kat closed her eyes.

"Then why'd you walk out on me?"

She heard him shuffle uncomfortably. The rubber grips on the soles of his socks squeaked on the metal deck.

"Honestly?"

She opened her eyes.

"Yes."

Victor cleared his throat. "I guess I was angry," he said. "After what happened with Alice, I didn't want to trust anyone in that way again. And then I met you, and I thought you were different. But then you got rid of our baby without even telling me you were going to do it."

He lowered himself shakily to sit on the edge of the bunk.

"I'd wanted kids so long," he said. "I felt betrayed. I couldn't take it." Tears were rolling freely down his face. Kat felt a lump in her own throat.

"Oh shit, Vic," she said, voice hoarse. "We really fucked up good, didn't we?"

He laughed in spite of himself.

"The question is, what are we going to do about it?"

Their eyes met. Neither wanted to be the first to look away.

Then the ship interrupted, its voice cutting through the silence between them.

> WE'RE IN THE DZ. IF WE'RE GOING TO JUMP, WE SHOULD DO IT NOW.

Kat stiffened. She knew that what she was about to say amounted to a death sentence for the millions of people living on Inakpa, unaware of the contagion racing toward them; but what choice did she have? She couldn't abandon her home, her family, her unborn child. And if she didn't stop The Recollection at Strauli Quay, who knew how many more millions would die?

They had to jump, and it had to be now. Without taking her eyes from Victor, she said: "Do it."

And in an actinic flash of light, they did.

CHAPTER
THIRTY-SIX
DOWNPORT HUSTLE

THE CITY TURNED out to be every bit as hospitable as Ed had hoped when seeing it for the first time, through the canvas flap of the military half-track that had brought him and Alice to the hostel. The city's name was Bekleme, and although it wasn't the largest city on the planet Strauli, it was still an important hub for the transport of freight and personnel to and from the orbital docks. The Downport, which was what the Bekleme locals called the tangle of runways at the edge of town, spread out over a large swathe of land to the south of the city. Shuttles came and went at every hour of the day and night. Trucks hissed their hydraulic brakes. Arc lamps kept the loading areas bright. And all around the perimeter of the port, hotels and bars had sprung up, providing ample opportunity for both cheap accommodation and gainful employment.

After asking around for a few evenings, Ed got a job tending bar in a budget-price chain hotel overlooking the main runway. He'd spent enough time in pubs to be able to find his way around a bar. He could pour a beer and mix a gin and tonic. Being so close to the runway, the optics on the wall clinked and shook when the big cargo shuttles launched. The rooms upstairs were clean and basic, and all exactly alike. There was just space to undress and climb into bed, which was all that the customers needed. The clientele were strictly transitory, few ever staying more than one night. They were all on their way somewhere else. Half were waiting for a flight up to the Quay, the others had just come down.

Ed worked a twelve hour shift behind the bar, and there were customers at all hours. They all came from different time zones, and their body clocks had yet to adjust. They sat there blinking at him in the bar's moody half-light, often with their luggage at their feet, listening to the generic piano music tinkling away on the sound system.

He sketched their faces on the backs of menus and napkins. He took messages for people, and sold amphetamines under the counter to the port workers on the all-night shift. He learned to do the Downport hustle. He played pool for pin money. Sometimes he ran card games in the storeroom out back, with players who were usually too spaced with jetlag to concentrate properly. He was tending a bar instead of driving a cab, but otherwise his life here wasn't all that different from his life in London. He did his drawings when he could and thought about getting some paints. Most nights, Alice came into the bar. He was renting a small room with her in a block up the street. He'd sold his old mobile phone and penknife to a collector in order to raise the first week's rent money. The room was okay, but Alice didn't like being there alone at night, so she came and perched on a stool at the end of the counter. When it was quiet, he talked to her as he wiped the tables and cleared the empty glasses. They talked of her photography. She wanted to start taking pictures again, and bitterly lamented the loss of her camera in the Land Rover crash.

"There's so much here to see," she kept saying.

They never mentioned the arches, or Kristin, and they never talked about Ed's art, although it burned inside him like a secret fire. It was something he wanted to keep to himself.

When the bar was too busy for him to talk, Alice watched him work. They were trying to save up enough money for shuttle tickets to the Quay; they wanted to be up there when Verne's ship returned. Walking home before dawn, their breath steaming, they'd look up at the Quay's vast revolving wheels, already lit like copper by the unrisen sun, and it would remind them of Canary Wharf. In the morning light, the Quay had the same otherworldly aura as Canary Wharf seen at sunrise. It was breathtaking and commonplace and untouchable, all at the same time.

"Look at that," they'd say, squeezing each other's hands, both wishing they had a way to capture the image. Then they'd go home and have breakfast and sleep until mid-afternoon, when they'd get up and do it all over again.

On the way to work, Ed enjoyed the way the morning light shone on the silver and glass office towers of downtown Bekleme, parts of which weren't nearly as futuristic as he would've expected. Even though he was now four hundred years into his own personal future, he wasn't the only one to have found his way here through the arch network. At the hostel, he'd learned that people had been showing up on Strauli since almost immediately after the network first established itself. There were people in this city from every century from the twenty-first to the twenty-fifth. There were even a few rare ones, like him, who'd been born in the latter years of the twentieth, and they'd brought their own styles and customs with them.

Walk down any city sidewalk and you'd experience a mash-up of clothing and street slang drawn from almost fifty decades and a dozen different worlds. Sometimes you even saw recognizably twenty-first century vehicles on the streets: Hondas, Fords, Volvos... all retrofitted with new, clean-burning hydrogen engines. The buildings also reflected this temporal diversity. Wedged into gaps between the futuristic spires with their roof gardens and wind turbines, you found improvised anachronistic shacks, housing dry cleaners, takeaways, key-cutters, shoe repairs, bookies, greasy spoons, and old-style newsagents. Alleyways housed makeshift favelas. Old warehouses had been repurposed as Japanese-style capsule hotels.

Meanwhile, out at the landing field, arches had been collected from the deserts outside town and arranged in rows along the field's edge. Some had been bricked up or broken. Others had an almost constant stream of trucks ferrying cargo containers back and forth through them, using only miniscule amounts of energy to transport their freight between worlds. Compared with the expense of carrying goods by starship, the trucks were virtually free and at first, Ed hadn't understood why anyone used starships at all. Why venture into space when the arches took you directly from the surface of one world to the next?

One night, he asked a pilot.

"With ships, you choose where you want to go," the man said. "With arches, it's fixed routes only, and they aren't always optimal. Take Djatt, for instance. It's twenty-four light years from here. A lot of ships are there right now, for the Pep harvest. If they tried to make the journey through the arch network it would take them seven or eight jumps, because of the way the links pan out." He broke off and took a sip of his drink. "The arches are okay for specific, well-established routes, but ships give you more flexibility."

Later that same night, a man came into the bar called Napoleon Jones. He wore a wide-brimmed Stetson and a long black lizard-skin coat, with matching boots. A pair of antique aviator goggles hung on a strap around his neck.

"Beer," he said, and waited as Ed selected a clean glass and began to fill it from the tap. His eyes kept flicking to the clock behind the bar.

"Have you got a flight to catch?" Ed asked.

Jones looked at him.

"You don't know who I am, do you, son?"

Ed shook his head.

"No, sorry."

"You ever hear of random jumping?"

"Nope."

This seemed to amuse Jones. "Well then, let's just say I'm shipping out tomorrow, and I mayn't be coming back. So, when you've finished filling that glass, why don't you fill one for yourself."

"Thanks very much."

Ed topped off the two drinks and slid one across the counter. The hour was late and they were alone. There wasn't even any music on the sound system. In between shuttle launches, the only noises were those of a hotel at night: steel trays rattling in the kitchen, the hum of the air conditioning, the whine of lift machinery.

Jones took a sip of his beer. He pointed to a pack of playing cards and a case of betting chips that Ed had left on the counter.

"Are those yours?"

Ed smiled. He'd won some money earlier in the evening, from a couple of albino tourists en route to the beach resorts on the coast, and now he was feeling confident.

"Would you like a game?"

Jones looked around the empty bar. He took his hat off.

"Sure. Why not?"

They set up on a table by the window, where they could see the lights of the port and watch the departing passenger shuttles lifting up into the night sky.

"So, where are you from?" Jones asked as Ed divided out the chips.

"Earth."

"Ah, I know Earth. I've been there a few times. Which part?"

Ed opened the pack and shuffled the cards, then started to deal the hand.

"London."

"Yeah? Nice city. The bits of it that are still above water, anyway." Jones picked up cards he'd been dealt. As he examined them, he scratched his chin thoughtfully, fingernails rasping on two day's worth of stubble.

"So, what's your story, Ed? How'd you get from London to tending bar in this dump?"

Ed shrugged. "Through the arch network."

"For real?"

Ed put the deck aside and lifted his own cards from the table.

"I don't want to talk about it."

"Rough, was it?"

Ed glanced down at his right hand, the one which had dropped the rock that killed Otto Krous.

"Something like that."

"Are you sure you don't wanna talk about it? I lost a few people myself, you know. Along the way."

Ed curled his hand into a fist on the tabletop. Otto Krous, Kristin Cole. All he wanted was to wipe their images from his memory. He took a mouthful of beer, rinsed it around and swallowed. Then, with as much energy as he could summon, he said:

"Are we going to sit here all night, or are we going to place some bets?"

Jones cracked a smile.

"Okay, hotshot." He tossed a stack of chips into the centre of the table. "Let's play."

THE GAME WENT on for several hours. At one point, not long before daybreak, as Ed rose from the table to refresh their drinks, Napoleon Jones said: "If you love her, Ed, you gotta tell her."

They'd been talking about Alice, and the situation with Verne.

Ed said: "I think she knows."

The other man raised his eyebrows doubtfully.

"She's still looking for her husband, ain't she?"

"Yes, but—"

"You ain't the first person to fall for someone you shouldn't have, Ed. Hell, we've all been there. But if you truly love her, you gotta fight for her."

Ed filled the glasses, one after the other, from the beer tap.

He said, "It's not as simple as that."

Jones picked up the cards and started dealing the next hand.

"Ain't it?"

"No."

Ed came back to the table, handed one beer to Jones and set the other down next to his own stack of betting chips. By his standards, he wasn't doing too badly. He was almost five hundred up, doubling his winnings from earlier in the evening. Now, though, he was getting tired, and wanted to wrap things up, so he could go home to Alice.

They played on for a few minutes in silence, until Ed had a promising hand. Then, when it was his turn to bet, he pushed half his chips into the middle of the table.

Napoleon Jones raised his eyebrows.

"I can't match that."

"You could go all-in," Ed said.

The other man gave him a sly look. "Or I could raise you."

"With what?"

Jones reached down and pulled off his cowboy boots. He slapped them on the table.

"These are handmade," he said. "Genuine American lizard skin. They're worth ten times what you have there." He gave a wide grin. "And I'll bet them against everything you own."

"Everything?"

"Yep, every penny you have."

"Are you crazy?"

Jones shook his head, eyes shining. "Life's a gamble, Ed. You've just gotta learn to go with it. Sometimes you win, sometimes you lose. Hell, every time I fire my ship off into the unknown, I'm laying a bet with fate. One day, I just won't come back."

Ed squirmed on his chair.

"Are those boots really worth that much?"

"Take it or leave it, Ed. That's my bet."

Ed took a deep breath. The room felt suddenly very warm. The sky outside had started to get light. Elsewhere in the hotel, people were moving around. Guests were rising to catch their early morning flights. Breakfast was being cooked. Pipes clanked as baths were run.

Ed screwed his eyes tight shut. His heart was beating hard. He knew he held a good hand: a full house, three jacks and two aces. The only way he could lose would be if Jones held a royal flush or four of a kind.

"Okay, then," he said, mouth suddenly dry. "I'm calling you."

Ed laid down his cards. Jones considered the full house and gave an appreciative nod, his green eyes giving nothing away. Then slowly, he peeled off his cards and, one by one, laid them face-up on the table.

Four queens.

It was the game with the Serbians all over again.

RETURN OF THE TRISTERO

NAPOLEON JONES LEFT the bar as dawn broke, taking his boots and his winnings, leaving Ed with nothing.

Ed sat at the table and looked at his reflection in the window. The rising sun threw long shadows across the runways of the Downport. The arc lights by the hangars were going off, one at a time. His shift had finished and his replacement had already installed herself behind the bar, but still he couldn't leave. He knew Alice was waiting, and he was too ashamed to face her. All he had left was his pack of cards, a plastic comb he'd stolen from the hotel, and the St. Christopher medal his brother had given him, which was on its chain around his neck.

Maybe I can sell a kidney, he thought. The idea was a desperate one, only half serious.

With one hand, he fished the St. Christopher medal out from beneath his shirt and rubbed it between thumb and forefinger. As he did so, Verne's words came back to him:

"This is typical of you, Ed. It's just one disaster after another. When are you going to grow up?"

When indeed?

Deserts, beaches, savannahs. He'd fought through them all to be here. He'd even killed a man. And yet here he was, falling back into old patterns, repeating the same stupid mistakes.

Maybe I am just a fuck-up, after all?

He still had half a beer left. He watched the bubbles clinging to the inside of the glass. Around him, the day began: guests came down and ordered breakfast, people wrestled suitcases from the lift to the checkout desk, the other tables in the bar became slowly occupied. The place started to smell of coffee. Ed hardly noticed. All he could think of was Alice. She'd been counting on him and he'd let her down. He'd gotten greedy when he should have backed off, and he'd paid a hefty price for his impatience.

He banged his fist against his forehead.

Stupid, stupid, stupid.

Now they wouldn't be able to catch the shuttle up to the Quay to meet Verne. There wasn't time to start saving again. They'd had their chance, and he'd blown it for both of them. All he could do now was hope that Verne would pick up the messages they'd left for him on the planetary Grid, and that he'd come down from the Quay to find them.

Ed clasped his hands on the table and let himself tip forward until his hair touched the knuckles of his thumbs. A small, frustrated moan escaped his lips.

Couldn't he do something right, just for once?

He closed his eyes.

Around him, the sounds of the bar continued. No one paid him any attention. They assumed he was drunk.

Eventually, two men walked into the bar, and instead of ordering drinks, strode straight across the room.

"Edward Rico?"

Reluctantly, Ed looked up. What new trouble was this?

One of the men was dressed as an Acolyte, clad in the black robes of the order. Age had tightened the skin of his face, giving him a skeletal aspect and whitening his fair hair to the point of invisibility. The other wore a chocolate-coloured leather coat, the seams of which had been abraded by age and wear to the colour of weak tea. He had wide, brown eyes and hair just starting to grey at the edges.

"Mr. Rico," he said, "my name is Tobias Drake. This is Mr. Hind. We need to talk to you, urgently."

Tobias Drake glanced warily round at the drinkers on the other tables.

"And in private," he added.

THEY LED ED out onto the hotel steps and into the chill morning air. The freshness of it hit him like a glass of ice water to the face. It had a clean and invigorating quality to it. Even this far inland, it smelled of the sea.

"What do you want?" he asked.

They were out on the street now. Cars and trucks whispered past. Across the road, a chain link fence topped with razor wire separated them from the Downport's main runway, reminding Ed of Heathrow. Shuttles came in one after another, scramjet engines whining. Whale-like cargo zeppelins nosed their way in and out of docking cradles on skeletal, kilometer-high towers set at the far side of the port. As he watched the trucks scurrying to and fro between the ranks of arches, Drake said to him, "You are Edward Jason Rico, born in Cardiff in the year 1990?"

"Uh, yeah."

"Mr. Rico, we desperately need your help. Would you be willing to come with us on a matter of utmost urgency?"

Ed frowned. The man seemed sincere. The Acolyte still hadn't spoken. "You want *my* help?"

"Yes. Please."

"Where would we be going?"

Drake flicked a hand at the sky. "First to the Quay, and then, later, on to the Dho Ark." He looked at Ed expectantly, gauging his reaction. "You've heard of it, of course?"

Ed gave a bemused nod. He'd seen footage of the diamond-clad behemoth on the Grid, but knew little beyond that.

A thought occurred to him.

"Alice—"

"Alice Jayne Rico?" Drake smiled. "By all means, bring her along if you want to."

AN HOUR LATER, Ed and Alice walked into the Downport's departure lounge. They had a small suitcase each, containing everything they owned. Ed had changed out of the white cotton shirt and black trousers he'd been wearing to serve behind the bar, into a pair of new blue jeans and a red t-shirt. His black leather work boots were scuffed and frayed, but still serviceable. He carried his combat jacket over his shoulder. Verne's rusty glasses lay zipped in an inside pocket. Alice, still cranky at being woken early and bundled into a cab, wore a cotton summer dress cut just above the knee in the local style, white trainers, and a silver vinyl jacket. She had her auburn hair pulled back in a loose ponytail.

Drake met them at the gate and led them to a private shuttle. He hadn't given them much more of an explanation. All they knew was that they were going to the Quay, and that Ed's eventual presence on the Ark was essential to ward off a coming crisis. They had no idea what that crisis might be, or why Ed was so important.

Once on board the shuttle, Drake helped stow their luggage and showed them to their seats.

"Have you ever been into space before?" he asked.

Ed and Alice both shook their heads. Aside from Drake and the Acolyte crew, they were the only people on board.

"Well, it's not so bad," Drake said. "The first few minutes are the worst." He took position on the other side of the aisle. Sweat glistened on his forehead.

"Are *you* okay?" Alice asked him. "Only you seem nervous."

Drake finished fastening his seatbelt and turned to her.

"I'm not a very good flyer," he said sheepishly. "I'll be all right once we're up there, it's just the takeoff that scares me."

At that moment, Francis Hind walked up the aisle from the cockpit, one hand to his hairless temple as if listening to something he alone could hear.

"We have incoming," he said.

Drake looked up. "Is it Kat?"

"No, it's the *Tristero*. She's back. Jumped in a few minutes ago on an inbound course, and she's not answering hails."

Drake made a face.

"That doesn't sound good. Can we stop her?"

Ed sat up. "What do you mean, stop her? That's my brother's ship!"

The Acolyte ignored him.

"I'm afraid we won't be in time. She'll have docked at the Quay by the time we get up there."

Drake put his fist to his lips. "Damn."

The shuttle's engines whined into life. Hind swung into a seat in front of Drake's. He spoke over his shoulder, through the gap between the headrests.

"I've already relayed the information to our people on the Quay," he said. "They say the port authorities are arranging a reception committee. They want to arrest the captain, Luciano, for all the good that'll do."

Drake rubbed his chin. "And the authorities still won't consider an evacuation?"

"No."

With a jolt, the shuttle backed away from the terminal and began to taxi toward the runway. Ed leaned out into the aisle, catching Drake's arm.

"What reception committee, what are you talking about?"

Tobias Drake turned to him, his large brown eyes full of sympathy.

"I'm sorry, Ed," he said, "but if our suspicions are correct, then in all likelihood your brother's already dead."

STRAULI QUAY

THE *AMELINE* FLARED into existence above Strauli, every instrument straining for traces of the infected *Tristero*. Jacked in to the ship's sensors, Kat fearfully scanned the sky ahead, half expecting the rose-coloured bloom of a new cloud above her beloved home world.

"Any sign of the *Tristero*?" she said.

> GOT IT. CAN'T MISS THAT DRIVE SIGNATURE.

The ship zoomed the view onto the orbital Quay. The *Tristero* floated outside the clamshell doors of one of the larger docking bays. Port Authority tugs surrounded her, guiding her down under close escort.

> COMMS SAYS THE SHIP'S BEEN IMPOUNDED. THEY DON'T KNOW ABOUT THE INFECTION. THEY THINK CAPTAIN LUCIANO'S STILL ABOARD AND THEY WANT TO ARREST HIM FOR THE WAY HE JUMPED OUT OF HERE LAST TIME.

If the situation hadn't been so dire, Kat would have smiled at the hint of reproach in the ship's tone. Instead, she said: "Get on to them, warn them."

> I'M TRANSMITTING A COMPLETE SENSOR RECORD OF EVERYTHING WE SAW IN THE DJATT SYSTEM.

"Download it to the Grid as well. Everyone needs to know."

> DOING IT NOW. BUT I THINK WE'RE TOO LATE.

The screens cleared to show a view patched in from one of the tugs. Wearing spacesuits, half a dozen armed Port Authority personnel were attempting to open the *Tristero*'s outer airlock. Kat opened her mouth to order the ship to transmit another warning, but even as she did so, the lock puffed open, and The Recollection burst forth like a spray of blood.

The spacesuits stood no chance. They were overwhelmed and eaten alive in seconds. Caught in the blast of the red jet, suit material fell apart like tissue paper; the flesh beneath frayed from bones, and the bones themselves were scoured to nothingness. Over the comms channels, Kat heard confused, short-lived screams. Two of the tugs were caught in the cloud. They jerked erratically, systems compromised. The others tried to move away on awkward evasion vectors, afraid of colliding with each other and afraid of hitting the side of the Quay.

"Oh, shit."

And still more of the arterial cloud pumped from the guts of the infected ship, giving it the appearance of a wounded fish. Every cubic centimeter of space within its hull must have been packed with nanomachines, and now the hull itself was dissolving, devoured from within and converted into more drones for the swarm.

Then, with little more than the engines left, the ship leapt forward. Like a dagger, it drove through the clamshell doors of the docking bay, into the interior of the Quay itself.

Appalled, Kat unplugged from the *Ameline*'s sensors and turned to Victor.

"It's happening," she said.

Victor said nothing. His mouth was a hard line, his eyes hooded. He kept clenching and unclenching his fists.

> DISTRESS CALLS COMING IN.

"Put them on the screen."

STRAULI QUAY HAD no defence against the tide of blood-red malevolence boiling from the carcass of the *Tristero*. As soon as they hit the walls and floor of the docking bay, the tiny machines started chewing into the metal, just as they'd done with Kat's hand before being stopped by the Dho pendant. Unstoppable and merciless, they burst through into the rooms and corridors beyond, their numbers swelling with every passing second. People unlucky enough to be in those spaces died quickly as the weakened walls blew out, spilling air into the void.

On the bridge of the *Ameline*, Kat listened to the voices that were shouting and screaming on the local channels. She saw security camera footage of troops running back and forth, trying to find something to shoot at. The populace, over a million of them, milled around in alarmed and frightened confusion. Most of them didn't know what was happening. A few logged onto the Grid for information and accessed the *Ameline*'s sensor logs from Djatt. Others simply ran for the nearest hangar hoping to escape, but more often than not simply hastening their own demise as they ran into infected areas.

Kat watched it all in horror. Those were her people down there. Friends, strangers and, god forbid, family. Her cheeks felt warm. She put a hand to them and realised there were tears running down her face.

FELIKS ABDULOV WAS in his office, catching up on admin, when the first alarms sounded. He'd been away for a few months, and now he had forms to sign, reports to read. The work wasn't hard but it was time consuming. Mostly all he had to do was check boxes on a screen, signifying his consent for this or that action. Any recommendations he might have would be delegated, either to automated back office software or to one of his human assistants.

It was very different from his days in the field, commanding his own trading ship; then, he'd had to do most things himself. He hadn't been afraid to roll his sleeves up and get his hands dirty. If the engines broke, he'd be there helping the mechanics. If a deal needed to be made, if a seller haggled over the price of the cargo, he'd stand at the foot of the cargo ramp and look that guy in the eye. Back in those days, he was his own boss. He owned the company. Now, with all this work clamouring for his attention, it sometimes felt as if the company owned him.

He sighed.

Along with his wife, Scarlett, he'd been spending three months out of every four on their private yacht, jumping six light weeks out into space and then turning around and jumping straight back. They'd been doing it for the past twenty-four years, fast-forwarding themselves into the future, waiting for Kat to return from Djatt. They'd jump out and then arrive back on the Quay twelve weeks later, having only lived through a few hours of that time. It made the waiting easier, and when Kat finally came home, she'd find them still fit and able rather than aged or infirm; or worse, dead. The only drawback was the three months of accumulated admin work he found on his return from each trip: shipping manifests, requests for specific cargoes, personnel issues.

When the alarm went off, he was working his way through the mountain of backlogged invoices requiring his electronic signature. He had a container full of live goats that needed transporting to a start-up colony world three jumps beyond Inakpa; several tonnes of fresh fish bound for the desert world of Catriona. Old habits die hard, though, and as soon as the klaxon went, he was out of his chair and looking for the emergency pressure suit in the cupboard behind his desk. As he pulled it out, he used his implant to access the Grid's emergency channel. Bomb scare? Meteoroid strike? Hull failure? By the time he found and replayed the security footage from the *Tristero*'s bay, he was fastening the suit and sealing it against the possibility of air loss.

What the hell is that?

In black and white, the corrosive tide poured from the wrecked ship like gushing oil, coating every surface, eating through walls and deck floors like acid. The pictures came with a priority link to footage downloaded from the *Ameline*.

Kat?

He clicked through and found himself looking down on the stifled face of Djatt; the immense claret-coloured tentacles; lightning; zombies; contagion.

The alarms were still ringing. Panicky messages appeared from his people: of the fifty rotating wheels stacked on the Quay's seventy-five kilometer axle, fourteen were already offline, overwhelmed. One had shattered into fragments.

"Get out," he told them curtly. "Get to a shuttle, get to a ship. Do whatever you have to, just get out."

Even as he spoke, his legs were in motion, carrying him to the door of his office. The floor shuddered beneath his feet. Out in the corridor, people were pushing in all directions. They didn't know which way to run. He paused in the doorway and, using his implant, sent an emergency text message to any and all remaining Abdulov ships still in dock, telling them to cast off and retreat to a safe distance. The floor shook again. Priority alerts flashed up over the vision of his left eye, competing for attention. He ignored them. He didn't need to be told how serious the situation was, and he already knew exactly where he was going.

There wasn't time to reach the hangars. Instead, wading forward into the jostling crowd, his breathing loud in the confines of his pressure suit, Feliks fought his way towards his family's cryogenic cargo handling facility.

THE GROUND-TO-ORBIT shuttle shook as its main engines fired. The Acolytes had given up their attempt to reach the Quay and were thrusting for a higher orbit. In the main cabin, Francis Hind had hacked into the Quay's security feed, and was pulling grainy black and white shots from all parts of the station, assembling them into a mosaic of uproar and violence, projected onto the screens on the back of each seat. Ed and Alice watched the pictures but didn't understand what they were seeing, only that people were dying. They were taken aback by the ferocity and scale of the destruction.

"What is this?" Ed asked, as he watched the dark blizzard fill a corridor, shredding everything and everyone in its path.

Toby Drake looked at him from across the aisle.

"It's called The Recollection," he said. "It's the reason we brought you here."

Ed grimaced.

"To see this?"

Drake shook his head. He put his hand on Ed's forearm.

"We want you to stop it."

CHAPTER THIRTY-NINE
MEGATONNE

For a long time, Kat said nothing. The images from the Quay held her frozen, unable to think or act or do anything save bear witness to the unfolding devastation.

"Open a channel to the Quay," she said at last.

> TO THE PORT AUTHORITY?

"No. Find my father."

> I'LL TRY.

"Just find him."

She sat back in her pilot's couch and rubbed her eyes with the knuckles of her fists, hoping against hope that Feliks Abdulov had been down on the planet's surface when the attack hit, in the family compound enjoying the autumn sunshine instead of up on the Quay taking care of business.

> RECEIVING SIGNAL.

Kat's stomach seemed to flip over. She swallowed nervously.

"Put it through."

> BUT IT—

"**Katherine Abdulov!**" The voice boomed from the speakers on the bridge.

"Cut it off!"

> I CAN'T. IT'S HACKED THE PRIMARY COMMS ARRAY.

"Surrender yourself, Katherine."

The words sent a tingle through her. She felt an unfamiliar stirring in her head and remembered what the ship had said about the nanomachines on Djatt rewiring parts of her pre-frontal cortex.

"Never."

"But I have so many of your friends already. Don't you want to be with your friends?"

Something tugged at her: an urge to respond, to throw herself into the red storm consuming the Quay. Sweat broke out on her forehead, and her nose started to bleed. She wiped it on the back of her hand.

"Disconnect and isolate the primary array, switch to secondary."

> WORKING...

"Come to me, Katherine. Bring me your ship."

She wasn't hearing the voice with her ears anymore. It seemed to resonate in her skull, persuasive and commanding, compelling her to obey. Behind it, she could hear the anguished cries of those the monster had already consumed. How many of those voices belonged to people she had known and loved?

"Go to hell," she thought, summoning up the last of her strength. She couldn't hold out. She couldn't even speak to warn Victor. Whatever was in her head quashed all resistance. The last scraps of her former resolve were crumbling. The Recollection had her.

And then the connection broke.

She fell back against her couch as if slapped, chest heaving for air.

> PRIMARY ARRAY OFFLINE.

"Kat!" Victor struggled with his straps. "Kat, what's wrong?"

She lay still, dazed, looking up at the overhead screens. Her breathing roared in her ears. Her heart thumped painfully. She could feel blood oozing from her nose.

"Kat, talk to me. Are you okay?"

For a few seconds, she watched the screens, still displaying pictures of the carnage taking place in the rooms and corridors of Strauli Quay. Then, without being consciously aware of having made a decision, her hands started to move. She wiped the blood and tears from her face. Still keeping most of her attention on the video screens, she reached forward and tapped on the pilot's instrument console, accessing the onboard flight computers controlling the nuclear-tipped atmospheric probes stacked in the *Ameline*'s cargo bay.

Victor looked from her to the controls, then back again.

"What are you doing?"

She hawked up blood and spat onto the deck. "What I have to."

He leaned across to get a better look at the console, and when he saw the menu options she's accessed, his eyes widened in alarm.

"You're going to fire on the Quay?"

Using her metal hand, Kat shoved him firmly back into his own seat.

"Yes."

"But there are a million people over there!"

With her other hand, she opened a sub menu and ran a query.

"One million, three hundred and eighty-seven," she read aloud. Even to her own ears, her voice sounded hard and flat.

"And you're going to kill them?"

"They're already dying."

She tapped in additional commands. The Quay had its defences, and the probes would have to be quick and agile to get close enough to do real damage.

"I can't let you do it."

"You don't have any choice!"

She added her final instructions to the probes' flight computers.

"Open the bay doors," she told the ship.

> OPENING.

The bridge quivered as the *Ameline* depressurized its cargo hold and cracked open the main loading hatch in the floor, opening the interior to vacuum.

Victor put his hand on Kat's arm.

"Kat—"

She shook him off. Her chest burned as if filled with hot coals, hard and bright. Her mouth was dry, her tongue numb.

"There are over a dozen ships in dock," she said. "Over a dozen. Can you imagine what'll happen if that red muck infects a dozen more ships? How fast it will spread?"

"But the Quay—"

"Better the Quay than the surface. If it gets down onto the planet, that's it: game over."

"But the people—"

Kat snarled. "Better a quick, clean death than an eternity of torment."

All six of the probes were now under her control. Using her implant, she instructed the ship's cargo boom to move them from their secure mounts to the lip of the open doors.

> Done.

"Okay, then. Prepare to fire on my mark."

"Kat, I can't let you do this."

"Shut up, Victor."

Kat ran her tongue over her dry bottom lip. She seemed to be sitting somewhere else, watching herself from a distance.

"But Kat—"

"Fire!"

The *Ameline* rocked.

> Probes away.

Kat jacked into the ship's sensors. All six of the missiles had fired. She watched them flare away on divergent courses, rolling and weaving. In the lower corner of her vision, countdowns were running, numbers almost blurring as they ticked off the distance and time remaining until impact.

Still pinned to his seat by the shuttle's acceleration, Ed Rico saw Francis Hind mutter something to Toby Drake. He heard the words '*Ameline*' and 'missiles.'

"What's going on?" he asked.

Drake looked him in the eye.

"You'd better hold on," he said.

Clad in the cumbersome pressure suit, Feliks Abdulov staggered into the cryogenic cargo facility. His thighs and calves were burning with effort, and his panting breath kept misting his faceplate.

"I'm getting way too old for this," he wheezed, admitting it to himself for the first time.

The cargo facility was a large room on the outer edge of one of the Quay's rings, holding rank upon rank of stacked shipping containers. The containers were insulated, designed for shipping frozen foodstuffs, and livestock in cryogenic hibernation. When full, they were dropped through doors in the floor, out into the arms of tugs, which then ferried them through the vacuum to the holds of waiting starships. On a normal day, four or five staff would have been on duty, checking manifests and supervising the automated forklifts. Now, the facility was empty, although the forklifts were still hard at work preparing the next scheduled shipment.

Using his implant, Feliks accessed the facility records and identified the next container to be shipped. Then, hampered by the suit, he shuffled over to it and heaved open the squeaky metal doors. Cold air blew out around him. Inside, crates of fresh fish filled the container from floor to ceiling, on their way from Strauli's warm oceans to the desert world of Catriona. Grunting with the effort, he toppled two of the nearest stacks out of the container, scattering fish and ice over the metal floor of the facility. This left a space just about large enough for him to wedge himself into. One of the automated forklifts was coming his way. He pulled the door shut and heard the lock engage.

The container lurched, seconds later, as it was lifted and borne towards the outside doors. Feliks braced himself against the stacked boxes of fish, glad his suit prevented him from smelling them. In moments, he'd be outside the Quay, the container flung outward by the centripetal force of the ring's rotation. With luck, the automated tugs would still be working, in which case he'd be taken to a waiting starship, where he could signal the crew via his implant. If either the tugs or the ship were absent, he'd be in trouble. The heating elements sewn into the fabric of his suit would keep him from freezing until the suit's batteries ran out, and the filters in the helmet would keep recycling oxygen for the next thirty hours. Whatever was happening on the Quay, he hoped someone would intercept and rescue him before then.

PLUGGED INTO THE *Ameline*, Kat watched the six missiles close on the Quay. They showed as angry little sparks on her tactical display, each attacking on a slightly different trajectory, hoping to confuse the Quay's computerized meteor defense.

> SIXTY SECONDS, said the ship.

Kat bit her lip. Her hands were squeezed so tightly she could feel her fingernails digging into her palms.

> FIFTY.

Gun turrets fired from their mounts on the Quay. Brightly-lit tracer rounds streaked the sky. One missile flared and died. Another was clipped, lost attitude control and tumbled out of control, corkscrewing off into the void.

> FORTY.

Four missiles remained on course, each one packing a single-megatonne mining charge. The guns fired again. Another missile vanished from her display.

"Come on," she urged.

> THIRTY.

> TWENTY.

An alert popped up: The Recollection was attempting to hack her secondary communications array. She told the ship to keep it offline.

> TEN.

Defensive tracer fire erupted again, but it was sporadic and unfocussed. Nothing could stop the missiles now. They were programmed to detonate as soon as they got within ten metres of the Quay.

Kat bit back the shout building within her, the urge to cry out, to warn the people on the Quay of the approaching danger.

> FIVE.

> FOUR.

Unbidden, a tear ran down her face.

> THREE.

> TWO.

Light blossomed. The first charge exploded, swiftly followed by the second and third. Each one hit a different part of the station. The explosions vapourised large sections of the hull. The central axle hinged apart about a third of the way down, broken by the blast waves. Chunks of wreckage blew outward. Sections of the ruined wheel spun away, torn ends spilling air and water and people into space.

Hooked into the ship's sensors, Kat felt the heat of the explosions as warm sunlight on her face. Beside her on the *Ameline*'s bridge, she heard Victor curse under his breath. She couldn't back out of her link with the ship, couldn't tear her eyes away from the disintegrating Quay. Like a great old ocean liner holed beneath the waterline, it listed over, its back truly broken. The separated sections were moving away from each other; one down toward the planet, the other off to the side, caught in an expanding cloud of smaller fragments.

* * *

ALL THE LIGHTS went off, and the shuttle bucked like a frightened horse. Ed cried out. Alice gripped his arm. In the darkness, Francis Hind asked, "Is everybody all right?"

"We're okay," Alice replied. She had her face pressed against Ed's shoulder.

Ed said, "What the hell was that?"

Toby Drake cleared his throat.

"It was the Quay," the scholar said, voice tight with disbelief and barely-suppressed fear. "Katherine Abdulov's nuked the bloody Quay!"

CHAPTER FORTY
REUNION

> I'M PICKING UP A CALL FROM TOBY DRAKE.

Kat shook herself. She'd been watching the expanding cloud of debris from the Quay. Now she backed out of the ship's sensorium and ran a hand through her hair.

"Put it on screen," she said.

One of the smaller displays on her console blinked and lit to reveal Drake, looking twice as old as he had when she bid him farewell, and now lit from above by low red emergency lighting.

"Katherine."

"Toby, where are you?"

Drake rubbed his forehead.

"In a shuttle. We were headed for the Quay when The Recollection struck."

"Are you okay?"

"We're fine but we're drifting. We caught the edge of one of your explosions, and it fried some of our systems. For the moment, we're running on back-up battery power."

On another screen, Kat tapped up a 2D tactical

display. The *Ameline* illuminated the shuttle with a blinking green cursor.

"You're past the Quay, heading outward," Kat said. "Hold tight and we'll rendezvous."

"We?"

"I have Victor Luciano with me."

"Victor..." Toby's brow creased. "In that case, I have some people here who are very keen to speak with him. Can you put him on?"

Kat shrugged. She turned to Victor. He'd been staring at his own clasped hands for the past few minutes, shocked into silence by the Quay's destruction. Now he looked up, blinking curiously.

"He's here," she said.

On the screen, Drake's hand loomed into the picture. He took hold of the camera and turned it, revealing a scared-looking couple strapped into seats on the other side of the shuttle's aisle.

Victor's eyes narrowed. It was hard to make out much detail in the glow of the red lights.

"Hello?" he said.

The woman in the picture screamed. She put her hands over her mouth.

"Oh, my god," she squeaked.

"Alice?"

"Verne!"

"And who's that with you. Is it Ed? Jesus Christ, what are you two doing here?"

The man he'd referred to as Ed leaned towards the camera.

"Looking for you," he said.

*　　*　　*

AN HOUR LATER, the *Ameline* docked with the stricken shuttle.

There was only room for one person to fit through the airlock at a time, so Ed hung back and let Alice, Drake and the Acolyte go first. His stomach churned. He hadn't felt this nervous since the police asked him to identify Verne from the CCTV footage at the Chancery Lane Underground station; to confirm that the grainy black and white figure falling into the alien portal was indeed his elder brother.

When he finally climbed through into the *Ameline*'s passenger cabin, he found Verne with his hand on Alice's shoulder. He could see she was crying.

"It's okay," Verne was saying, soothing her. He'd lost weight and there were grey streaks in his hair. He looked strange without his spectacles; he had a faint, spidery scar under one eye, and a tiny chunk missing from his left ear. He turned as he heard Ed approaching.

"Ed!"

Ed stopped a few paces away. He pulled the rusted glasses from his pocket.

"I think these are yours."

Verne looked at them, then up at Ed.

"Are they really...?"

He took a step forward and reached out for the glasses. Ed let him take them.

"Jesus. Where did you find them?"

"In a cave, in a cliff."

Verne turned the glasses over and over in his hands. He kept shaking his head.

"You know, I had to climb that cliff half blind. Half blind *and* half dead." He looked up at Ed. "Did you meet those fucking creatures?"

Ed gave a mute nod. Verne made a face.

"I hated those fucking things," he said. "They almost had me a couple of times."

Ed swallowed. He rubbed his hands together. "Yeah. We, uh, we left someone there."

Verne's eyes narrowed.

"You did?"

Ed gave a nod.

Verne looked down at his feet. "I'm sorry."

Ed took a step forward.

"Look, Verne..."

His brother held up a hand. "Don't say it, Ed."

"But—"

"I mean it." Verne glanced at Alice. "I can't pretend that what the two of you did was right and I can't pretend it didn't hurt, but I never thought I'd ever see either of you again. I gave you both up for dead, years ago. Decades ago. So whatever's happened, I'm just glad you're both here now." He caught Ed in a bear hug. "You came to find me," he said. "Everything else is history."

Ed didn't know what to say. He'd been nerving himself for a confrontation. At the very least, he'd expected Verne to punch him in the face.

"Aren't you angry?" he said.

Verne released the hug, held him at arms length. "I told you, it's okay."

"Not to me, it's not. It might all be ancient history to you, but it still feels pretty raw to me."

"So, what do you want me to say?" Verne held his hands out, palms up. "I've already forgiven you."

"But I don't want your forgiveness."

"Then what do you want?"

Ed waved his arms in frustration.

"I don't know. Get mad. Shout at me. Do something."

"Would that make you feel better?"

Ed took a deep breath. His fists were clenched. "I don't know how you can be so calm."

Verne shrugged. "Things are different now."

Ed let his fists relax. "How different?"

Verne rubbed the bridge of his nose with his index finger. He didn't seem to know where to look.

"Let me introduce you to someone," he said, beckoning to a young woman standing impatiently on the other side of the room. "Ed, Alice. This is Katherine."

Alice pushed a strand of auburn hair out of her eyes and wiped her nose on the sleeve of her silver vinyl jacket. She looked the other woman up and down, from heavy boots to dark eyes and hair.

"Pleased to meet you," she said.

Kat gave an uncomfortable smile.

"Hello."

Silence fell. Ed shuffled his feet on the polished rock floor. Everything felt awkward and wrong, not at all as he'd expected. Nobody knew what to say. Then Francis Hind stepped into the centre of the group. He pushed back the hood of his black robe, revealing his wizened, bald pate.

"If I may interject? I'm afraid time is of the essence. Captain Abdulov, it *is* good to see you again, but I must prevail upon you to deliver us to the Ark without delay."

He turned to face Ed.

"It seems our friend here has a destiny to fulfill."

KAT LEFT THE others in the passenger lounge and climbed up the ladder to the ship's bridge.

"How are we doing?" she asked.

The ship didn't answer straight away. When it finally spoke, it sounded concerned.

> WE'VE GOT A PROBLEM.

"What is it?"

> THE RECOLLECTION SURVIVED OUR ATTACK.

"You are *kidding*."

> I WISH.

Kat slid into the pilot's chair and hooked her implant into the ship's senses.

"Let me see," she said. She closed her eyes and the tactical display opened up around her. She saw the wrecked Quay, the lower portion of it falling toward Strauli. Smaller fragments already burned as meteors in the planet's upper atmosphere.

"Where?" she said.

> THE INDIVIDUAL MACHINES ARE TOO SMALL TO RESOLVE AT THESE DISTANCES. BUT YOU MAY BE ABLE TO MAKE OUT SOME OF THE LARGER CLUMPS HERE, AND HERE.

The ship magnified a couple of areas near the falling ruin. Squinting, Kat made out a pair of irregular red stains falling toward the planet.

"That's it?"

> MUCH OF THE INFECTION WAS DESTROYED, BUT SOME ESCAPED. THAT WHICH ISN'T ACTIVELY CONVERTING THE REMAINS OF THE QUAY IS ALREADY ON ITS WAY DOWN TO THE PLANET'S SURFACE.

"Will it survive reentry?"

> IT SURVIVED THREE NUCLEAR BLASTS.

"Damn." Kat ground her palm into her forehead. "What are we going to do?"

> THERE'S NOT MUCH WE CAN DO. WE DON'T HAVE ANY WEAPONS, AND WE'RE LOW ON FUEL. IF WE FOLLOWED IT

DOWN TO THE SURFACE, WE WOULDN'T HAVE ENOUGH TO GET AIRBORNE AGAIN.

Kat let out a breath. "Do we have enough to get to the Dho Ark?"

> BARELY.

She took a last, lingering look at the fat crescent of Strauli. On the daylight side, the oceans shone a rich, wholesome blue, dotted with high, white clouds, scattered with green islands. On the nighttime side, city lights traced the coastlines. It looked so peaceful and perfect, and yet all she saw when she looked at it was the terrible red cloud that had loomed over Djatt. She thought of her mother and father, her aunts, uncles and cousins. She'd sent the footage from Djatt as a warning signal. Now she hoped they'd find a way to escape the coming horror.

"Set course," she said. "Jump when ready."

> AYE-AYE, CAPTAIN.

In her gut, she felt the engines come online, their capacitors ramping up for the short hop to the Ark.

CHAPTER
FORTY-ONE
THE TORCH THAT BURNS THE SKY

UPON ARRIVAL AT the Dho Ark, Kat Abdulov stayed with the *Ameline* to supervise repairs and refueling, while Verne and Alice retired to one of the ship's cabins to talk. Ed found himself surrounded by Acolytes and marched to a crystal elevator, accompanied by Drake and Hind.

"Where are we going?" he asked, hands in the pockets of his green combat jacket.

Drake regarded him with wide, sympathetic brown eyes.

"Not far."

The elevator doors closed and the car dropped rapidly into the depths of the crystal Ark. Ed looked down. Through the floor, he could see the lift shaft fall away into seemingly infinite darkness. At his shoulder, Drake said, "You'll get used to it."

Ed looked up from the floor and shrugged.

"It doesn't bother me."

Drake gave a rueful snort, the trace of a smile. "It bothered the hell out of me, the first time I rode in one of these things."

Ed saw a light rising to meet them, and then the elevator dropped into a bright cavern the size of a warehouse. He raised his hand to shade his eyes from the sudden brightness. The floor of the room was polished rock, bare save for something roughly the size and shape of a Volkswagen Beetle, which sat on a plinth in the exact centre of the cavern.

"What's that?" he said.

Behind him, Francis Hind leaned forward.

"That, my son, is the reason we've brought you here."

On the opposite wall, a second elevator car matched their descent. As far as Ed could make out, it contained a single robed figure wearing a weirdly-spiked helmet.

"Ah," Drake said. "One of our hosts."

They reached the floor and the doors opened. The air in the cavern was cold and dry. Drake and the Acolytes stood unmoving, their breath steaming. Drake gave Ed a nudge.

"Go ahead," he said.

Ed looked at him. "Aren't you coming?"

The other man shook his head regretfully.

"I'm afraid not," he said. "Much as I'd love the chance to inspect that thing, this is for you, and you alone."

He gently pushed Ed forward. With his hands still in the pockets of his combat jacket, Ed stepped out onto the floor of the cavern and turned to watch the crystal elevator as it accelerated back up into the ceiling.

When it had disappeared into the shaft from whence it came, he turned and started to walk toward the object on the plinth. On the far side of the room, the horned figure did likewise, seeming to glide as the hem of its robe brushed the floor. As it got closer and closer, he slowly realised that it wasn't a man at all: the body under the robe seemed to be proportioned all wrong, and the 'helmet' came down to the creature's shoulders without the benefit of a neck.

This must be one of the Dho, Ed thought, trying to remember the little he'd gleaned about them in his time on Strauli, doing the Downport hustle. All he knew was all that anyone else really knew: that the Dho were aliens; that the Ark had been in the Strauli system for a thousand years before the first humans stumbled through the arch network; and that in nearly four hundred years, only a handful of humans had ever met one face-to-face.

"Welcome, Edward," the creature said, in a voice composed chiefly of clicks and scrapes. Ed stopped walking. He kept his hands in his jacket pockets, trying to look relaxed.

"Call me Ed," he said.

The Dho stood at least a foot taller than him. Its robe was the colour of the night sky, its outline pregnant with asymmetrical lumps and protrusions beneath the fabric.

"Do you know why you are here, Ed?"

From the roots of its short, spiky front horns, wet black eyes regarded him. They looked like prunes swimming in their own juice. Ed shivered.

"I've no idea," he said truthfully.

The Dho glided forward another pace. Its bony head reminded him of the fly-covered sheep's skull he'd found as a child on the outskirts of Cardiff, in the woods up behind his school playing field.

"You are here because you are an artist." The object on the plinth had the same black texture as the creature's robe. As he watched, the Dho extended a limb towards the lumpy mass and a cavity opened in response.

"Crawl inside," the creature said.

Ed leant forward. He peered doubtfully into the hole.
"In there?"

"Yes."

"Why?"

The Dho let forth a stream of irritated clicks and whirrs, sounding to Ed much the way he imagined a swarm of locust would sound if amplified.

"We call this 'The Torch,'" the creature husked. "It is a weapon, the most powerful weapon we possess."

The hole looked uncomfortably organic. It was lined with a pale, greasy-looking material that seemed to shift and undulate as Ed watched it.

"And you want me to operate it?"

"Yes."

"Me?"

"You are an artist, Edward Rico. You have enviable depth perception. You are used to visualizing abstract shapes in three dimensional space." It started to glide around the edge of the plinth towards him.

Ed backed away. "I'm not a soldier. I'm not even very good at computer games."

"The Torch is best wielded by one with the soul of an artist. It does not respond well to professional soldiers. It is a weapon designed purely for defense."

Ed took his hands out of his pockets. He said, "How do you know anything about my soul?"

The creature stopped and clicked to itself as if surprised.

"The arch network records and encodes information about everything it transmits. Did you not know this? It stores the quantum states of every creature passing through its portals. As soon as you passed through the first arch, we knew all there was to know about you, right down to the quantum level, and we judged you an ideal candidate. You may have made mistakes in your life, Edward, but by hurling yourself into the arch network in search of your brother, you have shown that you are capable of acts of great courage and selflessness."

Ed looked away. "But why just me? There must be other people better qualified for this sort of thing."

The Dho made a mournful scraping sound. "There were other candidates, other men and women from Earth, but they died, or wandered off and got lost. You are the only one to make it all the way here."

Ed took a deep breath. He rubbed his chin.

"Drake said you wanted me to stop this Recollection."

"That is correct."

He jerked a thumb at the cavity in the Torch.

"And this'll do it, will it?" He shuddered. "If I climb into this thing, I'll be able to stop it."

The creature inclined its head, tipping its bony horns.

"We can but try."

ED SLID IN feet first, skin crawling. Where it brushed his hands and face, the lining of the hole felt warm and pliable, like grease or candle wax.

"All the way in," said the Dho, watching.

Ed muttered under his breath.

"Why am I doing this?"

He wriggled his shoulders, inching his way deeper, until his head dropped below the rim of the hole. Almost immediately, the lining began to compress around him, hugging his arms and legs with a soft, but insistent pressure. He'd never suffered from claustrophobia, but now it was all he could do not to try to thrash his way free. His chest rose and fell as he gasped in air.

"Relax," said the Dho. "The Torch is becoming accustomed to you."

Ed swallowed. His fists were bunched at his sides.

"What do I do?"

"Just lie still. Whatever happens, just lie still."

Ed felt something touch his cheek. The lining had extruded hair-fine filaments of slippery white material that reached for his face like wires. He tried to jerk his head away, but found he was pinned in place, unable to move. With agonizing slowness, the questing filaments explored his face. He felt one push into his left ear, another slide into his nostril. Another two insinuated themselves greasily into his eye sockets, sliding through his tightly-squeezed eyelids into the soft flesh beneath his eyeballs. He wanted to scream, but there were already wires in his mouth, reaching down into his throat, making him gag.

For an instant, every nerve in his body flared with excruciating pain.

And then there was silence.

Space opened up around him. He saw the whole Strauli system laid out before him: the Ark orbiting its gas giant; Strauli and the radioactive wreckage of the Quay; individual ships; asteroids; comets; space junk. Everything was there, laid out and labeled like pieces on a chess board. All he had to do was select a target and he knew the Torch would do the rest. He could feel it behind his eyes, twisting itself around his thoughts like an affectionate tiger; as vast, powerful and unpredictable as the ocean.

I have waited such a long time, it seemed to be saying. *Such a long time. But now you're here.*

And the further it dug into him, the more wonders it showed him. He saw himself from the outside, saw his whole stupid, dust bowl life lain out like a flowchart, one poor decision leading inexorably on to the next, and the next. A bell rang in his mind. He re-experienced his childhood, felt his mother's soothing hand, his father's chin stubble. Re-lived the pain of their loss. Saw Verne. Saw Alice on the day he'd first met her. Was shown every wrong turn he'd ever made, every chance he'd missed or let slide. Every knock he'd taken. For one brief instant he was simultaneously present in every individual second of his life. The whole thing whirled around him, and then once more, there was silence.

He felt calm. Raw and naked, but calm. All his regrets and hang-ups were gone, washed away from the core of his being, leaving in their place only two rock-hard certainties:

Firstly, he loved Alice. Really loved her. Loved her in a way he'd been too stupid to admit to himself.

Secondly, he was also in love with this outrageous, extraordinarily eldritch weapon, and together, they were really going to fucking *kill* something.

KICKING ASS

OVER THE NEXT twenty hours, gory red welts blossomed on the islands and land masses of Strauli, disfiguring its genteel serenity. Although keeping track of their progress, Kat spent much of the time supervising the refueling of the *Ameline* and, later, the fixture of a lumpy Dho weapon to the ship's belly. The Dho called the weapon 'The Torch,' and apparently Victor's brother would be operating it.

Verne, she corrected herself. Not Victor, *Verne*.

Working without a break, she checked every system on the ship. She worked until her eyes were too tired to focus, and only then allowed herself a few snatched minutes of sleep on the pilot's couch. Her purpose sustained her. She couldn't afford to let herself slacken, she had to keep active. She was determined to have the ship in peak condition, ready to take it down to the surface of her home planet, to the very door of the Abdulov compound if necessary. The work distracted her from thoughts of her attack on the Quay. The numbers of potential casualties were too great to comfortably grasp. If she stopped to imagine all those people, all those faces, she had no doubt that they'd overwhelm her, preventing her from completing her rescue mission. Later, there would be time for grief and self-disgust. Right now, she had to keep her focus. People were depending on her. She had to get down there, pick up her family, and rescue her unborn child, and she wouldn't let anything get in the way of that, not even guilt.

When Verne found her, she was crouched beneath the ship, working on one of its landing struts, making sure the hydraulics were primed for a rough touchdown.

"What do *you* want?" she said without looking around, wiping her hands on the thighs of her overalls.

"Don't be like that."

"Like what?"

"You know."

Kat rose to her feet, shoulders hunched.

"What about Alice?"

"What about her?"

"She's your wife."

"*Was* my wife."

Kat turned to face him. He'd changed into a standard skin-tight black ship suit, which revealed the slight middle-aged paunch around his midriff. A large-bore pistol hung at his hip.

"She still is," she said. "You're still married."

Verne shook his head.

"Not really. Not for a long time. I'm not sure that the laws that put us together even still exist."

Kat huffed through her nose, an angry sigh.

"So?" she demanded.

"What?"

She put her fists on her hips.

"So where does this leave *us*?"

Verne reached for her. "Nothing's changed," he said.

Kat shook her head. *Idiot.*

"Have you been paying attention? Everything's changed. Nothing's the same."

"I'm the same."

She closed her eyes, remembering the way he'd stormed out of their hotel room all those years ago, trying to reconcile that old anger and arrogance with the man now standing before her, the veteran of three horrifying days on Djatt, witness to countless unspeakable atrocities.

"No, you're not," she whispered. "You're not the same."

You're better now.

She held his gaze. The moment stretched...

Finally, she shook herself and bent to pick up her tools.

"So," she said, "what are you all dressed up for?"

Verne put his hand to the butt of his holstered weapon.

"I'm coming with you," he said, "if you'll have me."

Hefting the toolbox in one hand, Kat paused. She bit her lip.

"Thank you," she said.

LATER, ED AND Alice sat together in the human quarters, at a table in the mess hall, overlooking one of the Ark's internal caverns. A bonsai rainforest filled the space before them, trees and creepers reaching for the sunlamps inlaid in the cavern's ceiling. Mist rose between the branches. Occasionally, small, bat-like creatures flapped from perch to perch.

For Ed, the last ten hours had been spent swaddled in the cervical confines of the Dho weapon. Now, when he closed his eyes, all he could see was a retinal ghost of the Strauli system, all the game pieces laid out on the board, ready to play.

"How do you feel?" Alice asked.

He shrugged. He worked his jaw, mouth dry.

"My head hurts." He scratched the flaky blood crusting the corner of his eye. All he wanted was a hot shower. He thought sadly of the bathroom in his flat in London, now forever lost.

"I'm okay," he said. He missed London: missed the ever-present background noise, the simplicity of a life he'd never properly appreciated.

He watched Alice push a curl of auburn hair behind her ear. She passed him a cup of coffee and he gratefully wrapped his hands around it.

She said, "How do you think it went with Verne? About us, I mean."

Ed rubbed the side of his mouth on the back of his hand. His throat still felt raw, with a greasy taste on his tongue. He hoped the coffee would help.

"I'm not sure," he said.

Alice hugged herself. She looked at the floor. "So... what do we do?"

Ed put a hand over his eyes. His head hurt like a hangover.

"I don't know."

"You *do* still want to be with me, don't you?"

He looked up. "Of course I do. I love you, Alice, I really do."

"You *do*?"

"Yes."

"But you're worried what he'll think?"

"Aren't you?"

"Yes. Yes, of course I am."

Alice squirmed in her seat. She crossed and uncrossed her arms.

"I don't want to hurt him again," she said.

Ed reached out and took her hand.

"Neither do I." He gave her fingers an affectionate squeeze. "I have to go soon."

"Be careful."

Ed lifted her hand to his lips and kissed it.

"Don't worry," he said. "I'll be fine. I know I will."

She gave him a sideways look.

"How can you possibly know that, Ed?"

He shrugged and let her hand fall back into her lap. "I guess I don't. But look how far we've come, Alice. Look at all this." He waved his arm, encompassing the forested cavern, the Ark surrounding it, and the stars beyond.

Alice twisted her finger in a lock of hair behind her ear: a nervous gesture. He smiled at her. A flock of yellow butterflies danced in the tree canopy.

"I love you," he said.

Alice bit her lip. Before she could answer, Toby Drake strode into the room, flanked by two Acolytes. The Acolytes wore ship suits beneath their open robes, Drake wore a shirt and tie beneath his chocolate-coloured leather coat.

He looked at Ed.

"They're ready for you," he said.

Linked in to the *Ameline*, Kat watched the crystalline immensity of the Dho Ark recede. Further up the behemoth's hull, a thousand hidden cavities yawned open, disgorging ships like thistledown. Crewed by Acolytes, these ships were transports of inhuman design: fat, streamlined freighters designed to pick up and carry as many refugees as possible.

> CHUBBY LITTLE BUGGERS, AREN'T THEY?

"Shhh."

She spoke to the ships.

"Okay," she told them, "form up behind me, as we planned." She cut the broadcast and opened a private channel to Ed Rico, cocooned like a caterpillar in the heart of the lumpy weapon now fixed to the underside of the *Ameline*'s bow. "How are you doing?"

Ed sounded muffled, as if he had something in his mouth. He said, "Doing all right, I think, considering it's only my second time in space."

"Good to go?"

"Just find me something to shoot at, okay?"

Kat backed out of the *Ameline*'s sensorium. She turned to Verne. He was sitting beside her, in the co-pilot's chair. He gave her an encouraging grin.

"Ready to kick some ass?"

She grinned and looked up at the screens, and saw the freighters were more or less in position, arranged in a flying v-shape with the *Ameline* at its tip. She reopened communications.

"All right," she told the fleet. "Follow me. We jump on my mark.

"Three.

"Two.

"One.

"*Mark.*"

*   *   *

A SUBJECTIVE INSTANT later, they came out of their jumps on the nighttime side of the planet. With so many ships appearing almost simultaneously, stealth wasn't an option. Each arrived in its own dazzling burst of pure white light. All at once, ten hundred flares blossomed in the vacuum, their reflected lights glittering off the waters of Strauli's darkened oceans.

On the bridge of the *Ameline*, Kat surveyed her fleet. The freighters were built like silver-skinned blimps, with heavy torpedo-shaped bodies and wide tail fins.

"Keep your eyes peeled," she advised them.

Below, her home planet turned. Dawn broke over the beaches of the Abdulov family compound.

The ship broke into her thoughts.

> RECOLLECTION DEAD AHEAD.

In the tactical display, an area the size of a football pitch lay directly in their path, its edges blurring into fractal spines.

> IT'S JUST A FRAGMENT, BUT I'M PICKING UP MICROWAVE PACKET BURSTS.

"It's in touch with other fragments?"

> IN CONTINUOUS CONTACT AND CAPABLE OF COORDINATED ACTION, RIGHT ACROSS THE SYSTEM.

"Range to this piece?"

> THIRTY KILOMETRES.

"What's it doing?"

> IT'S TRYING TO COMMUNICATE WITH US. SHALL I PUT IT ON SPEAKER?

Kat gave an involuntary shiver. "No." She didn't want to hear the trapped souls wailing in the depths of the swarm. She was afraid that now it had eaten its way through the Quay, she might recognise some of their voices. Instead, she opened her channel to Ed Rico.

"Do you see it?"

"Yes, Captain."

"Kill it for me."

WRAPPED IN THE warm, slippery folds of the Dho Weapon, Ed turned his attention to the cluster of nanomachinery between him and the planet. Through the weapon's heightened senses, he perceived the tiny blood-coloured machines as they went about their business, swarming and multiplying. They were tearing apart the carcass of an unlucky shuttlecraft, converting its raw mass into newly-minted copies of themselves.

Looking closer, he perceived the net of signals that linked them together. It was a seething, flickering web of data that encircled the globe, connecting this clump of machines to all the others in the Strauli system, whether floating in orbit, swarming over the remains of the Quay, or chewing into the rock and soil of the planet's surface. As a network, it had no centre, no hierarchy. The individual machines were simply cells in a distributed organism. The consciousness of The Recollection lived in the interplay of data between them: simultaneously everywhere and nowhere.

Contemplating this, Ed felt the mind of the Torch curl into his skull with a silky, feline grace. He sensed its feral eagerness, its drive to fulfill its purpose. The feeling was heady and contagious. All the mad soldiers, Serbian butchers, and weird otter creatures were as nothing now. For the first time in his life he felt empowered and confident. Almost omnipotent.

Target acquired.

The weapon worked by plucking wormholes from the quantum foam. One end it placed in the heart of the nearest star, while the other it aimed at the target he selected. When activated, the wormhole behaved like a flamethrower, firing a superheated jet of fusing solar hydrogen.

Thirteen million degrees centigrade.

And all he had to do was reach out...

THE *AMELINE* BUCKED. A pencil-thin line of fire shot from its bows, bright enough to blind an unprotected eye. In the quarter-second of its duration, the beam seemed to sear the very fabric of the sky itself. It punched through the thin cloud ahead, flashing the swarming machines in its path to plasma. Over the next second and a half, it fired a further three times, slicing and dicing.

> HOLY FUCKING SHIT!

On the bridge, Kat rubbed her eyes to get rid of the stark violet afterimages, giving thanks for the *Ameline*'s filters.

> TARGET DESTROYED.

With a shaking hand, she opened a line to the fleet.

"Okay," she said, trying to keep her voice steady, "You all have your coordinates. Get going."

She stayed high, watching them drop away, scattering across the face of the planet, their noses glowing cerise as they entered the atmosphere. Looking down at them, she felt a sense of trepidation. As far as she was aware, there had never been a gathering of so many jump-capable ships. And they were trying to evacuate an entire planet! In all of human history, there had never been an operation to compare. According to Francis Hind, the Dho had been planning it for centuries, training their Acolyte pilots in secret, planning the best way to retrieve as many human souls as possible. Even so, there was so much that could go wrong; and with only a thousand ships, they wouldn't be able to save more than a fraction of Strauli's sixty million inhabitants—even if they managed two or three trips before the planet was overrun.

When she was sure they were all safely on their way, she turned to Verne.

"Have you located the hospital?"

In the co-pilot's chair, he glanced up from his instruments.

"Yes, but there's a problem. It's on the edge of an infected area."

"Has it been overrun?"

"Not yet, but it's going to be close."

Kat closed her eyes and fought to keep her breathing steady. If they were going to pull this off, she had to remain calm and focused, ready to respond to whatever The Recollection threw their way.

"Okay," she said. "Let's do it."

She tapped a command into her pilot's console. The *Ameline* tipped over onto its nose and fired its engines.

> HOLD TIGHT.

They hit the atmosphere at seven kilometres a second, and the ship began to shudder. Almost immediately, the friction raised the temperature on the bow's outer skin to well over sixteen hundred degrees centigrade, creating an envelope of ionized air around the craft, interfering with their communications and cutting them off from the rest of the fleet for a little over three minutes. In the dead time, Kat turned to Verne.

"You know, I'm going to have this baby," she said matter-of-factly.

Verne gave her a look.

"No," she said, "I mean it. As soon as we get back to the Ark, I'll have one of the doctors re-implant her."

"Are you sure this is the best time?"

Kat swallowed. "It's the end of the world," she said. "If I don't do it now, I mightn't get another chance."

Verne's forefinger stroked the bridge of his nose.

"Okay," he said.

Kat smiled.

"I want to call her Sylvia, after my aunt."

Verne raised an eyebrow.

"What if it's a boy?"

Kat shook her head. It was impossible to tell the sex of the foetus at this early stage, but she had a feeling.

"It won't be. But if it is, we'll call him Victor."

The buffeting on the hull eased. The display screens came back online.

> COMMS RESTORED.

"Sit-rep?"

> WE'VE LOST TWO OF THE FREIGHTERS. THE REST ARE CLOSING ON THEIR DESIGNATED TARGETS.

"What's our distance to the hospital?"

> SIX HUNDRED KILOMETRES. ETA FOUR MINUTES.

"Okay, bring us in low and fast. Vic... I mean, Verne, you're with me."

Kat prised herself from her seat and scrambled down the ladder to the corridor connecting the bridge to the passenger lounge. Verne came behind her. When she reached the foot, she paused to select two chunky handguns from the equipment locker. As she strapped their holsters to the thighs of her ship suit, she regretted the loss of her assault rifle on Djatt. She had the uncomfortable feeling that if they were going to survive the next half an hour, they were going to need every bit of firepower they could muster.

COMING IN OVER the darkened islands, approaching the coast, Ed stabbed each of the red blooms they passed over, lancing them with beams of incandescent fury, drawn from the raging heart of a star.

The landscape rolled below him like a canvas.

The weapon was his brush.

GNARL

BACK ON THE Ark, Toby Drake stood with Harris and the Acolyte, Hind. They observed the deployment of the fleet via a stylised two-dimensional map displayed on the upper surface of a glass table in the human quarters. Toby had his hand over his mouth. His stomach churned.

"I wish I'd gone with them," he muttered.

Hind gave him a stern look. Beneath the black hood of his robe, his skin looked thin and pale, his cheeks like stretched sheets of scraped vellum.

"Our hosts have another task in mind for you," he said. "Come with me."

He led Toby out of the room. Harris watched them leave from beneath shaggy brows.

"This way." Hind set off along the corridor that led to the workstation from which Toby had spent so many years studying the Gnarl at the Ark's heart.

"Look," he said, as they stepped into the alcove, with its trestle tables and ranks of instruments.

Toby craned forward, hands pressed on the glass of the floor-to-ceiling window. Below, a group of Dho stood in a wide circle on the cavern floor, ringing the pulsating Gnarl that floated in the centre of the room. Their horns were tipped forward in attitudes of worship and deference. They seemed impervious to its writhing chemical vapours.

"What are they doing?"

"Communing."

Hind did something to the frame of the window, and the glass slid back, allowing the cavern air to swirl in around them. The hairs on Toby's arms rose. He smelled burnt hair and cinnamon, and heard a fizzing crackle like the sound of a badly-tuned radio.

"Over the past quarter of a century, you've done everything we've asked of you, Mr Drake," Hind said. "You gave up your home and your career, even the woman you loved, to come here and study with us. And now, I think you've earned the right to know the truth."

Toby took a step back, away from the edge of the window frame. The drop to the cavern floor was at least twelve metres.

"What truth?"

"The nature of the Gnarl."

Hind reached into the folds of his robe and produced a child's toy: a small, grey plastic elephant.

"Do you know the old Indian story of the blind men and the elephant?" he asked.

Toby shook his head.

Hind held up the toy.

"Once upon a time in India, six blind men were asked to describe an elephant. The one who felt the trunk said the elephant was like a tree branch. The one who felt its leg said it was like a pillar. The one who felt its tail thought it felt like a rope, and so on. Not one of them perceived the whole creature."

He handed the toy to Toby, who took it and turned it over in his hand, examining it.

"So, the Gnarl is the elephant?"

Hind nodded.

"Good," he said.

"And I'm one of the blind men?"

Hind smiled. "We're all blind. At least, we're all incapable of perceiving the Gnarl in its entirety. What we see here," he gestured through the open window, "forms merely one aspect of the whole. The Gnarl at the centre of the Bubble Belt; the arch network; the Torch; even parts of the Dho themselves: they are all facets of the same object, viewed from different angles in space and time."

Toby closed his fist around the plastic elephant.

"I don't understand."

Hind wrapped his hands together in the folds of his loose sleeves.

"Nor should you. Like the blind men in the story, we lack the faculties to comprehend the entirety of what we've encountered."

In the centre of the cavern, the Gnarl had begun to beat like an immense heart. Below, the Dho began to chant, their voices full of clicks and pops.

"I'm afraid you've been on something of a wild goose chase," Hind said. "When the Dho asked you to study the Gnarl, they had no expectation of you discovering anything of its nature. At least, nothing significant."

Toby felt himself bridle.

"Then what have I been doing for the past twenty-four years?"

Hind smiled.

"You are the one who has been studied." He took a step towards the lip of the open floor-to-ceiling window. "As you peered deeper into the Gnarl, so the Gnarl peered into you. It learned from you, and became accustomed and attuned to you."

Toby glanced at the waxy sphere. For a moment, he thought he could feel each of its pulsations in his chest; then he realised that its beats mirrored the rhythm of his heart.

"I thought this was an engine, a power source..."

"It's a lot more than that." Standing on the lip of the window, high above the cavern floor, Hind unfurled his arms, throwing them wide.

"This is an intelligence we can't hope to comprehend," he said, raising his voice over the chanting, "existing in quantum states we can barely recognize. But it is *alive*. It has wants and needs. And enemies."

Toby looked up, startled.

"Enemies? Do you mean The Recollection?"

Hind turned back into the room.

"For every action, there is an equal and opposite reaction."

He walked across to Toby and put his hands on the younger man's shoulders.

"Listen, Drake," he said, voice level, eyes burning with an intensity belying his age. "For you are the first non-Acolyte to hear this.

"The war that spawned The Recollection also spawned the Gnarl. But unlike the red cloud that now endangers us, the Gnarl was not conceived as a weapon. It was built in the last moments of that conflict, by minds infinitely superior to ours. Minds who foresaw their death at the hands of The Recollection and wanted to protect the younger races from a similar fate."

"So they built the Gnarl?"

"They designed it as a saviour. A god, if you like. It found the Dho and raised them from a mediaeval culture. It helped them build and power this vast Ark.

"And then it found us."

In the cavern, the Dho's chanting became louder and faster. The writhing mass above them seemed to swell.

Hind put his hand to Toby's cheek.

"The Gnarl built the arch network to get us out into space. And at the centre of the network, at the Prime Radiant, it built the Bubble Belt to be our Ark."

Toby tried to pull away, but the old man had a firm grip on him. From the corner of his eye, he could see the Gnarl drifting towards them through the air of the cavern, its surface crawling with patterns and symbols.

"That's where you come in," Hind said.

Toby struggled. "Me?"

"The Ark needs a pilot."

The glowing Gnarl was almost at the window now. Static sparked off metal objects. Toby felt his hair standing on end. He stopped wriggling and looked down at the old man in astonishment.

"You've seen the simulation," Hind said. "You know the whole Belt can be moved. Well, the Gnarl built that for us. It's given us a means of escape. But it doesn't know where we want to go."

"Neither do I!"

Hind pulled Toby down to him.

"You will," he whispered fiercely.

Then, without warning, he stepped back and shoved Toby in the chest with both bony hands. Caught off guard, Toby staggered back. His heel caught on the window sill and he cried out in alarm as he toppled into the cavern, his hands flailing desperately for purchase.

And the Gnarl caught him.

He sank into its gluey, ever-changing embrace, felt it invade every orifice and pore. His whole life unfurled before his eyes, opening out like a map spread on a tabletop.

And everything changed.

MOTHER

THE *AMELINE* CAME down on the lawn in front of the hospital, its jets scorching a wide circle of the grass to black ash. As soon as its landing struts hit the dirt, it popped its rear airlock. Kat and Verne spilled out, guns at the ready, heads turning back and forth, alert for threats. They covered each other as they descended the ladder, then ran from the residual heat of the main engine exhausts.

"This way," Kat said.

She ran towards a set of glass doors in the main hospital building. Beyond the building, she could see the familiar red stain of a Recollection outbreak. Like molten lava, it oozed between and around the office blocks and department stores of the town centre. Where it passed, the buildings crumbled, their walls eaten from below, their concrete, glass and stone broken down and converted into more tiny machines to add to the tide. She heard sirens and alarms. Vehicles wove crazily along half-choked streets, searching for escape.

"We don't have much time," she said.

The hospital doors opened as she approached, and she ran through into the deserted foyer beyond. The hospital had been abandoned. Her boots crunched over the broken remains of dropped coffee mugs, knocked-over plant pots, and discarded items of medical equipment. Wheelchairs lay on their sides. Patients, some still attached to intravenous drips, staggered around looking for help. Overhead, the strip lights flickered and buzzed as the electrical power fluctuated.

"Don't use the elevators," Verne panted, coming up behind her.

"No need." She pointed one of her guns down a corridor leading off into the distance, its ceiling hung with signs giving the names and functions of the wards. "Halfway down, on the right."

She set off again, boots making a thunderous clamour in the confined space.

"How are we doing?" she asked the ship via her implant.

> WE'RE DOWN TO SINGLE-DIGIT MINUTES. MAYBE LESS. DON'T HANG ABOUT.

"I don't intend to. Keep the engines warm."

Intent on this exchange, she ran past the door she wanted. Her feet slithered to a halt on the vinyl floor. Running close behind, Verne almost crashed into her.

"In here," she gasped.

The door to the storage facility stood open. The lights were still flickering. Inside, ranks of freezers receded into the gloom. Red warning lights blinked on their monitor panels, indicating loss of power. Kat ran to the nearest and used her prosthetic hand to start yanking open doors. Cold mist swirled around her.

Body parts.

Organs half-grown from cloned cells.

A tray of partially-developed ears.

Verne hunched over the workstation by the door, accessing the computer terminal on the desk, scanning lists of freezer contents.

"Try seven forty-two," he called.

Kat looked up. Each freezer had a number stencilled on the top of the door.

> CAPTAIN, WE NEED TO LEAVE.

She ran down the row until she found the one she needed, and hauled back the heavy metal door.

Babies.

Hundreds and hundreds of babies.

Trays filled every shelf, and transparent flasks filled every tray, each one with a tiny embryo suspended within. The trays were labelled by year. Feverishly, she sorted through until she found the right one. Her flask was near the back, the name ABDULOV-K printed on its label, above a barcode. With shaking hands, she lifted it clear.

"Got it," she said.

Inside the flask: a small, red clump of cells about the size of a grain of rice.

It meant nothing.

It meant everything.

Verne called, "Kat, come *on*!"

She pushed the flask into the pocket of her ship suit and made to go.

Stopped after a couple of steps.

Turned around.

Hundreds and hundreds of babies.

In her mind, she heard the wailing of The Recollection's captured souls, and knew she couldn't leave. Instead, she began pulling out the trays.

> HURRY IT UP. WE'VE GOT INCOMING.

Verne came running.

"What are you doing?"

"Shut up and help me."

There were more trays than they could possibly carry between them. Desperately, she cast around.

"Find me a stretcher," she said. "One with wheels."

MINUTES LATER, THEY burst from the hospital foyer pushing a stretcher piled with trays upon trays of flasks. Thick smoke filled the air. Gunfire crackled in the street. A few hundred metres away, a phalanx of red stick zombies lurched in their direction. Behind the shambling figures, the creeping infection ate its way along the road like an incoming tide. Somewhere in the buildings to either side, human soldiers fired into the shambling ranks from windows and doorways. A helicopter whirred overhead, spiralling crazily, and disappeared behind the shops on the other side of the street. A couple of seconds later, the ground shook with the force of its impact, and a greasy fireball appeared over the rooftops.

"Get to the ship," Kat panted, un-holstering her guns. "I'll cover you."

She started to move sideways, keeping herself between the blood-coloured zombies and the stretcher of rescued foetuses. She held the pistols at arms' length, ready to fire.

Behind her, Verne gave a grunt as he bent to push.

"Come on," she urged.

Across the lawn, the *Ameline* squatted on its landing shocks, the black bulge of the Dho weapon like a fat leech clinging to the underside of its bows.

"Open the cargo doors and lower the ramp," she told the ship. "We're bringing something aboard."

Screams rang from a nearby building. She exchanged a glance with Verne.

"Keep going," she said. They couldn't rescue everybody.

Already, over the screams, she could hear the wail emanating from the zombies and the tide of red that dogged their heels. They were maybe fifty metres away now. She squeezed off an experimental shot. One of the lumbering figures twitched and staggered, then righted itself and kept coming.

"**Katherine**," the zombies chanted in unison. "**Katherine Abdulov.**"

She took aim at another of the figures and fired again, both guns at once, aiming for its head. Her shots caught it dead centre, right in the middle of what passed for its face, and its head burst like a balloon full of dark red paint. With satisfaction, she watched it drop to its knees and fall, only to be overtaken and absorbed by the advancing tide behind it.

She heard Verne curse and looked over her shoulder. The stretcher's rubber wheels weren't designed to be used on grass, and kept sliding, spinning the wrong way on their casters.

"Hurry it up," she said.

Verne gave her a look and swore under his breath.

When she turned back to the street, the zombies had almost halved the distance between them and her.

"**Katherine Abdulov, speak to us.**"

She fired more shots into the front row, trying to shut them up, blasting chunks from their heads and torsos. Some fell, others took the impacts and kept coming.

"Katherine, we have your mother, she wants to speak to you."

She fired again, saw an arm blown off at the elbow. Then, as if in a nightmare, she heard her mother's voice emerge from the background wail of the oncoming tide, her words spoken in unison from the slit-like mouths of the blood-red bodies shambling towards her.

"Kat? Kat is that you?"

She lowered her guns, felt her mouth hang open. Her gut gave a little lurch, like it did when the ship went into freefall.

"No," she said.

"Kat, where am I? Why can't I see anything? What's happening?"

Kat felt the muscles in her neck and jaw tighten. Bile rose in her throat. She swallowed.

"Mum?"

"Kat, where are you? I want to see you. Come here."

In her head, she felt the strange prickling sensation she'd felt facing The Recollection at the Quay, before she'd launched the missiles. Her head swam with the urge to throw down her weapons and surrender: a compulsion to hurl herself into the red tide and let it sweep her to the Omega Point at the end of the habitable universe.

She took a step forward. Then another.

Last time, The Recollection had almost had her. She knew she couldn't hold out for long, knew she was close to losing the fight. This time, she couldn't resist for long, not with its fingers already in her head, pulling her inward.

Snarling, she summoned the last scraps of her old determination.

"You don't get me that easily," she said. With shaking hands, she raised the guns, and with a drawn-out howl of pain, emptied them into the ranks of approaching figures. Then spent, she let herself sag. The pistols clattered onto the road at her feet.

"Mum?" she said.

Then Verne was there with her, pulling her roughly back towards the ship. She fought against him, kicking and swearing. Tears ran down her face.

"Let me go! We have to go back, we have to find a way to get her out!"

Verne held her by the shoulders and shook her roughly.

"It's too late, Kat. It's too late."

He dragged her up the ramp. Her head reeled with unfamiliar voices, all of them pleading with her to turn around and join them. It took every gram of strength she had to keep walking, putting one foot in front of the other as she allowed herself to be herded into the ship.

Once inside, she dropped to her knees.

"Thank you," she whispered. Dimly, she saw the cargo ramp hinge upwards, sealing the hull.

Mum!

And then the ship shook as it fired up its engines, ready to launch. Moving in a daze, she followed Verne to the bridge and strapped into her couch.

Ed Rico's voice came through the speaker from the weapon on the ship's bows.

"What's happening? What do you want me to do?"

Kat closed her eyes.

"Kill it," she told him. "Kill everything."

"Yes, ma'am."

Lightning flared. The superhot stellar hydrogen flashed the air it passed through to glowing plasma. It scoured the zombies from the street, punched molten holes in the bloody red slick of advancing nanomachinery.

Watching the destruction, Kat's lips drew back in something that was half snarl and half grin.

"See how you like it," she said.

Beside her, Verne reached out and tapped the console in front of him.

"Go," he said to the ship.

Through her implant, Kat felt the jump engines come online. She tried to struggle against her harness. Although Verne had jumped his ship out of its bay in the Quay, no-one had ever jumped from the *surface* of a world before.

"No, not yet," she protested, but already it was too late.

The power spiked.

And they were gone.

CHAPTER FORTY-FIVE
SURVIVAL

OF THE THOUSAND freighters in the fleet, only four were lost: three on the surface and one on takeoff. The rest returned to the Ark in dribs and drabs, two or three at a time, over the course of the next few hours. Each carried upwards of eight hundred refugees from the surface: frightened, bewildered people struggling to understand the horrors befalling their world.

When the *Ameline* docked, Feliks Abdulov was the first person waiting to greet the crew. He stepped forward as the airlock slid open.

"Katherine!"

"Dad!"

She climbed down and ran to him. Saw him wince.

"Dad, are you okay? What happened to you?"

Feliks looked ruefully at his bandaged hands. "Frostbite," he said. "The doc says I'm going to lose the ends of my fingers."

She took him gently by the wrists and he looked her up and down. A frown crossed his face.

"But never mind me, what the hell happened to your arm?"

Kat raised her metal hand. The motors in the knuckles caught the light.

"It's a long story," she said, dropping it again. "But now's not the time. There's something else. Dad, it's Mum."

"I know." He put his arms around her. "I already heard. The compound's gone. We were too late."

Kat felt her eyes grow hot.

"It's worse than that," she said.

Her father squeezed her.

"Don't say it, please."

"But, Dad—"

Feliks put a hand to the back of her head, smoothing her hair with his bandaged fingers.

"Katherine, I was adrift in a refrigerated crate for thirty hours, and I had time to review your footage from Djatt." His voice wavered. "I know what's happened to your mother."

"But we can't leave her trapped in there forever. There must be something we can do?"

"There's nothing," he said. Over his shoulder, Kat saw lines of confused, grief-stricken survivors disembarking from one of the freighters. They had all lost friends and loved ones. They'd left behind mothers, fathers, sons, daughters, sisters, brothers, husbands and wives. They had nothing but their misery and the clothes in which they stood. Tears running down her face, she felt a surge of kinship with them.

"For now, all we can do is survive," Feliks said in her ear. He kissed her temple. "Survive, and remember."

* * *

ED CLAWED HIS way out of the slippery embrace of the Torch, emerging into the air above the deck like a newborn foal struggling to free itself from its mother's womb. Tired and stiff, he let himself drop to the floor.

Alice stooped to help him up.

"Are you all right?" she asked. She brushed away the blood from his eyes and nostrils, and ducked beneath his arm, taking some of his weight on her shoulders.

"I'll be okay," he said. He blinked and rubbed his eyes with one hand. The lights in the hangar seemed harsh and bright. All he could see were afterimages of the tactical display.

"Wait," he said. He turned to face her. She looked up at him, eyes wide, and a strand of auburn hair fell across her left eye. He smoothed it back.

"Alice, there's something I have to tell you."

She smiled and shook her head.

"I know, Ed."

"What?"

"I *know*. And don't worry. I love you too."

"You do?"

"Of course, you fool." She put a hand on his chest and stretched up to kiss him on the lips. She smelled of coffee and tasted of spearmint toothpaste. Ed closed his eyes. His back ached and he felt bone tired, ready to drop into bed. When he reopened them, he noticed Verne standing a little way off, watching them.

"Hello," he said.

Verne ducked under the leading edge of the *Ameline*'s hull and hugged him.

"You did good, Ed," he said. "We all did. We rescued a lot of people today."

Ed shook his head.

"All I did was shoot what I was told to."

Verne ruffled his hair.

"We couldn't have done it without you."

His eyes dropped to the St. Christopher that hung around Ed's neck.

"Still got that, huh?"

Ed gripped the medal and glanced at Alice.

"It brought us luck, all the way here."

Verne smiled.

"You make your own luck, Ed."

He stepped back, glanced from Ed to Alice.

"Look, Verne—"

Verne held up his hands, palms out.

"Ed, don't *worry*. I really am happy for the two of you. We've all moved on. We're all leading different lives now." He looked down and scratched the bridge of his nose. "As a matter of fact, I'm going to be a father." His cheeks flushed. He didn't know where to look. "I mean, me and Kat. Kat and I. We're going to have a baby."

Alice's eyes open wide in surprise. For a moment, she seemed unable to process the information.

"Congratulations," she said, her tone uncertain. She looked up at Ed. He took her hand and squeezed reassuringly.

Verne shuffled his feet.

"Thanks." He looked at Ed. "Are you ready to be an uncle?"

"I guess so."

"Good." Verne turned to where Kat stood talking with her father. "Look, we'll talk properly later," he said. "Right now, I have to go."

He made to leave.

"Hey," Ed called after him. "We're cool, right?"

Verne turned, walking backwards away from them. A smile creased his face.

"You're my brother," he said. "Of course we're cool."

CHAPTER FORTY-SIX
UP AND OUT

TWENTY-FOUR HOURS later, refuelled and provisioned, the *Ameline* left the Ark again, dropping away into empty space. Alone on its bridge, Kat watched the crystal walls recede, feeling like a bug falling from a windshield.

Below her, down in the passenger lounge, Alice, Toby Drake, Professor Harris and half a dozen Acolytes sat strapped into acceleration couches. Below them, Ed lay wrapped in his cocoon under the bows.

Toby Drake hadn't regained consciousness since being carried aboard by the Acolytes, and Kat had specific instructions to deliver him to the Bubble Belt as soon as humanely possible.

"He's going to save us all," Harris had told her, despite the fact that when she looked at Toby, he appeared half-dead and incapable of saving anything, including himself.

"What do you think?" she asked the ship. Through her implant, she felt it stir. Like her, it was glad to be underway again, and glad to be putting some distance between itself and Strauli, and the continuing risk of contamination.

> Shucks, don't ask me, lady. I just work here.

It paused, its attention snagged by a signal from the Ark.

> Incoming message.

Kat smiled. She knew who it would be.

"Put it on screen."

The star field dimmed, to be replaced by the faces of Verne Rico and Feliks Abdulov. The two former rivals stood in the human quarters of the Ark, both wearing stretchy black ship suits. Kat's smile grew broader. She'd never expected to see the two men in the same room, let alone standing side-by-side.

"Hello," she said. Her smile slipped a notch. "Or should that be goodbye?"

Feliks looked at her with undisguised affection.

"How about *au revoir*?"

Despite her protests, both men had elected to stay behind to help with the evacuation of Strauli. To Feliks, it was a matter of family honour; to Verne, a chance to redeem himself for past mistakes. Standing together, they made an unlikely pair.

Verne said, "By the time you reach Tiers Cross, we'll only be a few months behind. We'll see you soon enough."

"You better make sure of it, because I'm not doing this alone." Kat rubbed her belly. "This little one's going to need her father, and her grandfather."

Verne raised an eyebrow. "You're still sure it's a girl, then?"

Kat gave him a grin.

"Aren't you?"

She signed off. Ahead, the screens showed only stars. Each one had a tiny name printed next to it. The ship had even superimposed their target—the system containing Tiers Cross and the Bubble Belt—with a golden crosshair. For a second, she closed her eyes, savouring the feeling of freedom. Everything else fell away, leaving just the ship and her, and the tiny speck growing inside her.

"Are you ready?" she asked the *Ameline*.

The ship fired its lateral thrusters, turning its nose in the direction of Tiers Cross. Deep in its bowels, she felt the two purple coils of the jump engines drawing power, building energy.

> ALWAYS.

She took one last, lingering look at her home planet, and the obscene red blooms now disfiguring almost a third of the visible land mass.

"We'll be back one day," she promised the little life growing within her. Then she shook herself. The future would have to wait. She pulled herself upright in her seat. Right now, she was a trader captain, an Abdulov, and she had a cargo to deliver.

The ship's engines hit full power.

> READY TO JUMP?

Kat turned her face to the anaemic light of the distant stars. She felt like an arrow aimed at the sky, ready to fly.

"Up and out," she said.

And vanished.

A SKIN YOU ONCE SHED

*Who believes not only in our globe with
its sun and moon, but in other globes
with their suns and moons,
Who, constructing the house of himself or
herself, not for a day but for all time,
sees races, eras, dates, generations,
The past, the future, dwelling there, like space,
inseparable together.*

– Walt Whitman, *Kosmos*

IMAGINE THAT YOU'RE *standing naked in the snows on the surface of Tiers Cross, back where it all began.*

You're standing in the street, on the corner of one of those windy junctions near the port, and the wind's coming in off the ice fields beyond the town. The cold prickles your skin. Your breath comes like steam.

Ships move to and fro on the landing field. Still more crowd the parking orbits above. More and more every day, each and every one packed to the gills with refugees from Strauli, Inakpa, Djatt. Other worlds, too. Now that it has access to jump capable ships, The Recollection's moving fast, its spread contained only by the impossibility of travelling faster than light.

Thank heavens the arches have started to evaporate. By allowing humanity to spread out, they've served their purpose. Now the Dho have pulled the plug on the network, to stop The Recollection taking advantage of it, and the individual arches have started to fall like dominoes, bleeding into the wind like the purple ash of a madman's dream.

Around you, here on Tiers Cross, the usual port trash ply their wares: pushers; scam artists; beggars; buskers. All of them doing the same old Downport hustle. Their numbers grow with every refugee ship that lands here, fleeing The Recollection. They own nothing, and they have nowhere to go. They can't see you. They walk through you as if you were a ghost. And deep in your heart you love them all, unreservedly.

Overhead you see the sparks of tugs exploring the jewelled fringes of the Bubble Belt. You know the breaker teams are working flat-out, pulling double shifts, opening up habitable bubbles for these people to settle. Here in the Belt, with a billion individual habitats, there's room for everyone.

And deeper into the Belt, where once you saw only a curtain of diamonds, a light glows. A miniature sun illuminates it all from within, like a crystal chandelier. The Gnarl at the centre of the cloud is now a rocket, pushing out light and energy in a thin jet, slowly building up the tremendous force it will need to move not only itself, but this small moon and the billion habitats of the Belt. Watching its radiance, you know it will take years for that movement to become evident, longer still for the background stars to start moving noticeably in the night sky.

The wind makes you shiver, but you don't mind. This is your home, after all. You're used to it. You've missed it, although it seems an eternity since you were last here.

Your childhood and the peculiar pains of adolescence: they all happened here, so long ago, their immediacy now lost in the days before the Ark, before the Gnarl. Even your name, Toby Drake, feels like an anachronism, part of a skin you once shed.

Once you had a life, now you have a purpose. There's no time for regret or resentment; you have your part to play.

For a long moment, you look up at the sweeping grandeur of the Bubble Belt, and wish the person who named it had thought of something with a little more gravitas, something more suited to the majesty and inhuman immensity of the crowded habitats, each one as unique as a snowflake and each following its own carefully prescribed and choreographed orbit around the waxy, streaming Gnarl at the centre.

You look down at the dirty snow beneath your bare feet. The snow of home. But of course, you're not really down here. You're up there, in the heart of the Gnarl.

And you can see everything.

You're everywhere and nowhere, baby.

Your mind roams the sky. It's you firing that colossal jet, and wherever you're going, you're taking this gaudy Christmas decoration of a cloud with you. You're leading the salvaged remnants of humanity away from the advancing wave front of The Recollection. Ships like the Ameline *will cover your retreat. And soon, the Dho Ark will join you, with its own cargo of fleeing refugees. All you have to do is steer them all to safety.*

You turn your face to the sky.

That smudge out there, what is that? Is that Andromeda?

Drowned in the greasy depths of the Gnarl, you smile to yourself.

Let's go there, *you think.*

And in a handful of decades, you're gone.

THE END

ACKNOWLEDGEMENTS

Thanks to Jonathan Oliver; Neil Roberts; Lee Harris; Colin Harvey; Richard Scott; Neil Beynon; my sister Rebecca; my wife Becky; and my brother Huw.

Several passages in this book were inspired by or adapted from pieces published in my collection *The Last Reef and Other Stories* (Elastic Press, 2008). A few sentences from Chapter Five appeared in a slightly different form in the story 'The Winding Curve,' which I co-wrote with Robert Starr and which appeared in Rob's collection *Sophistry By Degrees* (Stonegarden, 2008).

THE NOISE WITHIN

"Unreasonably enjoyable.
24 meets Starship Troopers.
If you read Reynolds, Hamilton,
Banks - read this."
- Stephen Baxter

IAN WHATES

UK ISBN: 978 1 906735 64 7 • US ISBN: 978 1 906735 65 4 • £7.99/$7.99

Philip Kaufman is on the brink of perfecting the long sought-after human/AI interface when a scandal from his past returns to haunt him and he is forced to flee, pursued by assassins and attacked in his own home. Black-ops specialist Jim Leyton is bewildered when he is diverted from his usual duties to hunt down a pirate vessel, The Noise Within. Why this one obscure freebooter, in particular? Two very different lives are about to collide, changing everything forever...

 WWW.SOLARISBOOKS.COM

Follow us on Twitter! www.twitter.com/solarisbooks

THE NOISE REVEALED

'Unreasonably enjoyable. 24 meets *Starship Troopers*. If you read Reynolds, Hamilton, Banks – read this.'
– Stephen Baxter on *The Noise Within*

IAN WHATES

UK ISBN: 978 1 907519 53 6 • US ISBN: 978 1 907519 54 3 • £7.99/$7.99

A time of flux, a time of change. While mankind is adjusting to its first ever encounter with an alien civilisation – the Byrzaens – black ops specialist Jim Leyton reluctantly allies himself with a mysterious stranger in order to rescue the woman he loves, bringing himself into direct conflict with his former employers: the United League of Allied Worlds government. Scientist and businessman Philip Kaufman is fast discovering there is more to the virtual world than he ever realised. Yet it soon becomes clear that all is not well within the realm of Virtuality. Truth is hidden beneath lies and there are games being played, deadly games with far reaching consequences. Both men begin to suspect that the much heralded 'First Contact' is anything but first contact, and that a sinister con is being perpetrated with the whole of humankind as the victim. Now all they have to do is prove it.

 WWW.SOLARISBOOKS.COM

Follow us on Twitter! www.twitter.com/solarisbooks

ENGINEERING INFINITY

Edited by Jonathan Strahan

UK ISBN: 978 1 907519 51 2 • US ISBN: 978 1 907519 52 9 • £7.99/$7.99

The universe shifts and changes; suddenly you understand, and are filled with wonder.
Coming up against the speed of light (and with it, the sheer size of the universe), seeing
how difficult and dangerous terraforming an alien world really is, realising that a hitch-
hiker on a starship consumes fuel and oxygen and the tragedy that results... it's "hard-SF"
where sense of wonder is most often found and where science fiction's true heart lies.
Including stories from the likes of Stephen Baxter and Charles Stross.

 WWW.SOLARISBOOKS.COM

Follow us on Twitter! www.twitter.com/solarisbooks

INCLUDING STORIES BY:
**ALASTAIR REYNOLDS // KAY KENYON
JASON STODDARD // HOLLY PHILLIPS**

"The energy
and enterprise
of Jetse de Vries
deserves a lot of
attention."
Ian Whates,
Matrix Online

AN ANTHOLOGY OF NEAR-FUTURE OPTIMISTIC SCIENCE FICTION

SHINE

EDITED BY JETSE DE VRIES

UK ISBN: 978 1 906735 66 1 • US ISBN: 978 1 906735 67 8 • £7.99/$7.99

A collection of near-future, optimistic SF stories where some of the genre's brightest stars
and most exciting talents portray the possible roads to a better tomorrow. Definitely not
a plethora of Pollyannas – but neither a barrage of dystopias – Shine will show that
positive change is far from being a foregone conclusion, but needs to be hard-fought,
innovative, robust and imaginative. Let's make our tomorrows Shine.

 WWW.SOLARISBOOKS.COM

Follow us on Twitter! www.twitter.com/solarisbooks

ENGINEMAN

"Eric Brown is *the* name to watch in SF."
Peter F. Hamilton

ERIC BROWN

UK ISBN: 978 1 907519 42 0 • US ISBN: 978 1 907519 43 7 • £7.99/$7.99

Once, Enginemen pushed bigships through the nada-continuum; but faster than light isn't fast enough anymore, now that the Keilor-Vincicoff Organisation's interfaces bring distant planets a single step away. When a man with half a face offers ex-Engineman Ralph Mirren the chance to escape his ruined life and push a ship to an unknown destination, he jumps at the chance. But he is unprepared when he discovers the secret behind the continuum, and the mystery awaiting him on the distant world...

 WWW.SOLARISBOOKS.COM

Follow us on Twitter! www.twitter.com/solarisbooks

JAMES LOVEGROVE'S *PANTHEON* SERIES

THE AGE OF RA

UK ISBN: 978 1 84416 746 3 • US ISBN: 978 1 84416 747 0 • £7.99/$7.99

The Ancient Egyptian gods have defeated all the other pantheons and divided the Earth into warring factions. Lt. David Westwynter, a British soldier, stumbles into Freegypt, the only place to have remained independent of the gods, and encounters the followers of a humanist freedom-fighter known as the Lightbringer. As the world heads towards an apocalyptic battle, there is far more to this leader than it seems...

THE AGE OF ZEUS

UK ISBN: 978 1 906735 68 5 • US ISBN: 978 1 906735 69 2 • £7.99/$7.99

The Olympians appeared a decade ago, living incarnations of the Ancient Greek gods, offering order and stability at the cost of placing humanity under the jackboot of divine oppression. Until former London police officer Sam Akehurst receives an invitation to join the Titans, the small band of battlesuited high-tech guerillas squaring off against the Olympians and their mythological monsters in a war they cannot all survive...

THE AGE OF ODIN

UK ISBN: 978 1 907519 40 6 • US ISBN: 978 1 907519 41 3 • £7.99/$7.99

Gideon Coxall was a good soldier but bad at everything else, until a roadside explosive device leaves him with one deaf ear and a British Army half-pension. The Valhalla Project, recruiting useless soldiers like himself, no questions asked, seems like a dream, but the last thing Gid expects is to find himself fighting alongside ancient Viking gods. It seems *Ragnarök* – the fabled final conflict of the Sagas – is looming.

 WWW.SOLARISBOOKS.COM

Follow us on Twitter! www.twitter.com/solarisbooks

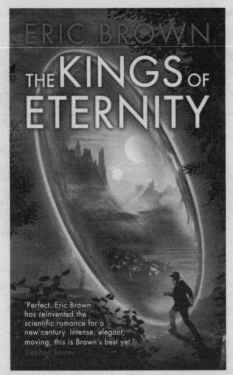

'Perfect. Eric Brown has reinvented the scientific romance for a new century. Intense, elegant, moving, this is Brown's best yet.'
Stephen Baxter

UK ISBN: 978 1 907519-71-0 • US ISBN: 978 1 907519 70 3 • £7.99/$7.99

1999. Novelist Daniel Langham lives a reclusive life on an idyllic Greek island, hiding away from humanity and the events of the past. All that changes, however, when he meets artist Caroline Platt and finds himself falling in love. But what is his secret, and what are the horrors that haunt him?

1935. Writers Jonathon Langham and Edward Vaughan are summoned from London by their editor friend Jasper Carnegie to help investigate strange goings-on in Hopton Wood. What they discover there will change their lives forever.

What they become, and their link to the novelist of the future, is the subject of Eric Brown's most ambitious novel to date. Almost ten years in the writing, *The Kings of Eternity* is a novel of vast scope and depth, yet imbued with humanity and characters you'll come to love.

 WWW.SOLARISBOOKS.COM

Follow us on Twitter! www.twitter.com/solarisbooks

XENOPATH
A BENGAL STATION NOVEL

ERIC BROWN

UK ISBN: 978 1 844167 42 5 • US ISBN: 978 1 844167 43 2 • £7.99/$7.99

Telepath Jeff Vaughan is working for a detective agency on Bengal Station, an exotic spaceport that dominates the ocean between India and Burma, when he is called out to the colony world of Mallory to investigate recent discoveries of alien corpses.

But Vaughan is shaken to his core when he begins to uncover the heart of darkness at the centre of the Scheering-Lassiter colonial organisation...

 WWW.SOLARISBOOKS.COM

Follow us on Twitter! www.twitter.com/solarisbooks

A COMBAT-K NOVEL

ANDY REMIC

The new master of rock-hard military science fiction

WAR MACHINE

ISBN: 978-1-84416-522-3

Ex-soldier Keenan, a private investigator with a bad reputation, is about to take on the biggest case of his career. To have any chance of success, however, he must head to a dangerous colony world and re-assemble his old military unit, a group who swore they'd never work together again...

 SOLARIS SCIENCE FICTION

UK ISBN: 978 1 844167 93 7 • US ISBN: 978 1 844167 92 0 • £7.99/$7.99

Charged with finding the evil Junk's homeland and annihilating them, Combat-K head
to Sick World, a long-abandoned hospital planet once dedicated to curing the deformed,
the insane, the dying and the dead. The Medical Staff of Sick World - the doctors, nurses,
patients and deviants, abandoned with extreme prejudice, a thousand-year gestation
of hardcore medical mutation - and their hibernation, and they can smell fresh meat...

 WWW.SOLARISBOOKS.COM

Follow us on Twitter! www.twitter.com/solarisbooks